There were then five Lords of Darkness. Uhlume, Lord Death, was one, whose citadel stood at the Earth's core, but who came and went in the world at random.

Another was Wickedness, in the person of the Prince of Demons, Azhrarn the Beautiful, whose city of Druhim Vanashta lay also underground, and who came and went in the world only by night, since demonkind abjured the sun (wisely for it could burn them to smoke or cinders). The earth was flat, and marvelous, and had room then for such beings.

But it is not remembered where a certain third Lord of Darkness made his abode, nor perhaps had he much space for private life, for he must be always everywhere.

His name was Chuz, Prince Chuz . . . And who was Chuz? **His other name was Madness.**

# *Delusion's Master*

## TANITH LEE

**DAW BOOKS, INC.**
DONALD A. WOLLHEIM, PUBLISHER

1633 Broadway, New York, NY 10019

FIRST PRINTING, SEPTEMBER 1981

5 6 7 8 9

PRINTED IN THE U.S.A.

# TABLE OF CONTENTS

# PROLOGUE

## The Tower of Baybhelu

A mile from the enameled walls of the city, where the desert lay gleaming like golden glass, a beautiful woman sat in a stone tower, and she played with a bone.

"Will he come to me today?" she asked the bone, rocking it in her arms like a child. "Or will he seek me tonight? All the stars will shine, but he will shine more brightly. For sure, he dare not come by day, for he would outshine the sun. The sun would die of shame, and the whole world grow dark. But oh, he will come. Nemdur," said the beautiful woman, "Nemdur, my lord."

Her name was Jasrin; Nemdur was the king whose city stood one mile to the east. Once, he had been her husband. No longer.

When the day began to go, folding its robes around it, slipping from the desert silently, Jasrin called for her women. There were only two attendants now, one very old, and one a young girl. Both pitied her, but she barely noticed them. Nor did she notice the loathing behind their pity. At the door below, brawny men, armed with swords and axes, maintained watch, charged to keep danger out, or in. Palm trees, with fronds of brazen green, enclosed the tower, and a little pool was spread there like a piece fallen from the sky. At sunset, the girl ran down to the pool and drew water for her mistress's bath. Presently Jasrin bathed, and was perfumed and anointed. The old woman combed Jasrin's desert-colored hair, and plaited jewels into it, as Jasrin instructed her. A garment of silk was put on Jasrin's body and golden slippers on her feet. All the while, Jasrin kept a firm hold of the bone. She had some cause for this. It was the bone of her child.

"Prepare the feast," Jasrin said to her attendants. "Soon my lord Nemdur will arrive."

The attendants obeyed her, as best they could. They laid the tables with embroidered napkins and set out plates of silver, and put cooked meats on them, bread, fruits and sweetmeats. They placed wine ready in silver vessels packed about with ice.

"Make music," said Jasrin.

The girl took a stringed instrument and plucked notes from it like sharp crystal sighs.

Jasrin leaned at the window. She looked toward the city a mile away along the darkened slopes of the desert.

Above, the still stars blazed. Jasrin looked for blazing stars which moved, lamps and torches proceeding from the city of Sheve, the procession which would bring her lord to her.

"Soon," she said to the bone of her dead child, "soon he will return to me. His hair like bronze, his strength like the sun, his eyes like the stars. He will lie with me, and his mouth will be wine, his loins fire. Oh, the music he will make in me, and I will be only an instrument for that music. And in that music, I shall conceive. I shall become big with you, my child; you will be born again."

But if the bone heard her, it paid no heed. If the night heard her, it paid none. And if Nemdur, the king, where he sat in his palace with his new queen, if he heard her, then he stopped his ears.

At midnight, Jasrin screamed. She flung the bone from her into a corner. She began to tear her skin and her hair, and her two attendants ran to her, and they prevented her. Jasrin had grown so weak even an old woman and a slender girl could restrain her—they were, besides, well practiced. This happened every night.

And, as on every night, Jasrin wept for many hours. Every night was wept away in her tears, till in the pastel moments before dawn she slept a little, and waking, called for her child. And then the girl would bring her the bone and Jasrin would rock the bone and hold it to her breast.

As the sun rose, Jasrin asked the bone again: "Will he come to me today? Or will he seek me tonight?"

But Nemdur would never come to her.

She had been sixteen when she was wed to him. She had lived till then in a kingdom of many waters, of rivers, lakes, waterfalls, fountains. Green hills were piled above green valleys, skies overlaid a mosaic of green foliage. When they told her she must go from this green velvet land to a land of raw amber, Jasrin had wept, in the manner of one at ease among waters, facile with their use. Obedient, wretched and afraid, she had gone to the man who was to be her husband, and she had fixed her eyes on the green ground she must leave. While with gentle strong fingers he lifted the veil from her face, it was as if the sun shone in on her. Slowly she raised her eyes, and beheld Nemdur was the sun, and the sun dried her weeping with his smile.

Nemdur was beautiful, a young lion. His hair glinted bright as metal shavings, his eyes were the pale burning slate of desert air. When he saw his bride, he had smiled at her because he was pleased by her loveliness. He had wished to be pleased; now, she wished only to please him.

She rode to Sheve in a carriage that tinkled with silver discs, her hair cascading, her eyes brimming not with tears, but love. She was the princess of all waterfalls. In the palace, behind the doors of the bedchamber, Nemdur taught her of another land where fire and liquid mingled.

Soon, she was heavy with his child. Nemdur loaded her with other gifts, necklets of gold, silver mirrors, bracelets of sapphire, ropes of pearls. He had made for her a garden where lotuses lay like swans on the shallow pools, a water garden in the midst of a desert. He sent her the pelt of a lion he himself had slain, a mantle in which to wrap his son when it was born. So much he sent, but he himself did not come to her any more. The child made her big, cumbersome and ugly. Nemdur, free as sand or sunlight, went in to other women. His appetite was large, and his tastes various. The child had merely hastened an inevitable desire in him for change. Certainly, there was yet room in his heart for Jasrin, but also room for others, and in his bed, room for a world of women.

She saw his eyes turn to saffron-haired maidens with skin pale, like cream, and maidens colored dark as molasses with hair like smoky fleece. She smelled these skins, this hair, on him, their perfumes and their lust. Her soul shrank inwards and grew little. At last her soul grew small enough to fit inside a coriander seed.

Then she looked at herself in the lotus pools and in the silver mirrors. And she divined that Nemdur's child made her hideous, and she began to hate the child. Until that moment, she had scarcely considered her life, or rather, she had not considered that she might have any say in her life. But now a great terror filled her. Huge things had happened to her, and none of them at her ordering. Exile, love, pregnancy and desertion. Next came her labor. Others had suffered worse, but who is to say for Jasrin, at that time, the pain and fear did not appear the most awful ever visited upon woman? Her body seemed split; her brain was cloven. She was delivered of a son and they laid him on the lion's skin, but Jasrin was laid on molten lava. Yet she thought, *I am free of it, and now he will love me again.*

Nemdur sent gifts. For his wife, earrings and necklaces of lapis lazuli, for his son, a jade apple. When Nemdur entered the chamber, he lifted the baby high in his arms, as once he had lifted the veil of his bride, and Nemdur laughed with pleasure at his son. He had only smiled at Jasrin. This time, he barely glanced at her.

In a while, a woman wandered from Jasrin's apartments. She had a soul small enough to fit inside a coriander seed, a brain cloven in two parts. One part said to her: *See where my husband plays with his son.* The second part said to her: *See how my husband has eyes only for the child and none for me.*

Nemdur gave the child robes of silk, toys of ivory, an anklet of gold. Nemdur came to Jasrin's bed.

"Am I beautiful?" Jasrin questioned him.

"Beautiful as a lotus, and you bud beautiful children. Let us make another, you and I."

"My lord," said Jasrin, "I am sick tonight. Do not ask me. Go instead to one of your snowy women, or your inky women."

"Come," said Nemdur, "it is you I want."

Then her cloven brain put words in her mouth, like honey:

"I have yearned for you—"

Like aloes:

"But I am the last you turn to."

Nemdur saw her hurt, and he said: "I have been thought-less and will amend it. But I never honored you the less."

"I am just another of your sluts," said she.

"You are my wife and the mother of my heir."

Then Jasrin would say nothing else, and she stretched her-self out like a stone. When he could not move her, Nemdur left her. His garden was full of flowers, he had no need to wait for one. If you had opened the coriander seed at that hour, you could not have found any longer the soul of Jasrin, for it had shrunk to a speck no bigger than the point of a pin.

That month, the shallow waters of the water garden failed and the lotuses died. *There*, said the second part of Jasrin's brain, *that is what they have done to you, Nemdur and Nemdur's son.*

And the first part of her brain whispered: *If you had not borne a child, Nemdur would love you still.*

The child was sleeping on his lion skin in the shade, and nearby his nurse lay sleeping too, and all about were scat-tered the tiny ivory animals that the king had sent the child, and on his ankle was the golden anklet.

Jasrin noiselessly took up the nurse's outer garment that the woman had cast off in the heat of the day. Jasrin wrapped herself in the garment and pulled its folds over her head, and next she took up the child in the skin. Then she be-gan to cry, for the child was innocent and beautiful; but even so he was her enemy.

Jasrin passed through the palace yards, and no one ques-tioned her, thinking her the trusted nurse. When she went out and through the city, she became only another woman with her child carried close. And sometimes indeed Jasrin saw other women with their babies, and she was sad for them, be-lieving every woman who had borne a child had lost thereby the love of her husband.

Down wide streets and narrow, across the great market-place where the brown camels glared like lords, and the blue-black figs sweated and the red meat swung and boys danced to a pipe and a snake rose from a copper urn and spread his heart-shaped hood. So Jasrin came to the tall enameled walls of Sheve. She did not see the pictures there of beasts and flowers. She ran out through the broad gate whose shadow was like black death. She ran into the desert.

About a hundred paces from the walls, where there was a well, clustered an encampment of wandering people. Jasrin walked boldly among the tents, and none challenged her since she was a woman, and in those parts they did not fear women much, or did not suppose they did.

At last Jasrin came on a group of several young children and babies sleeping or sleepily playing together in the shadow of a tent. Nearby a pair of large hunting dogs reclined, their tawny masks upon their paws.

Now Jasrin was beyond reason almost, but not quite. It seemed to her that she might leave her child here undetected, among so many others. And when the mothers came and found an extra child, no doubt they would take it in, concluding themselves repaid by the golden ring about its ankle. Once noon was done, the camp would be disbanded, for such nomads rarely stayed long in any place, let alone beside the cities of the desert country, which they considered devilish and decadent. By nightfall, then, if not sooner, Jasrin would be free of the thing which had, so guiltlessly, robbed her of all happiness.

As she was standing there musing feverishly on these things, one of the dogs raised its head, snuffing the air, and growled softly at her. Plainly, these animals had been set to guard the children, and would guard hers as well when she was gone. Yet the dog's merciless eyes filled Jasrin with sudden alarm. In a frenzy she put the bundle of the child from her and let it fall gently on the sand, beside the other infants. It had not cried; perhaps instinctively it had known her for its mother, while unable instinctively to guess her purpose.

The dog surged abruptly to its four slim feet, and now its eyes were hard charred glasses, fired by the relentless desert sun. Jasrin turned and fled, expecting the dog's fangs to fasten any moment in her robe or her flesh, but its growling only died behind her, though over it she heard all the sleepy children wake and begin to wail and shriek, as if accusing her, and thus she ran the faster, from the camp and back through the city gateway. Up the streets, wide and narrow, she ran, and near the palace she checked, and threw the nurse's robe on the ground. The guards, seeing her reenter, stared, for she was the Queen of Sheve and she had come in without attendants from the streets; but they did not question her.

She went to her apartments and sat down there. Her head ached, her very mind ached.

Nemdur would come to her and say: "Our son has disappeared, none can discover him. Do you think the woman who was his nurse killed him?"

And Jasrin would answer: "Spare her, my lord. She is demented. She is jealous that she has no child of her own, for her own child died . . ."

Noon had come, and afternoon, and then the time of redness, the blood-red splashed on the walls, the scarlet aftermath of the sun changing swiftly to magenta and to indigo, and the stars appeared, the lamps of the cities of heaven. Jasrin had heard no outcry and no search through the palace. Nemdur had not come to her.

And then he came.

He stepped quickly into the unlit chamber, and for once he did not light the room with his presence, nor did he speak as she had anticipated.

"Jasrin, my wife," said Nemdur, "I have heard three stories. The first is that someone thieved the robe of a woman as she slept in the garden shade. The second that this same woman, muffled in her robe against the heat, stole out into the city, but that she never returned. The third story is that Jasrin, the Queen of Sheve, came back from the city unescorted, though none had seen her go there."

Jasrin's aching cloven brain could not deal with this.

"These are all lies!" she cried. "You should whip such liars."

But Nemdur said gently to her: "There is a fourth story. Listen, I will tell it you. Nomads pitched their tents by the walls of Sheve, in order to draw water from the well outside the gate, and to sell produce of theirs in the market. But a woman came and left a child lying among the children of the tents."

"It was the nurse," Jasrin blurted.

"No," said Nemdur, "for she was that very hour searching for our child, mine and yours, and she has witnesses to her search."

"They are all liars!" cried Jasrin once more.

"There is only one liar."

Immediately Jasrin's strength went from her like blood from a mortal wound.

"I confess it," she said. "The child took away your regard

for me. I would send away the child instead. Do not blame me. I could not help myself."

"I do not blame you," said Nemdur. His voice remained quiet, she could not see his face in the dark.

"And has the child been returned to you?" muttered Jasrin.

"Returned," said Nemdur, and then he shouted across the chamber: "Bring in my son." The doors opened again, and certain servants entered, and one carried a burning torch, and another a bundle. "Set him down," said the king, "and let this poor madwoman behold the fruit of her planting."

So they placed the bundle before the Queen of Sheve and unwrapped it in the torchlight.

For a while she stared, and then she screamed, and the two parts of her brain shattered in a hundred fragments.

The people of the tents had known the infant by his gold anklet, and out of respect for Nemdur and out of horror, they had brought home to him, risking his vengeance, what was left of his son. For the dogs had torn the child in pieces. Generally, such dogs would not have harmed a baby, but they were hunting hounds, and they had scented lion the moment the woman approached. When she had dropped the child in the sand, wrapped in the lion skin, the dogs had rushed to it. As Jasrin fled, the dogs had fallen on the skin and coincidentally on the baby inside the skin. Truly, Jasrin was rid of her son, truly she had conquered her enemy.

Nemdur showed none of his grief or his revulsion, nor did he sentence his wife to any punishment. He put her aside merely, and had her locked in a lavish pavillion adjoining the palace. He went on sending her gifts, costly hangings, succulent meats and ripe fruit, jewels. He was good to her, his tolerance was wondered at. In fact, he would have been less cruel if he had given her instantly to the executioner. Instead, it was a living death he shut her in, worse, far worse, than the scourge, the fire, the clean stroke of a sword.

In the third month of her imprisonment, the month when the king was to be married again, somehow Jasrin escaped. She was so mad by then that she half believed she was a bride, that this was the water country, and Nemdur, the bridegroom, was about to receive her and unveil her for the first time. The notion had obsessed her, however, that she would be barren, unless she could find a particular magic token, the promise of the gods to her that she should bear a

son. This token was none other than the body of her child. So
she reached the tombyard and wandered about there, and at
length she came upon a gardener. He, knowing her and
seeing no help near, took pity and led her to her son's tomb,
and let her go in. Finally, those who pursued her came on the
scene, and perceived her sitting in the twilight of the tomb,
with the poor body, all gone to bones, in her arms. In her
fragmented mind, she believed she had found the key and
symbol of her security and future joy. But in some wellspring
of herself no doubt she knew it was her frightful guilt she
rocked, and her guilt she would not be sundered from. Re-
peatedly, those who had come after her attempted to prize
the dead from her grasp. Eventually she had relinquished everything save one bone, and this they could not get away, try
as they would.

So Jasrin and her bone were removed altogether, to a stone
tower in the desert one mile west of the city of Sheve. And
here her living death went on, and the routines of her
madness never varied, her looking for Nemdur, her speech
with the bone, her agony, her fury, her despair, her weeping,
on and on. Till all about her grew also a little mad, catching
her sickness, and even the tower was steeped in the anguish
of her insanity, even the trees, the sands, the stars, the sky.

There were then five Lords of Darkness. Uhlume, Lord
Death, was one, whose citadel stood at the Earth's core, but
who came and went in the world at random. Another was
Wickedness, in the person of the Prince of Demons, Azhrarn
the Beautiful, whose city of Druhim Vanashta lay also underground, and who came and went in the world only by night,
since demonkind abjured the sun (wisely, for it could burn
them to smoke or cinders). The earth was flat, and marvelous, and had room then for such beings. But it is not
remembered where a certain third Lord of Darkness made his
abode, nor perhaps had he much space for private life, for he
must be always everywhere.

His name was Chuz, Prince Chuz, and he was this way. To
come on him from his right side, he was a handsome man in
the splendor of his youth. His hair was a blond mane couthly
combed to silk, his eye, being lowered, had long gilded lashes,
his lip was chiseled, his tanned skin burnished. On his hand
he wore a glove of fine white leather, and on his foot a shoe

of the same, and on his tall and slender body the belted robe was rich and purple-dark. "Beauteous noble young man," said those that came to his right side. But those who approached him from the left side, shrank and hesitated to speak at all. From the left side, Chuz was a male hag on whom age had scratched his boldest signatures, still peculiarly handsome it was true, but gaunt and terrible, a snarling lip, a hollowed cheek, if anything more foul because he was fair. The skin of this man was corpse gray, and the matted hair the shade of drying blood, and his scaly eyelid, being lowered, had lashes of the same color. The left hand lay naked on the damson robe, which this side was tattered and stained, and the left foot poked naked from under it. When Chuz took a step, you saw the sole of that gray-white foot was black, and when he lifted that gray-white hand, the palm was black, and the nails were long and hooked, and red as if painted from a woman's lacquer-pot. Then again, if Chuz raised his eyes on either side, you saw the balls of them were black, the irises red, the pupils tarnished, like old brass. And if Chuz laughed, which now and then he did, his teeth were made of bronze.

Worst of all, was to come on Chuz from the front and see both aspects of him at once, still worse if then he raised his eyes and opened his mouth. (Though it is believed that all men, at one time or another, had glimpsed Chuz from behind.) And who was Chuz? His other name was Madness.

Like Lord Death, maybe Prince Chuz was simply a personification that had come to be, a fluid concept that had hardened into a figure. For sure, his appurtenances were as conceptually they should be. Sometimes he carried the jawbones of an ass, and when he cracked them, they gave out the braying crazy noises of the living beast. Or sometimes he carried a brass rattle, and shook it like the sistrum, and from it came a clatter as if a brain were being shaken into bits. But sometimes, he wore an overmantle of black-purple, embroidered with splinters of glass representing malign configurations of the stars. . . .

Jasrin's six guards had laid aside their axes. With their six swords in their belts, they crouched at the foot of the stone tower in the cool of evening, throwing dice. The moon had risen, one white fruit on the black-leafed tree of night. By her shine and the flare of a torch sunk in the sand, the guards kept score.

The first man threw, and the second. Next, the third, and the fourth, and the fifth. Next the sixth. And then the seventh.

The seventh?

The seventh man's dice fell; they were yellow and had no markings.

"Who is this stranger?" demanded the captain of the six men. He clapped his hand on the stranger's shoulder, snatched the hand back with a curse. The seventh man's mantle was strewn with bright scintillants that drew blood. "How did you come here and what is your business?" barked the captain.

The six men peered, and in the torchlight they glimpsed half a face, the other half hidden by the cowl of the mantle. A glamorous young man sat among them, his eyes—or the one visible eye—demurely lowered so the long blond lashes rested on his cheek. With a closed mouth, he smiled. Then suddenly a white-gloved hand appeared and in it an ass's jawbones that clicked, and let out a raucous braying. And for a second the one eye flashed up, a confused dart of the impossible, before it was lowered again.

The stranger did not speak, but the ass's jawbones spoke abruptly between his fingers. They said, "The moon governs the tides of the sea, the tides of the wombs of women, and the tides of the humours of the mind."

The six men sprang to their feet. They drew their swords, but also they backed away. Jawbones which spoke were new to their experience, though not unheard of.

Continuing to smile, his eye meticulously lowered, the stranger rose. Gathering his blank yellow dice, he walked straight through the wall of the tower and was gone. A sound flowed in the air, it might have been a crazy laugh or the screech of a night bird over the desert.

The captain pushed open the tower door, and led his men in a search of the stair and the lower rooms. Soon Jasrin's attendants, in alarm, ran down the old woman and the young girl.

"Have any passed this way?" demanded the captain.

"No one," said the old woman. She started to berate four of the guards, who cowered foolishly like small boys.

"Your hand is bleeding," said the young girl shyly to the captain. For a year, the only man she had seen close to had been these six, and this was the year she had become a woman. As she took the man's hand, she saw he was strong and comely, and he, as she bathed the wounds the stranger's cloak had made, realized she was gentle, and that the moon shone through her thin garment on her gentle breasts, and all her gentle hair the moon had changed into a cloud of silver.

Outside, the sixth guard lingered on the sand, amazed, watching the torch which had been knocked into the pool. There beneath the water its flame burned on, as bright as day.

In the chamber above, Jasrin was in her stage of leaning at the window looking toward Sheve. Dimly discerning the commotion below, she said to the bone: "There are the messengers to say my lord is setting out. In less than an hour he will be here."

So she moved about, and so she found a young man seated cross-legged on the carpet, half his face hidden in his mantle, half his body turned from her.

Jasrin gasped, and held the bone protectively to her.

Proudly and angrily she said to the stranger: "My lordly husband will soon be with me, and he will slay you for venturing into my apartments."

Chuz did not reply, but again he cast his dice. This time they were black as two coals, and where they fell, the carpet smoked.

Jasrin clutched the bone more tightly.

"You will not dishonor me before my child," she said.

Suddenly the bone began to struggle in her grip. It thrashed and wriggled and ripped itself from her fingers. It tumbled to the ground, and hopped horribly away from her.

"Dogs ate me!" screamed the bone in a thin high voice. "You gave me to dogs to be eaten," and it threw itself into the folds of the mantle of Chuz, as if it sought refuge from her.

Jasrin covered her ears with her hands. The tears burst from her eyes though it was not yet midnight, not yet the season for her tears.

But a very tender melodious voice began to speak to her. It was the voice of Chuz, one of his voices, for he had many.

"Jasrin of Sheve is my subject, therefore let her approach me and be comforted."

And Jasrin discovered she was creeping to the stranger, and when she was near, he threw off the mantle with the glass splinters strewn on it. So she beheld the entire aspect of his face, one half youthfully bronzed, one half haggardly gray, the rusty hair and the blond, but it seemed to her it was the most natural face she had ever looked on. Chuz drew her into the shelter of his arms and he rocked her softly and he kissed her forehead with his strange, strange mouth. And for the first it seemed to her, as he had told her, she was comforted.

At length, Chuz, Prince Madness, said to her: "Those who are truly mine may ask a request of me."

Jasrin sighed sleepily. "Then grant me my sanity."

"That I cannot do, nor would I if I could. And if I did, sane, you could not bear what you had done, and what you have become."

"True," said Jasrin. "It is true."

Then Chuz produced the rattle of brass and shook it, and he gave a dreadful laugh, raucous and profane, and Jasrin wildly laughed with him, and she reached for the rattle, but in her hands it altered to the jawbones of the ass. These she commenced to clack and to click, till from them exploded a shout: "If I, Jasrin, must be mad, then make also my husband Nemdur mad. Madder than I. Let his madness destroy him."

Jasrin started in distress.

"I did not say this thing," she avowed.

Chuz answered in another of his voices, high and coarse.

"These were the words your brain would speak."

"But in my heart I love Nemdur still."

"And in your brain you hate him."

"Again," she said, "it is true. And will you send him mad?"

"His madness shall become a legend," said Chuz. He spoke as a murderer would speak in the dark.

But this time they laughed together delicately and low, like lovers. And presently Chuz vanished.

There were several doors by which madness might enter any house. One was rage, one jealousy, one fear; there were others. But Chuz, who could walk through a stone wall if he chose to, must select his entry into the human soul with more care. Jasrin's lunacy had summoned him, or tempted him, or actually evolved him from the shadows. The impetus of her lunacy was like a psychic fuel, a flow of energy along his quite incorporeal nerves. Though fashioned as a kind of man, he did not reason like one. Nor is it necessary to assume that he, the master of madness, was himself positively mad. Therefore he understood—though understood is an inadequate word—that it was not enough for Nemdur to glimpse him from the back alone. Nemdur must meet Chuz face to face, and so encounter destruction. None of this was like a game to Chuz. It was something like a duty, a service which he performed with dedication.

What then were the chinks he spied out in Nemdur, the crevices whereby madness might enter? It was simple. Nemdur was at the peak of all his life. He was powerful, rich, handsome and secure. He was proud and lustful, and his appetites were large. Nemdur the lover of women, the creator of sons, the King of Sheve. Without vast intellect or imagination, it required a snake beneath the flower to hiss at him, *Now you are vital, now you are mighty. But tomorrow, tomorrow.* . . . Nemdur had not really considered that today he was a lion, tomorrow, like his hapless dead first son, he would be bones.

Chuz did not exactly take other forms. His art was rather in the way he played upon the extraordinary form he had, like variations on a familiar melody.

Nemdur met him first, leaning in a great door of the palace, his damson overmantle wrapped close. But Chuz did not look particularly like any sort of figure at that moment, more like the shadow of a coming night. "Who are you?" said Nemdur angrily. "One who will outlive you," said Chuz, and was no more. Later a beggar ran beside the king's stirrup as he rode out to hunt. The beggar extended a white-gloved hand, and shards of glass, like the quills of a porcupine, glittered along his back. "Give me a coin," squeaked the beggar. "For when you lie in your tomb what use will your coins be to you?"

As Nemdur sat idly glancing at a book, leafing it impatiently to see if it would please his second wife, who was still new and interesting to him, a wind or a hand brushed the pages. And there before Nemdur was the story of the hero Simmu, who had feared Death and elected himself Death's enemy, and stolen from the gods a draught of Immortality to save himself and mankind from the tyranny of decay and ending.

"Some say," murmured a voice at Nemdur's ear, "that at that era, no longer was Death's Master the title of the Lord Uhlume, who is the Master of the dead, but that Simmu bore the title Death's Master, seeing he had mastered Death—"

When Nemdur's dark wife came, walking with white gauze upon her fragrant somber skin, Nemdur said to her: "Here is a book which has the story of the hero Simmu in it. It is a trifle, to delight your femininity. No doubt you believe that there is a well in the sky, with a water of Immortality in it."

"No doubt I do," acquiesced the woman with a sable laugh.

But when Nemdur lay with her in bed, the glimmer of the lamp made her lovely face into an ebony skull.

Soon the harsh yellow winds of the winter season swept over the desert. The sands blew against Sheve, and the cold frost dripped by night upon her walls and minarets. One came to Nemdur as he was sleeping.

"In a hundred years, Sheve will lie beneath the sands of the desert. In a hundred years, who will remember the name of Nemdur?"

When morning returned over the edge of the world, Nemdur stood at his high window, gazing across his city. He had lost his color, and his hands were clenched with anger. He recalled his dream, how Sheve had been buried under the nomadic sands as if drowned beneath the sea. He had observed his own ghost wandering the world, and many were spoken of, but no one spoke of Nemdur.

There came a sharp sound from the terrace below, like two dice striking the pavement. Nemdur stared down. No one was there. But now, when Nemdur ate a roast fowl, he brooded over the bones.

Strange things happened in Sheve about this time. Lamps would come alight and burn with no oil in them; butchers told of severed heads which spoke, reprimanding the slaughterers. Sometimes a woman would powder her face with pearly powder, and it would turn black as soot, or a kid would be born with five legs, or hens would lay wooden eggs, or doors which had always opened inwards would open outwards, and water that ran from a public fountain would suddenly flow upward into the air. Such events were, of course, due to the presence of Chuz. Additionally, the citizens of Sheve became generally unlike themselves, over-industrious where they had been lazy, lackadaisical where they had been busy, snappish, waspish, prone to stupid mirth, quarrels and fits of weeping.

For Nemdur himself, he too was not quite as he had been. His second wife did not conceive, but she laughed her dark laughter at him. His other women were fanciful and spoke of spirits, ghosts and demons. He was uneasy with bones. He thought of the stone tower one mile to the west, of the tomb of his son, and of his own tomb. He thought of Simmu, the fire-haired youth who sometimes, it was said, had also been a maiden. The Well in Upperearth, (the country of the gods), had a cistern made of glass, which, due to the sorcery Simmu worked on it, had cracked. Drops of the fluid of Immortality had rained to earth and become the property of Simmu. The end of the story—the failure of Simmu's enterprise—Nemdur had forgotten. Uhlume, Master of Death, Simmu, Death's Master, and Sheve buried nameless in a sea of sand, these were the fancies of Nemdur.

In the dark before dawn, he sat alone in his chamber and he called for wine. The servitors came, three of them, simply to pour the wine of the king for him. One laid a silk napkin, the second set down a bowl of polished crystal with a stem of gold, the third uncorked a flagon of black ceramic. The wine was poured into the cup, Nemdur raised the cup to his lips, but when he made to drink, no wine would run from the cup into his mouth.

The three servants stood petrified. Nemdur himself upended the cup to see if the wine would run out that way, but though the drink roiled in the crystal, it would not leave the bowl. Then the cup spoke to Nemdur.

"Kindly replace me on my foot," said the cup.

Nemdur was struck as immobile as his servants.

"You are uncivil," said the cup clearly. "Would *you*, when wine had been poured into you, disgorge it in the mouth of the first wretch that set his lips to yours? No, I will retain the liquor and become tipsy." Here the cup belched, at which Nemdur, with an oath, let it fall. The crystal smashed on the paved floor into countless pieces, and from each of them came a dreadful crying, and the wine spilled like blood.

At this, the fourth servitor (the fourth?) made a swirling motion of his mantle. The bits of crystal instantly became one with other bits of glass upon his cloak, and the crying ceased.

No longer heeding Nemdur, and wailing, three servants fled. The fourth servant, who was Chuz, raised a white gloved hand. Nothing of his face was visible. The hand pointed at Nemdur.

"What?" demanded Nemdur in trepidation.

Chuz did not speak. He swung his gloved hand toward the wide window. Behind the drapery, which all at once drew itself open on its rings, the night had begun to lose its darkness. The stars were dull as wax, and a fringe of red had appeared on the hem of the sky.

Nemdur rose automatically, and as the peculiar muffled figure beckoned, Nemdur walked to the window. Without moving then, the figure was at Nemdur's side.

Oddly, as the light began to come, the figure grew more solidly and impenetrably dark. Oddly, Nemdur conceived the notion it was a priest, cowled and folded in deepest purple, one who might guide him.

"This business," said the priest, "which troubles you, this problem of death and an unremembered name. The answer is straightforward."

The sun filled the sky and the dawn wind unbound its hair. Great measures of sand were stirred into the air, and Nemdur beheld a mirage.

"What is that tower?" said Nemdur.

How huge it was. It stood some miles to the east, yet it had blotted out the sun. The base seemed broad as the city itself, and from this base it rose in many tiers, each a little less broad, but rising upward, upward on each other, out of sight, into the very topmost regions of the ether—and so disappeared.

"Do you see a tower?" inquired Chuz the priest.

"A tower of several tiers, so tall it pierces heaven."

"Here is your oracle," said the priest. He extended to the king the jawbones of an ass. Nemdur foolishly accepted them, and instantly the jawbones cried aloud, just as the wine cup had cried, but with different words.

"The cistern of Upperearth may not be relied upon a second time to crack. So, if a man wishes to gain a draught of

Immortality from the well of the gods, let him build a high
tower, the highest the world has ever known, its base on the
earth, its summit in the sky. Let new tiers be added until the
top of the tower thrusts through into Upperearth itself. Then
let the armies of the king scale the tower. Let him make war
on heaven, raid the gods, seize by force the thing they will
not grant to prayer. That done, Nemdur may live forever.
Nor need he fear that any will forget his name, for who has
forgotten the name of Simmu, and how much greater than
Simmu shall be Nemdur, who takes by might rather than
stealth."

Nemdur grinned, and as he did so, the mirage of the
gigantic tower faded. No matter, he had seen it.

Then he turned and saw another thing.

Chuz was at the king's side, face-on to him, uncowled, un-
cloaked, his horrid duality quite plain. Nemdur stared, his
eyes fixed, his mouth wide. In answer, the eyes of Chuz
stared back and his lips parted. Quietly, Chuz retrieved the
jawbones from Nemdur's grasp, and then he drew off the
white leather glove from his right hand. The right hand of
Chuz was constructed of brass, but the four fingers of it were
four brazen serpents that snapped and hissed. The thumb was
a fly of dark blue stone, which, released from the glove,
slowly spread its wings of azure wire and clicked its mandi-
bles together noisily.

Nemdur fell back with a cry and covered his face. When
he looked again, he was alone. Nemdur grimaced and
trembled—till he recollected the colossal purpose he might
accomplish. Then he roused the palace with his shouts, and
next all Sheve was made to listen.

From throughout the land of Sheve, men were summoned.
First summoned, presently enslaved and dragged in chains.
The soldiers of Sheve pressed far into the deserts. They took
captive the nomad peoples, the wanderers, the inhabitants of
tiny villages. Sheve made war on neighboring kingdoms, brief
holy wars. Many thousands were brought to a place seven
miles east of Nemdur's city, and here they were set to labor,
day and night, under sun, under moon and under no moon,
through storm and drought, and leaden heat and biting cold.
Their labor was to build a monstrous edifice, a pyramid of
steps to touch the sky, the world's roof, and beyond.

Nemdur's dark queen came to him at dusk with all her

most subtle allurements, but Nemdur was like a child. There
was no longer anything lusty in him, his spirit now was fever.

"My lord," said the woman, "why will you waste yourself
on this blasphemy? I long to bear you a son. There is another
tower you might raise, better than that thing of brick and
wickedness in the desert. Raise me the tower of your love,
my lord, and forget the other."

But though Nemdur heard her voice, her words were like
gibberish. It was to him as if she spoke in another tongue.

And when his councillors ventured to persuade him from
his madness, they too spoke in this alien tongue, or another
tongue even more alien. And when Nemdur's people ran to
him as he rode through Sheve and out of the gate and over
the dunes toward the Tower, when they sobbed and begged
him to be merciful, not to send their men to die from the
harsh unremitting labor, to consider the times of planting and
harvesting which in the desert must be observed particularly,
Nemdur paid no heed. It was like a howling of dogs, growling of lions, screeching of wild birds.

And the Tower grew. Three tiers it raised, and then a further three. Its base, they say, was almost a mile square and a
tenth of a mile high—only its base. In that season, to ask
how high might be the sky was no idle question. The base of
the Tower was of sun-baked clay on a frame of stone and
palm wood. Three score oases lost their trees to support that
base. Those kingdoms Sheve had recently conquered must
send tribute of wood and stone to Nemdur.

The second tier of the Tower was also of wood and brick.
For this, two score oases gave up their shade.

The third tier was reinforced with the bones of men. There
were sufficient by then, those who had died during the building, their hearts burst, their blood thinned or dashed out of
them when they fell. Sometimes, in their dizziness and
sickness, men fell like rain from the tiers of the Tower.

Three tiers, a further three, a further three upon those
three and three.

And further tiers, and further. Until there is no knowing
the count of the tiers of the Tower of Nemdur.

To begin with, Nemdur would walk up the broad zigzag of
the stairs which made ladders on the Tower, now slanting
from left to right, and now from right to left. But deliberately
these stairways were formed wide enough to accommodate

chariots and horses, camels and carriages, elephants if need be, and possibly even creatures that were not of the natural order. Mounted, Nemdur would race up the steps of the Tower, heedless of the drop that gaped below now on his left hand, now on his right. And the king's household must follow him, in litters and in wheeled vehicles drawn by toiling horses.

As they went up, the desert sank away. The desert became a tawny chart, where features were marked in blots and smudges, here the charcoal line of a road, there the bright dab of water, and there the mosaic of the city, poured to the horizon. But ascending higher, the horizon extended itself to contain the city. Blue-rimmed the sand, as if the sky had stained its edges. And now the air was more immediate than the earth.

How high now, on the mountain of the Tower? High enough that eagles soared level with the heads of the nervous horses. Looking up, to the levels above, men might see a cloud or two braceleting with amber those levels. The land was like a mist below, the land looked insubstantial as once the sky had looked. And the sky was hard and solid.

The atmosphere changed, was thin and rare. Men panted and felt drunken. The horses crept, blood beaded their nostrils. Sometimes, a horse crashed over in the shafts. Once or twice a chariot, losing balance, tilted over the side of the mountain, riding the thin air to death.

The color of the Tower, faced with clay brick, was the color of the desert sand. The sun struck on it and it seemed to glare and to glow like molten gold.

And now the scaffolding rose ahead. Here the king's party would pause beneath canopies, wine would be sipped and stringed instruments would play haltingly, as the slaves teemed, small as beetles, over the architectural embryo above.

By night, the stars shone large and blinding. At length the Tower must thrust up through those star gardens, tearing the silver roots. At last the Tower must penetrate the sacred sphere of heaven. Rape.

"When will this be?" Nemdur would ask of his sorcerers.

And they, shuddering, would shake their rattles and cast their horoscopes.

"Soon, oh king."

But they spoke in another language to Nemdur. Only certain words could he understand: Today. Now. Victory. Conquest.

In all the lands about they knew of Nemdur's scheme, and they were afraid. The Tower had a name. It was called Baybhelu, that is: The Gate to the Gods.


What were the gods doing all this while? Did they perceive or guess the work of Nemdur and his madness? Were they at all apprehensive about his ambition?

Pale and nearly transparent as glass, fragile as the most delicate sticks of the most enduring steel, awash with the blanched violet ichors that swam about in the veinless petals of their genderless bodies, cold-eyed, self-absorbed, introspective, (almost mindless) the gods had gone on in their timeless, inanimate contemplation of infinity. But, they had noticed. At some hour in the Future, or in that timelessness of Upperearth, the Past, these ethereal beings would consign the whole of the world to death, vowing man was nothing to them. And truly, they were indifferent to him, to his deeds and his prayers, his hopes and his anguish. And yet, once before (or in years to come) they had grown irritated and had opened the valves that held back the rain. They had drowned the earth in a flood, either because the earth had utterly forgotten them, or because she had remembered them too much. So it is to be seen, the gods were not entirely as aloof as they might claim.

And now a madman built a Tower intended to shatter the floor of Upperearth, and he planned to lead an army into it. The Guardians of the Cistern of Life he meant to overwhelm, he meant to steal the Elixir from the Cistern. And worse, he would cause men, horses, chariots, *humanness* to trample through the icy tranquility of that celestial country. Sweat and blood and shouting on the frigid blue pastures, horse dung about the harpstring palaces.

Was such an event even likely? It is debatable. Few traveled to Upperearth, and they by curious methods. Once Azhrarn, Prince of Demons, had come there, or would come there, in a winged ship. Uhlume, Lord Death, had never visited, for then the gods did not die. The way into Upperearth, besides, was obscure, oblique. Higher than the moon, beyond the sun. A door that was not a door, an entrance that did not properly exist. . . . Could Nemdur ever have breached

heaven in such a forthright logical fashion as a Tower tall as
the sky?

And yet. Perhaps the rude blast of mere *intent* troubled the
gods, like the blowing of a foul wind. Even a man may kill a
gnat that has not stung him.

The gods appeared ineffectual in their effete beauty, but
they were not. Their indifference had, to a great extent, saved
men from their supernal abilities. Now, they did not exchange a word or a glance. Did one lift his head, or several?
Or did the impulse simply flow jointly from all their pure and
bloodless intellects?

Their Will, so minuscule a speck a grain of sand would
hold it, so vast it could engulf the world, seeped from the
nowhere-otherwhere of Upperearth, and drifted like a feather
to the Tower of Baybhelu.

By now, the journey from the base of the Tower to its temporary summit required most of a day.

Upon the topmost tier, beneath the scaffolding that portend-
ed the next topmost, King Nemdur had encamped his court,
and one tier down from them, the chariots, the animals, the
soldiery also camped.

The tier where the court rested was perhaps seven hundred
feet square, and a movable garden had been laid out on it to
enrich the slender atmosphere. Huge tanks of water or soil had
been borne to the place, hauled by groaning camels, wretched
horses. Green showerings of foliage sprang from these tanks,
and vines, fruits, blossoms and grasses overhung the lip of the
tier that the beasts tethered below might feed on them. In their
upper shade were erected Nemdur's dark tents, embroidered
with crimson and hung with medallions of gold. From their
looped-back portals, Nemdur's women peeped out prettily,
but they were sallow and uneasy. In a green bower, beneath a
parasol, itself like a giant flower, Nemdur sat in a carved-
bone chair. (His story is packed with bones—of children,
fowls, asses, slaves.) About him his sorcerers crowded and his
priests, divining endlessly, but their hands quivering, their
eyes bulbous. They had difficulty understanding each other
now, just as Nemdur had difficulty in understanding them.
Indeed, each who perched on Baybhelu had begun to lack
comprehension of all others. Only on the scaffolding did this
not matter. There the overseers lashed with their toothed
whips, the slaves strained at their tasks like automata. They

had never understood each other; nothing was changed. But yet, everywhere the thin air was thick with blurted sentences without meaning, and the shutting of deaf ears, such items veiled by magicians' smokes, scents of roses and palm oil, and faltering musics. While now and then, above, a shriek, as another slave plummeted from his precarious vantage. As they tumbled, hideous joke, they passed the dark Queen of Sheve, who was ascending the long stairs to her lord.

She wore a gold crescent moon in her smolder of hair— Nemdur had ordered that she wear it, for soon, he shouted, the Tower would stand as high as the moon itself, and her white face would burn against the brickwork bright as day. Later, the Tower would stand higher than the moon. The moon would lie below like a round dish of milk.

Gold was also painted on the lids and nails of the queen, and rubies were wound over her smooth black skin, but diamonds trickled from her eyes.

Nemdur saw her coming from far off. Gradually her retinue emerged from the mist that was the land, and grew visible as tiny figures winding up a steep mountain. Now her chariot climbed through a ring of eagles. Now she could look down and see the eagles bank and float on their serrated wings a quarter of a mile beneath her feet. Then she would climb, hidden for a moment, through a ring of cloud like an unraveling gauze. Sometimes the entourage would pause on the broad terraces to breathe.

All day, Nemdur watched them climbing toward him, and as the sun set, a low river of flame to the west, the second queen of Sheve was carried into the upper sky.

The stars came out like splashes of quicksilver. The evening wind soared over Baybhelu and the darkness bloomed grape-black, and the moon commenced to rise.

The Queen of Sheve stood very still to watch the moon, and she was not alone. The soldiers and the beasts on the tier below were transfixed in a strange silence. Nemdur's court hushed and pointed. A little bell flickered in the silence somewhere, a woman's anklet or the bridle of a horse; only these things were heard. Aloft, the hopeless slaves craned from their ominous skeleton of scaffolding, and the white radiance of the rising disc limned their gaunt bodies even as it limned the troughs of bricks, the struts of bones. All now in utter soundlessness.

And then a sound began. It was like smoke and lifted like smoke. It was the voice of Nemdur's dark and second weeping queen. It curled into the sky, dark as she, dark as the sky, the voice of her sorrow and her beseeching.

"O moon who governs the tides of the sea, the tides of the wombs of women, the tides of the brain's madness, carry my message with you to the door of the gods. By your pallor I swear I fear them, and by your brilliance I plead for their clemency. Take away madness from the Lord of Sheve. My soul bows down and my heart sinks upon its knees, and my mind humbles itself. My blood is water and my flesh is dust."

"What does she say?" Nemdur demanded of one of his sorcerers.

"My lord, I do not understand you," gasped the sorcerer.

And Nemdur reviled the man for speaking in a foreign tongue.

And then the moon brimmed over the improbable length of Baybhelu and the feather of the gods' Will brushed it.

Recall then that terrible law—the lowly shall be exalted, the ambitious shall be cast down. Conjure the last vision of Baybhelu, for now it passes away.

The Tower was so tall, truly it had at no time any warranty to stand. Maybe all that had kept the Tower upright indeed had been the frantic aspiration of Nemdur, the Tower being the channel into which he had poured all his strengths, those energies of life, of sex, of power.

Now, quite suddenly, the whole edifice vibrated, as if it were a string stretched taut between heaven and earth, that had been elusively plucked by a master's hand.

The vibration was gentle, harmonious, soaking through the core of the Tower, until it reached the ground. There it became a deep sullen rumble. The rumble flowed into the arteries of the desert. And then the earth shook.

The earth shook itself like an animal on whose back a predator has lodged. It spasmed, curvetted, tossed and writhed, to throw that malignity from its shoulders. Enormous fissures cracked and gaped. The sands spouted like jets of water or steam into the throbbing air. Then the noise of tearing cloth, the fabric of the Tower's foundations dividing. The cracks in the ground ran on and up the framework of the lowermost tier. Its bricks shot out, the joints and bars of

palm wood arched themselves like bows and fired off splinters
at the stars.

Abruptly that whole tremendous base glided apart from itself. Away into the dark on every side the huge walls rushed
as if on wheels, and into the chasm thus provided, falling like
an inward-gushing fountain, cascaded Baybhelu.

On the upper three tiers, the stable, the court, the tier as
yet unfinished, the ultimate madness fastened. Beasts, swept
into the moment of panic, flung themselves forward and leapt
into space. The scaffolding of the slaves utterly collapsed,
hurling its human cargo to the levels below. The cracks
which spread like a tide from step to step, from tier to tier,
were all at once negated when the central floors of each terrace began to give. Partly hollow, even as it gushed down the
Tower dropped inwards upon itself, yet casting as it did so its
outer skin away in bricks, in mortar, in screaming whirling
figures, flying hair and limbs.

Such a dew then was sprinkled upon the desert, and far
and wide, over the night-waste, the shuttered city, twenty villages. Into courtyards as among the dunes, into the cradles
of trees, upon the killing beds of roofs, through apertures,
into wells and dry canals, across the air like shooting stars, all
over the board of the night. Bricks, bodies, jeweled ornaments; flowers from the hanging garden spun like a bridal of-
fering. Broken swords, vessels of religion and magic, horses
affixed to chariots, a woman's hand with a bangle sparkling
on its wrist, a parchment which read: *I, Nemdur of Sheve,
shall conquer the gods. Who now shall unremember the name
of Nemdur?*

For sure, his name would be remembered, and used—to
frighten children with and warn them from the dangerous
path of pride.

When the thunder and the crying ended, the silence came
again, snowing down in huge soft flakes upon the wounded
land.

Nemdur was dead, buried by flesh and clay and stones and
bones. They were all dead, all but one, Nemdur's dark queen
who had abased herself before the gods. But it is doubtful
whether the gods, impartial and vaguely, almost absentmind-
edly ruthless as they had revealed themselves, would have
reacted to her supplication, or saved her because of it.

As the Tower fell, and Nemdur's second wife fell with it, an eagle came flying straight into the turmoil and bore her away with it to the west. Now there were eagles in plenty in that region, circling the Tower by day. Perhaps this eagle spied the jewels of the Queen of Sheve, the rubies, the golden crescent, flashing on her somberness. Then again, she was lovely, most lovely, and it is said that as she was, so the eagle was: black. And for amusement, sometimes, there was one who would take on him the shape of a black eagle. Azhrarn, Prince of Demons, one of the Lords of Darkness.

Whether or not it was he is unknown. The selective rescue, certainly, was more like the prank of an Eshva, the unspeaking, dreaming, lesser demons, servants of the Vazdru—of which Vazdru Azhrarn was one. Nevertheless, someone or thing bore the black woman to safety, or to a kind of safety.

Near midnight, stumbling alone and dazed across the sand, and occasionally over terrible debris loosed on the sand, Nemdur's second wife came to an oasis whose palm trees were yet standing, and in the middle of them, a yet-standing tower. It was the prison of mad Jasrin she had reached.

However, no one any longer guarded the door. Since Prince Madness had entered the walls, there had been bizarre events. A weird mooning love affair had occurred between the captain of the guard and Jasrin's girl attendant. The elder attendant had browbeaten four of the guard and they had grown like babies, sniveling when she berated them, cavorting idiotically to please her. The sixth guard had perished by drowning in the pool. After staring interminably at a torch which, though lying under the water, continued to burn, he declared: "If a torch may burn under water, may I not live under it, as the sea people do?" At which he jumped in and stretched himself on the bottom and breathed the water and died. After this, the pool being fouled, the inhabitants of the tower had been able to drink only wine, which had sent them madder than they were to begin with.

At the awful thunder of falling Baybhelu eight miles away, and the hail of ghastly remnants which followed, the five guards and the two attendants fled into the desert uttering an extraordinary clamor.

The insane former Queen of Sheve, Jasrin, who by that time was the least insane of all the persons in the stone tower, remained companionless in her chamber, dumbfounded with fear.

When she heard a step upon the stair, a distorted ghostly memory of a blond prince or a rust-haired devil stole over her. Her fear took another direction at the thought, but she was unsure whether to defend herself or to plead his friendship. Altogether her memory was unreliable. She had almost forgotten her husband since Chuz had promised her Nemdur's destruction. Possibly she had not wished to suffer further guilt. Most definitely she did not rock a bone anymore in her arms. She had become for herself a woman with misery in her past, but all amorphous, nameless. She had never wed, never been delivered of a child, never conspired with a Lord of Darkness.

In much the same way, Nemdur's second wife had also erased the shock and horror of the collapse of Baybhelu. Something had happened in the desert—what? A sharp pain in her soul warned her not to search it out. The vile objects which lay about the desert she avoided with feet and eye and reverie. The flight of the eagle had faded to a rushing of stars. If Azhrarn had taken her or consoled her or done with her anything at all, he had removed her knowledge of the event.

So she entered the stone tower, climbed the stairs, because, after Baybhelu, climbing up stairs had become the most normal of activities to her, and found Jasrin in her chamber.

Both were startled, both exclaimed. Nemdur had inconvenienced them both in greater or slighter ways. They were, in a curious fashion, bound. And in their abject strait, mortal restraint dismissed, they presently ran together and sadly comforted each other. In that embrace, their tears mingling, one who had been sane lost a fraction of sanity's burden, one who had been a maniac grew calm.

That blending, more than duty accomplished, drove punctilious Prince Chuz from the vandalized kingdom of Sheve.

But just as Chuz, one of the Lords of Darkness, was departing from that place into whatever incomprehensible place he meant to go, he met another in the midnight desert. And by the moon's cool torch, Chuz perceived that other to be also a Lord, one of his un-kindred.

Uhlume, Lord Death, Chuz might have anticipated, but not necessarily Azhrarn.

Neither was Azhrarn solitary. Behind him, ranged on the dark powder of the sand, were some of the princes of the demon Vazdru. The moon lit perfectly their pale and marvelous faces, the black-burning coals of their hair and eyes. They rode, as frequently, on the macabre elegant horses of the Underearth, of Druhim Vanashta, black horses with manes and tails like clear blue gas, and everything, of horse and rider, aclink and aglitter with gems and silver. These were demons, artisans of wickedness, yet they held their handsome features a touch aslant from Chuz, Prince Madness. They were being careful, even they, how they glanced at him, lest they see more than they desired. But as they did it, they pretended they had other reasons for the angle of their heads and eyes, toying with their rings, petting their steeds, perusing the sky. For these were demons whose pride was such that mortal pride beside it was like a blade of grass beside a cedar tree.

Only Azhrarn himself. Prince of the princes, looked directly at the hooded blond half-face of Chuz, directly in the uncanny single eye. Azhrarn the Beautiful (and beautiful he was, beautiful being a poor description) was one of the few who dared outstare Chuz; and come to that, Chuz was one of the few who dared outstare Azhrarn. Their stares were, nevertheless, wary, contemptuous, interested and enigmatic. So Lords of Darkness responded to one another. Somewhat attracted to, rather offended by, each other's existence.

Presently, Azhrarn the Beautiful (beautiful being a poor description, but the wondrous words of the flat, four-cornered earth, that did him, even so, the barest justice, are no more), presently Azhrarn spoke. He spoke in a voice that lay like dark music on the air. Chuz smiled, mouth courteously closed in Azhrarn's presence, at the sound of it. Probably Chuz was learning the voice by ear, in order to add it to his other sweeter vocalisms.

"This desert," said Azhrarn, "is strewn with dead. Your doing, un-brother?"

"Yes," said Chuz, in his nicest current voice, be it admitted, nearly as fair as Azhrarn's. "And no."

"But if no, then what are you doing here, un-brother?" inquired Azhrarn, with a display of most chillingly ironic ingenuousness.

"I might ask the same," murmured Chuz, Prince Madness.

Now Azhrarn, and all demonkind, came often to earth by night. But what had drawn them to that exact spot and in that exact hour, could only have been Baybhelu. Maybe the odor of the Tower's peculiarity had enticed them for a long while, and maybe they had been regularly in the vicinity, intrigued and titillated, as ever, by the self-destructiveness of men. Watch and proximity might support the idea of the black eagle who had rescued Nemdur's second wife. On the other hand, the eagle could have been coincidence or a phantasm of another type. It is conceivable the demons had not involved themselves in the Tower of Baybhelu until this very night, had not even learned of it, their genius concerned with unrelated evils. It might be that they had only come up here from Underearth now in the investigating manner of tenants in the basement who had heard a prodigious bang on the floor above.

"My business is my own," said Azhrarn. "Yours seems somewhat broadcast." And he nodded to a bloodstained brick not two paces from his horse's silver hooves.

Chuz tossed his dice, and caught them. They were gray by this moonlight.

"Madness called me. Madness I brought. Men wished to invade the apartments of the gods. The gods threw them down."

"The gods?" said Azhrarn. A couple of the Vazdru spat upon the sand, and the sand shone like fire for a second where they had spit. "The gods are stale."

"Stale or not, the story of this night will linger. You shall see new altars raised and new temples built and much reverence offered in panic to the stale gods, after this night. Shall you be jealous, un-brother Azhrarn?"

"What is a mortal century to our Lord of Lords?" called out one of the Vazdru scornfully, but still not quite looking at Chuz. "In the blink of a long-lashed eye in Druhim Vanashta, that century is gone."

"In a century," said Chuz, "humanity may forget—many things."

"What is keeping you, Chuz?" said Azhrarn. "You must be

irked, being from home so long. I will not detain you further."

"Nor will you dismiss me," said Chuz. "Even you, my dear, have had, or will have, a taste or two of me."

Then Chuz vanished.

The Vazdru maintained a distraught quietness, awaiting, disturbed, their Lord's reaction. But after a little, Azhrarn said softly: "The stink of madness is unsubtle here. Let us be going."

And like a stormy dream, the Vazdru also disappeared, leaving the desert empty, but not empty enough, under the cruel moon, forever above and never below the scope of men.

# PART ONE

## *The Souring of the Fruit*

# CHAPTER 1

## Storytellers

There was strong music in the sky: the music of sunset. In the west, a wall of clear red amber through which the sun went blazing down. The remainder of the sky was smoky rose, a color like a perfume—musk. The earth had given up its tinctures. Heights and depths and long dunes were melting into the air. But there was another music on the earth, a music of drums, tabors, bells and pipes, a music of voices and shouts, the churn of wheels and the stamp of feet. And presently, too, as the limitless lamp of the sky burned low, the small yellow lamps burned up on the plains beneath, a swarm of fireflies, all moving, and all one way. The music of the setting sun and the music of men flowed together into the west.

"Where are you going?" They had asked on the broad roads, the slender tracks, at the gates of oases and by village fences. "Where are you going with so much song?" And the answer was returned with the song: "We are going to Bhelsheved, to worship the gods!"

And the question, being as much a tradition as the answer, was the signal in the places by the way. The people here put aside their buying and selling, their husbandry, their toil, gave over their quarrelling and their deeds of love, and followed the procession, adding to it their own music, with the flames of new lamps in their hands. On this route alone, seven thousand went dancing, to the beat of drums, over the desert to mystical Bhelsheved.

When the sun was gone, the seven thousand halted, though

the sound of their music intermittently continued. To such an accompaniment, a sprawling campment was made, and fires were kindled, scattering the sands, as if droplets had rained from the falling sun. The scents of roasting meat and baking bread rose with the melodies and the lights. But there was scarcely any order in that camp, and scarcely any watch was kept. What need? Religious fervor was the motivation of this people who danced across the desert. The cold of the night could not harm them, nor the predatory roaming of wild beasts. No thieves or villains of any sort could linger in such a company. No hint of deceit or wickedness.

And the sky faded, became a pale glimmering blue, like the ashes of a flower. The stars appeared from behind the sky. And from the desert, a man, tall and slim, came walking like a panther among the tents and fires.

A girl was kneeling in the pool of the dusk, feeding three or four black sheep. She raised her head, and looked after the man as he passed. When her tan-haired sister came from the tent, the girl pointed. "See, Zharet, *he* is here again."

"Indeed, one cannot mistake him, even from the back," said the second girl, and her eyes shone like still flames. "He walks like a king."

"But he has no servant with him, and no guard."

"Perhaps he has no need of them, being his own state."

"But who," whispered the first girl, "has ever seen him pass among us by day?" Tan-haired Zharet thought, *I should be happy enough to see him by night.* She was to be married to a cousin she had scarcely met. She pictured the stranger as her bridegroom, and closed her eyes.

But by now, the stranger, in his inky cloak, had disappeared from their view, though others saw him, looked at him, whispered similarly, dreamily:

"Who is he?"

"Who has seen him under the sun?"

"I saw him by moonlight."

"Was he a ghost, or a spirit?"

"Only if they are very handsome, for he is so."

Others were less pensive.

"There goes that dark one. On such a journey as ours, there should be no malcontents, but *he* is bent on mischief, I believe."

"In all the years I have gone to Bhelsheved there was never

anything stolen or any trouble, yet three nights ago my cousin's black goat vanished from its pen. Only the bones were found—"

"He has a murderer's stealth."

"He walks like a shadow."

And some who were not elegant said: "He is too elegant to be honest." And some who were not tall said: "He is too tall to be trusted," and some who were intuitive shuddered, though they were not sure why.

Other things happened, as the stranger passed. A pet bird pecked through the last bit of wicker on its cage—it had pecked at the wicker very earnestly for three successive nights, each time the stranger had gone by—and flying out of the cage and through the tent opening, it darted after the black-cloaked man, and fluttered round him. Though he did not slacken his pace, the man reached into the air and took the bird in his hand. It was a notable hand, articulate and strong, with long, long fingers. The nails were also rather long, like those of some mighty ruler who need do no work, yet not pointed, but squarely and smoothly tipped, and with each a silver crescent marked on it. The bird trembled in this cool and gentle grip, and stared up into the face which was visible only to itself, for a fold of the man's cloak otherwise obscured his countenance. A moment later, the tiny bird soared into the deepening sky. It seemed to think itself an eagle, or some great mythical fowl of night. It cast itself toward the vault of heaven with an impassioned inspiration surely too fierce for its fragile wings to sustain.

(In just such a way, the black goat had eaten an exit from its patched-together pen. It had followed the stranger into the desert, and a lion had crept up on both of them. Seeing the man, the lion had thrown itself down, rolling on its back like an enormous kitten, growling and purring. But when the man had gone, the lion remembered the goat, and turned immediately to kill and devour it. The man had looked over his shoulder once. His eyes, appearing for a second from the midnight of his cloak, gleamed like two black stars, with a cruel pity, an ironic, sympathetic, merciless regret.)

A skin of wine stood in the sand before a pavilion. The cork leapt from its mouth as the stranger's shadow slid over it, upsetting the skin, so it toppled. The wine gushed into the sand, like a libation.

A lean dog howled for no apparent reason, and burrowed under the cushions of its master's bed.

A mechanical doll, which for a year had not stirred, suddenly began to march up and down on a child's knee.

A rose, in a pot, shed all its petals.

A dead twig, in a bundle ready for the flames, put forth a bud.

At one large fire, near the center of the camp, certain philosophers and elders, and men in authority of various kinds, sat about, and nearby there were professional storytellers seated under their scented lamps. Many of the people who had come on the joyous religious pilgrimage to Bhelsheved, were gathered here, to listen. As was suitable, the tales were all concerned with the glory and beneficence of the gods.

At this hour, just before the moon's ascent, they were telling the antique and relevant history of the foolishness of Nemdur, the king of Sheve. How, seeking to belittle the gods, he had built a blasphemous tower of many tiers, destined to pierce heaven. But the gods, aware that such knowledge and such powers as the Upper Regions might afford men would be damaging to them, had prudently cast down the tower. Only Nemdur's queen, who had implored the pardon of the gods, they had saved. Thereafter, the area had been sacred. Men would come from far and wide to witness the ruins of the mighty tower, and the ruinous city nearby, forsaken Sheve, and to make sacrifices and offer prayers to the masters of heaven.

At this point in the story, a child interrupted from the crowd, asking fearfully and loudly if the gods were terrible to behold. The storytellers smiled, and bowed to the philosophers. One of these, a venerable elderly man, spoke gravely to the child. "No, indeed. The gods are beautiful, and just. Those who reverence and obey them need fear nothing from the gods. The gods reward those who adhere to them. Those who stray, they punish. Then they are terrible, terrible in their perfection and magnificence."

"But," said the child anxiously, "what do they *look* like?"

The philosopher was done, however, and the storytellers proceeded with their tale. "Hush!" said the child's nurse sharply.

"But," said the child, "if I cannot tell them from their

looks, how am I to know them and beware of offending them?"

Then a voice spoke to the child, a voice which brushed the insides of the child's ears, wonderfully unexpected, like the sound of the sea inside a shell.

"The gods are colorless as crystal for they have no blood in their veins. Neither do they possess breasts or genitals. Their eyes are cold as their country where everything is tinted by frost. But you will probably never meet them; they have no liking for the world."

"Oh," said the child, and looked up and saw the pale face of a man bending over it, a face so astonishing it dazzled the eyes of the child like the moon.

Then the child, dazzled, blinked, and in the little interval of that blink, the man was gone.

The storytellers were telling now of how some hundreds of years came and went across the desert. Of how divination excelled prophecy, and omen excelled divination, and visions excelled everything. A group of holy men dwelling in the ruins of Nemdur's Sheve, began to exhort others that came there to build a second city upon the wreck of the first, a city every stone of which was to be laid in praise of the gods.

Men will do much in hate. In love they will do more, much more.

They worked under the lash of love, as the slaves had worked who built the tower of Nemdur's madness, under the lashes of agony and death. What time had left of Sheve was razed. From the broken stones, like a mirage, the second city bloomed into the air. A strange city, a small city. A rare city, unlike all others. For this was to be no home for commerce or domesticity. Along its colonnades, and beneath its cupolas, the tide of men should pass only at one season of the year, when the people came in to worship, and so lay down the fruits of their year of life elsewhere. A city which was to be kept pure—a temple: Bhelsheved.

As they worked on it, digging through the crusts of the antique streets of Sheve, they struck water, the desert's blue gold, a secret lake. And this turquoise eye, gazing back into heaven, was, to the builders, a seal of the gods' favor upon their enterprise.

The crowd drifted out a sigh. They began spontaneously to sing, one more song of their journey. How, at this apex of

each year, the peoples would turn toward Bhelsheved. From
the west, from the north, from the south and from the east,
flowing inward like sheep toward their pen, like wine into a
bowl, as a tired man into sleep, so naturally did they move
toward the sacred city. And we, the people cried, who come
from the east into the west, follow every night the sun, which
itself flies to Bhelsheved to honor the gods, Bhelsheved, where
all sorrow is forgotten, all pain is healed.

When the song ended, the crowd was happy and boister-
ous, and someone called for the story of how the gods had
saved the world when the Evil One, the Prince of Demons,
would have destroyed it.

The storytellers chuckled, for this tale was well-thumbed in
their minds, being ever popular. They took it in turns to
relate the legend. Night's Master, they said, the Black Beast
who lurked underground (so hideous to look on that he himself avoided at all times mirrors or any reflective surface)
saw the piety and comeliness of humanity, and geared a force
of evil sufficiently gigantic that the earth was overwhelmed.
Yet, in its death throes, the gods heeded the prayers and
pleadings of men. They cast a golden bolt out of the sun itself that scorched the demon so terribly that he was obliged to
withdraw, and his disgusting energies with him.

At the riotous description of this singed monstrosity scram-
bling underground, the crowd roared with laughter. There
was only one in all the throng who did not laugh. At the edge
of the inner ring now, the man in the black cloak was standing. The glow from the lamps of the storytellers caught him,
and the fold of material had slipped away from his face. He
was not merely pale, at last, the stranger, but whiter than
chalk, and his mouth whiter yet. His eyes seared with a dry
and inextinguishable black fire. He was so still, so silent, that
gradually stillness and silence spread from him, through the
circles of the crowd, as if his immobility had become one re-
sounding chord struck over and over against the night.

Even the storytellers came to hear this noiseless chord.
They too fell quiet, turning to gaze at him, shading their eyes
against their own lamplight. Even the philosophers stared.

Finally, when the soundlessness had spread all through the
congregation, the man spoke.

"It seems," he said, and his voice carried, as a wave will

run across the sand, "that if the creature you speak of is so vile as you insist, you had better beware of him."

The crowd muttered. The philosopher who had addressed the child now addressed the man.

"Sir, we need not fear the Demon. We are but a day's journey from Bhelsheved. Here, of all places, the gods will protect us from him."

"Will they indeed," said the stranger. Then, for the first time, he smiled. The eyes of the philosopher briefly faltered, but he was on his way to the holy city, and the appearance and demeanor of a man could not undo him.

"Should it happen," said the philosopher, "that the Evil One finds himself able to harm us, then we should understand that we had in some way offended the gods—that we had *deserved* any evil that thereafter came upon us."

"Ah," said the stranger. He lowered his lids as if he mused. When he looked up again, it was like a dawn, a sunless dawn, but of colossal radiance. "I, too," said the stranger, "will render you a story."

So beautiful he was, and his voice so beautiful, very few in the crowd were able to recognize the extent of such beauty and such marvel. As a man would look at one quarter of the night sky, and wonder at the stars, putting from his mind all those myriads of stars his eyes, at one glance, could not take in, just so they looked at and attended to the stranger, thinking to themselves that he was very handsome, and spoke very well, putting from their minds that in every respect he was beyond them, scalding them, drugging them, stunning them, with his mere presence.

The man walked straight into the center of the lampglow and the storytellers made way rather nervously for him, envious of their trade. A little night breeze came and went across the desert and the camp, fluttering the soft fires in the lanterns. The stranger's cloak blew back from his shoulders, as if the wind stirred it, though it was not the wind. That cloak folded itself behind him like two black wings, and the blue light of many distant stars was on his hair. A great pulse seemed to beat through the atmosphere, the very ground. The wind lay down on the sand at his feet like his dog, and he began to tell the story.

It was this: A prince happened to be walking in the cool of the evening, along the border of the country which abutted on his own estates. There was no law in this country, and so the prince was not greatly amazed when he discovered that all the people in the place were being slain systematically by a fearsome monster which had evolved in their very midst. Now the prince had always been interested in the antics of his neighbors, and seeing their trouble and that they were likely to be annihilated, he took it on himself to seek out the monster and get rid of it.

Accordingly, he left his own estates, and wandered across the lawless land, through all the ghastly disruption which the monster had caused. At length, he located the creature's lair, and standing on the barren rock outside, he called it forth. Forth it came, and awful it was, obese and bloated with the blood and distress of men, and swollen with its strength. But the prince did not falter. He drew from its silver sheath the only sword he possessed. He went forward and began to hack and slash at this grisly foe. Lightnings wailed and thunders bellowed. The earth was riven and split. The monster exhaled poisonous fire and rains of steel splinters. The prince was burned and torn, thin needles pierced him; his eyes, which had been most beautfiul, were put out. But blinded and in agony, he did not forego the fight. For centuries, or so it seemed to him, in the supremest anguish and horror, he battled, and at last, at last, the loathsome beast lay dead. But, on its carcass, the body of the prince fell down, equally lifeless.

At this point, the stranger turned slowly about, looking at all the crowd, and into every face it seemed, and into every pair of eyes with his own curious and unfathomable glance. His voice had cast a spell on them. The story seemed quite real. It hurt them to hear him tell it, as it seemed also to hurt him, though they could not reckon how they knew so much, for his tone was harmoniously even, his face clear of all expression.

It transpired, the storyteller said, the subjects of the prince came to look for him, and eventually they found his corpse. Then, knowing something of sorcery, they went about the task of restoring him. But one ingredient of his restoration was nothing else but tears. This appeared, under the circumstances, an easy element to obtain. The prince's subjects went instantly to the folk of the neighboring country, for whom he had sacrificed himself, and asked them to weep for him. But these good neighbors averted their faces, and declared: "We know who you mean, and we do not credit you. We shall not shed one tear for the prince of such liars."

"And was that not strange?" said the storyteller to the crowd. Some shivered as they heard him. In some there came a bizarre welling of guilt, of shame and fear. . . . "But the strangest portion of the story is to come."

The subjects of the prince shed their own tears, and these proved adequate to raise him at last out of the gray limbo in which he had lain all this while imprisoned. But, being restored, as he was traveling back to his kingdom, he chanced to look over into the neighboring land. All was lawless as ever, but now a massive festival was in progress. Moved by curiosity, the prince drew near, and presently he saw and heard these things. His neighbors had erected a formless stone, and were dancing around it to the joyful noise of pipe and drum, and now and then someone would embrace the stone, or pour oil or wine or aromatics over it. Fascinated— for he truly was fascinated—the prince inquired what rites were in progress.

"We are venerating this incredible and kind god," the neighbors replied, "who saved us from a fearful monster."

The prince observed the stone for some while, but that was all it was—a stone. Rugged, passionless, insensible.

Presently, he remarked, "Pardon my foolishness, but I had heard it was a lord from over your border, who sought out the monster with a sword, and slew it."

At this, the neighbors spat. "We have heard that lie, too," they said, "but that ugly and misshapen fiend from the next estate is more foul to us than the monster itself. Pray do not mention his name again."

For a long while after the stranger had ceased speaking, the crowd sat on in silence. Almost every head was bowed, as if in deep thought—or in humiliation. Yet the crowd did not comprehend what had come over it, this unpleasing doubt in the midst of celebration.

Then the philosopher spoke primly and loudly to the stranger's back.

"A peculiar notion, sir, if I have your drift. It seems you instruct us that the Unspeakable One, the Lord of Shadows, was, at some time, savior of the world."

The dark storyteller did not look about. He said: "You

have presumed the gods value man so much that they will hurry to his rescue. I think you misjudge the gods."

"And you," declared the philosopher sternly, "suggest that they are merely as stones."

"There, I admit, I have maligned them. For if you strike a stone, it may disgorge a stream of water, or a precious jewel. Or you may build a house from it, or scratch words on its surface with a knife. *Stones* can be serviceable to men."

"Your blasphemy is uncouth," said the philosopher, and the crowd began sulkily to grumble and mutter, taking its cue from him. "You had best remember Baybhelu, and how the tower was shaken down by the gods, to cure mankind of its pride."

"Pride?" asked the stranger caressingly. "What have you to be proud of? Your lives, which perish in the blink of an eye? Your memories which are shorter still? Your brains which are so empty of wits that spiders may spin there? Or is it your religion which makes you proud, that sweet and succulent fruit of faith? A fruit may sour. Whatever else, if any Lord of Darkness was unwise enough in the past to have saved you from yourselves, he will not do it ever again."

It was only much later that they noted he had spoken of mankind as "you," and not as "we."

When he had finished, an uncanny thing occurred. Although the air was still, a wind came, without sound and hardly any motion, and blew out the lights in each of the lamps, and smothered all the flames round about, so that suddenly the whole area was in blackness, but for the glints of the stars, millions of miles away.

In the blackness, he was gone. And, relighting their fires, they were glad of his departure, though they did not know him for Azhrarn. Some indeed, weighing their rage above their unease, set out to search for him, for the philosophers vowed such a blasphemer must be scourged.

It is conceivable that they had already scourged Azhrarn, centuries of this particular scourge, they and their forebears. Although it is unarguably true he had no right to take the attitude with them that he did. No rights at all to his righteous anger, he who had played games with humankind for eons, and before humankind, who knows but that he had not played games with the little creatures that crawled from the seas of chaos aboard the flat, four-cornered earth, the minus-

cule sparks and atomies with which mortal life had begun.
And having played so often with them—like a child who
fears to lose its toys—so he had seen the loss of them. He
had once sacrificed himself to save the world because without
the world to torment and tangle, he knew his own immortality would be dull. Or so they said, the poets, the songs, the
stories.

Certainly, he had known for centuries that his act had
been mislaid, set at the wrong door, that of Upperearth.
But certainly now, demonstrated so vigorously, their forget-
fulness stung him, the shock all the more violent for being
delayed, perhaps. If he beheld this frenzied worship of the indifferent gods and was jealous, how much more bitter to find
himself unremembered—worse—remembered wrongly. Azhrarn the Beautiful, to be recalled as *shambling* and *hideous*. Maybe it was this slight upon his vanity that had the
most incensed him.

Or could it be that this Lord of Fear had committed, for
whatever selfish reason, an act of unique and total love, and
some part of him had expected to be loved for it? And now
he discovered he was not. Discovered that he was laughed at.
Discovered, more terrible than anything, his own unrealized,
erroneous expectation.

Several bands of young men went searching through the
campment for the blasphemer. They carried staves and sticks,
and some had knives ready, and one or two had the long
bull-hide whips they had brought with them on this journey
to alarm lions and men alike.

"How shall it be," they had said to each other, "that we
should gain the holy city with this wretch walking free in our
midst? Does the city not sing a welcome as men approach it?
And surely will it not groan with anger if this devil goes
near? Let us hurry after him and beat him."

So they searched up and down and round and about,
causing a great commotion, overturning cooking pots and the
fragile supports of tents, blundering among the goats and the
sheep, frightening the children and the young girls, and all
the time uttering furious oaths and threats.

At first, there was not a sign of the stranger. He might
have dissolved into the air or been changed into sand. Then
they began to catch glimpses of him—at this turning, or that;

among the shadows between two pavilions; crossing through a pen of animals, not disturbing them any more than the passage of night itself. Yet, whenever the pursuers pursued, the stranger was no more to be seen.

There were three brothers, full of wine and religion and with a whip apiece, and soon they lost patience with their fellows and broke away to hunt on their own.

"I believe," said the youngest, "the old venerable philosopher could get us some special relic of Bhelsheved from the priests, some gold talisman, perhaps, if we bring this villain to justice."

"Very unlikely," said the middle brother. "But who knows what blessings the gods themselves will heap on the heads of whoever champions them?"

"One thing," said the oldest brother, twitching the whip he carried, "I have a suspicion the blasphemer is also a mage, and a shape-changer. How else has he eluded us so long?"

Just at this moment, they entered an open unfrequented place between the tents. There in the starlight, on the charcoal darkness of the sand, stood the one they sought.

At sight of him, the youngest brother immediately uncoiled and lashed out with his whip. As if it were a falling scarf, the stranger raised one hand and caught the whip's savage tongue, and so held it.

The young man was astounded. No shout of pain had attended the stranger's weird action, and now another astonishment was in progress. A cool wild light had sprung from the stranger's grip, and began to glide, pulsating, down the length of the whip. The youngest brother glared at this light, perceived its direction, which was toward himself, and made to let go the whip's handle, at which he found he could not. Learning this, he was the one to yell aloud, but no sooner had he yelled than the thread of light ran into the handle. Intuitively he braced himself for pain, for the glow along the whip resembled a sort of stilly pouring lightning. But then the force of the light passed into his hand, and at once he knew it to be no pain at all, but an exquisite pleasure. Through knuckles, wrist and forearm, elbow joint and upper arm the sensation raced like silver wires, so into breast and torso, into limbs and loins and spine and skull. With a moan, the youngest brother fell to the earth, and presently his ecstasy caused him to faint.

At that, Azhrarn let go the end of the whip and the light died in it.

The two older brothers, gaping, now at their swooning kindred, now at the magician, declined any further aggressive moves, and lowered their arms, so the lengths of hide straggled in the sand.

"You observe," said Azhrarn eventually, "that I have returned you delight for injury."

"We observe," said the oldest brother, "that you are a sorcerer."

"Oh, how you flatter me," said Azhrarn. His voice was cold, too cold for them to understand how cold it was, seeming warmer than it was, just as ice can burn.

"A magician would travel in state," protested the middle brother stupidly, "with his servants and his riches. Or come riding through the sky on a black horse winged like a raven."

On the sand, the fainting brother revived, and murmured, "He is not a magician, but a god."

Such are the credentials of pleasure.

But Azhrarn turned his shoulder, and walked through the fabric of the evening as if through a narrow door, and was gone again.

The oldest brother went to the spot where the Prince of Demons had disappeared, and, looking down, he saw three dark glowing gems lying on the earth. Like the blackest of rubies they lay there, already harder than obsidian, and he, with an embarrassed terror he could not explain, hastily kicked sand over them, burying them. He could not have said what these jewels were, yet surely some part of him had known they were no less than three drops of precious Vazdru blood spilled from the fingers of Azhrarn. For when he reached and caught the whip, he who could have shielded himself from any weapon or force, save that one sheer force that was the sun itself—by which he had once died to save the world—had not shielded himself, but taken the ringing blow, cutting as any knife, across his palm.

It was a symbol, possibly, his token to the earth that she herself had cut at him. Truly, truly, he had been wounded that night, and not alone in the hand.

# CHAPTER 2

## All About Bhelsheved

The sweet and succulent fruit of faith:

From east and west, from north and south, once a year the peoples came, and gathered all about Bhelsheved. The old had seen it many times, the very young recognized it from hearsay. Ancient Sheve, which lay beneath it, had been called The Jar, for its sources of water. Bhelsheved was "The city the gods made from a jar." Yet some also named it Moon City, for it was white as the moon.

By day, in the distance, across the tawny sand and against the blue of the ether, the whiteness of Bhelsheved was like a glorious omission of color, so children, seeing it for the first, sometimes inquired, "Who has torn the sky?" By night, burning like a cliff of salt, across the dunes, the city seemed to emit its own radiance. Only those who approached it from the west, the true moon rising behind it, saw Bhelsheved darker, as if in eclipse, yet even this was the darkness of pure silver.

Being approached and used by men only at one brief season of the year, the few days of the festival of worship, the city had never been soiled. The smokes that rose there, of incense and holy fire, were not enough to smirch it. Even during the ingathering, none entered the city to profane it with the common practices of living. Instead, the camps of humanity were spread out in vast and multitudinous disorder, each and all terminating no less than a hundred paces from the outer walls. The gates stood open then at all hours of day and night, but those who came through them came as guests merely, calling on the gods in their home, bringing gifts and compliments. Never overstaying their welcome. The feastings and sports and contests that took place were conducted always outside, always one hundred paces or more from Bhelsheved's whiteness. She was so lovely, and so choice, that city, they never argued against the ban. And she repaid them, in her way. Every year, when they returned to her, it seemed she had grown lovelier.

About a mile from the city paths welled like water out of the desert. These paths were broad, all alike, and all paved with curious stones, regular, smooth and glistening. Sand blew now and then across these paths, but always it cleared itself again. No path which led to the city was ever buried in the drifts, nor even partially obscured for more than a moment. Half a mile from the city, lines of trees, perfectly shaped and manicured, sprang up beside the paths, so that suddenly those worshippers who traveled in the bald heat of the day progressed along avenues of green and liquid shade. A quarter of a mile from the city, little fountains appeared at the wayside, and little cisterns, in the forms of dainty indigenous animals or peculiar beasts out of myth, and all carved from the milk-white stone of Bhelsheved itself.

By now, the city's walls dominated the horizon. The slopes of a mountain covered with snow, such was the impression the walls gave. At their feet, luxuriant groves of trees, at this season all in blossom, nearly as white as the walls. Above the walls, the cones and steeples seemed to tremble like white towers of hibiscus, white hyacinths, and the white birds streamed from tower to tower, like bees in search of nectar.

There were four great gates, facing to the four quarters of the world. These gates were each of three shades of whiteness: the harsh white of steel, set with panels the gentle sallow white of ivory, and studded with enormous polished pallid zircons.

As the people approached, the city sang to them. Initially, in the distance, a faint, faint sound which, as they drew nearer and nearer, grew louder and louder, swelling to greet them. The song was a melodious yet uncanny thrumming—a thunder which whispered, the buzzing of a thousand wasps in a hive of glass—

The processions poured in across the shining sandless paths to Bhelsheved, and the extraordinary hymn foamed from the pristine cauldron of the city. When they reached their hundred paces of proximity, the hymn dissipated in the sky.

They stood in wonder, the visitors, a wonder which was never decreased, listening to the quiet which followed the song, beneath the unmelting hill of desert snow, birds flashing over the hibiscus minarets.

"It is like a city of the gods," men declared, unaware the gods possessed no cities, nor wished to possess them.

And those who reached Bhelsheved by night also heard the song unfold from the city into the sky, like a pillar of invisible, audible steam. And by night, the domes were lit, great ghostly pearls, and the night flowers bloomed in the groves, and the air surged with perfumes, which came and went like spirits.

Thus, the exterior of Bhelsheved.

Within, it was this way:

Entering at one of the four tall gates, the worshipper found himself on a wide straight concourse, paved on this occasion in mosaics of the most pastel marbles, none of which depicted either scene or pattern, but nebulous swirlings, like those of vapors or clouds. Such an ethereal road led from each of the four gates, toward the heart of the city. And on all sides of the four roads stood temples pressed close to each other, as in a mortal city houses would have pressed close. Some of the buildings were massive, pouring up their flowerlike snow domes into the sky, shot with windows internally lit and of a heavenly blue glass, each window itself set in the form of a flower or a leaf or some abstract shape that hinted at supernal reveries. Some of the buildings were delicate and small, alabaster figurines, crystal pinnacles. Pleated stairways went up and down like the keys of strange instruments. Colonnades led in and out, their pillars carved like women or like trees. Trees which were real blossomed inside the city as out. If a wind blew, a snowstorm of petals fell.

At the core of the sacred city, the four roads ended on the rim of the miraculous lake, that turquoise of water which had seemed the seal of the gods' approval. And up over the turquoise arched four white bows of bridges, making ovals with their white reflections below. The four white bridges met in a diadem of light, the central fane of Belsheved, which was not of white stone, but plated over, like a fabulous liz-

ard, with scales of palest gold. The rich kernel of the sweet
fruit of faith.

Men declared: "See, it is like the mansion of a god."

But it was not, for the mansions of the gods were shafts of
psychic material which probably no man could have seen,
even had he been able to enter the Upperearth and gaze
thereon.

Standing on the bridges, which were ornately carved, the
golden architecture before them,. the shining orb of water
beneath, those who came to worship presently beheld white
robed figures moving, like sprites, through the misty interior
of the fane.

While the people lived elsewhere, returning to this, the
fount of their religion, once only in a year, some few dwelled
always in Bhelsheved, to tend it, and to keep alive the flames
which burned there, and to nurture the flowers which
bloomed there, to the glory of the gods, and to see to all the
other esthetic tasks of the city.

They were chosen, these few, from a certain type. Somehow, some idea of the physical appearance of the gods was
already current, and had been tailored to mortal standards.
All who served the city were good to look upon, very slender
of build, and of a pale translucence of skin which was perpet-
uated by the rigorous fasts, diets and medications of their order. Their hair, both male and female, was of a general hue,
a gold blanched almost to platinum.

Their characteristics were select, their glances obscure,
their gestures flowing. They seemed sublimely unaware, removed from the roughness, the sheer red meat of humanity.

Yet, it was from among the people that they were chosen,
those elevated ones. Although the people deliberately forgot
the origin of their priests and priestesses, just as they forgot
that the city had been built by their own wealth, designed by
their own mathematicians and scholars, and imbued with sorceries by their own mages.

When the priestly servants of heaven approached them,
they bowed and trembled pleasantly with respect and awe.

At the heart of the golden temple, mounted on the backs
of two vast golden beasts that had the heads of hawks, the
fore-bodies of lions and the tails of gigantic fish, was an altar
of translucent sky-colored crystal, in which opaline clouds
and constellations seemed to float. When the temple had been

filled with people, the doors were closed, and in the honey gloom, the astrological altar began to blaze. The servants of heaven sang in sweet thin voices as they stood fearlessly between the paws of the two beasts, which would then suddenly open their beaks and cry, in a brazen resonance: *Who loves the gods shall know everlasting joy!*

Then a second sun would seem to explode slowly outward from the altar, a glare which must surely blind, yet did not, for in the midst of it were seen visitations which came and went. None after could describe what they had witnessed. Some spoke of the forms of the gods themselves passing luminously to and fro in a sort of gorgeous fog. Others spoke of scenes of happiness from their own lives reenacted, or prophecies of good things to come. Some coyly mentioned glimpses of a paradise, or visions of other worlds. Many wept and many laughed aloud, and a few collapsed on the mosaic floor where the tightness of the crowd permitted.

But when the great brilliancy faded, they gathered themselves, moved dazedly to the reopened doors, and filed away meekly to offer blood or precious gems or wine in the glittering temples that stood everywhere about the lake. And through filigree screens, to half-seen confessors beyond, they would recite their sins and their apprehensions—which, in those moments seemed unmomentous, easy both of telling and of future avoidance. For it appeared to them their souls had been washed clean and sponged with glorious elixirs. So they sawed through the throats of little lambs and burnt their flesh on blue fires, sobbing at their luck, that they, and all things, were in the care of the merciful and gentle gods.

The dunes of day drifted over the sky and were blown beyond the edge of the western earth. The darker sands of night piled up on the threshold of the sunset, and eventually buried it.

A young man came walking slyly, with an oddly hesitant yet urgent step, between the clusters of the tents. Fires and lamps and stars were blooming on the dusk, and the pale ghost of the city, like the sail of some anchored ship, rested over the many-ringed campments. The young man, a youngest brother, had come far from his own camping place, across the makeshift byways, and far around the city walls, though keeping always the prescribed one hundred paces out from them. A cloak was folded around him, though the night was warm.

Presently he reached a grove of scented trees, where some girls were drawing water from one of the ornamental troughs.

One by one, these girls caught sight of the youngest brother far from his own camp. They saw him to be a stranger, and one or two, for the barest instant, held their breath, for there had been another stranger who sometimes walked about the camps by night, but he had been cloaked as if with inky wings. . . . This one was no one of importance, his manner diffident, his face muffled, and the maidens began to giggle at him somewhat behind their sleeves.

At length, the young man beckoned to one of the girls, and when she approached him, said: "Pardon my interruption of your duties, but I am searching for the tent of the satchel-maker."

"Would that be Grizzle-Beard the satchel-maker that you mean? Or the other, with the limp?"

"Or," chimed in another of the girls boldly, "do you mean old Twisty-Nose, whose wife resembles a goat?"

The young man lowered his eyes, and pulled his cloak yet more tightly around him. He seemed to be carrying something beneath the cloak, perhaps a satchel that required mending.

"I think it must be he you call Twisty-Nose," said the young man. "If he dwells at the edge of the camp, nearest to the dessert."

"There is no satchel-maker there," declared another girl.

"Then I have mistaken—" began the young man anxiously, and broke off as another girl interrupted.

"He is looking for the limping one who pitched his tent farther out yesterday, saying our noise disturbed his religious meditations. I doubt," she added, "he will do any satchel business with you, he wishes to think only pious thoughts."

"Nevertheless," said the young man, "may I ask you to guide me to the spot?"

The girls tossed their hair at him like a pride of lionesses.

"It is not so far. Can you not find your own way, a big strong ox like yourself?"

"Alas," said the youngest brother, "I am at a disadvantage, being quite sightless in one eye."

At this, the girls were abashed. They might have been expected, in the vicinity of the holy city, to have behaved better to a disabled man, and indeed spoken more graciously altogether.

"I will guide you," the bold girl said quickly. And she hurried to the part-sighted man, and took his hand. "It is this way."

Leaving the others to their unexpiated discourtesy, the girl led the traveler between the trees and the tents, and soon into that more isolated area of the camping grounds, where the shelters were infrequent and scattered.

The shadows were thickening on the land, though the sky was taking on the lambent sheen of starshine. The disabled traveler paused abruptly, shifting about as if troubled.

"What is the matter?"

"I had a purse to offer the satchel-maker and just now I felt it fall from my belt."

"I heard no chink of coins."

"No surprise in that. My coins are too sparse to make much noise. Please look on the ground, and see if you can find my money, for I can make out little in the darkness."

So the girl bent to the ground, seeking the purse she had not heard fall. As she did this, the disabled traveler grasped her all at once in a dreadful grip. His hands clamped over her nostrils and her mouth, oblivious to her frantic clawing and struggling, until, from lack of air, she grew insensible.

Lions patrolled the desert. Now one more lion was abroad. It bore the dangling figure of a maiden, not in its jaws, but across it arms. It had, besides, certain aids and tools a lion did not resort to—a length of rope, a length of cloth, another length coiled over and over, the length of a whip.

Out across the night-stained sands, much beyond the fringes of the various campments, their lights, their songs, their religion, and farther still beyond the notice of the gods of Bhelsheved. Here, by a rock, the youngest brother bound the girl with rope and cast her on the earth. Here he stoppered her pretty mouth with the ugly gag. And here he uncoiled and flexed that whip of his, that whip which he had raised against Azhrarn, and which the Prince of Demons had captured in one hand. Cool lightning had poured up the length of the whip, through the handle, into the body of the youngest brother, and become a delirium. He had not ceased remembering it. It had become a sweet torture. Ultimately, a solution insinuated itself.

He raised the whip now, and brought it down. At the impact of its wicked edge on flesh, cutting as a knife, he felt the light—invisible, yet positively experienced in every nerve—begin to come to him along the swinging bull's hide. At the second stroke it sank up through the handle. At the third stroke, pleasure, like a branch of silver, flowered along his arm, and he groaned.

At the ninth stroke, with a scream, the youngest brother dropped unconscious on the sand.

Later, when the moon was rising, he roused, with a ghastly apprehension, a weight of lead upon limbs and heart. He crawled, as if abject, to regard the object of his affection. He leaned to her bloody shoulder, but she had died at the seventh blow, a vital vein severed, before she woke—in that at least her fate had been kind to her.

As the moon stole up the sky, spying on his deed, the madman buried his victim in the dunes, and smeared her blood from his hands with their powders. Tears of horror bathed his cheeks, he was sickened to his soul. But at the memory of the whip, and the light which had flowed from it, his pulse quickened, and in despair he knew he must kill again and again. Such was the visitation of love he had received, and such the black-haired "god" who had brought it.

As the young man returned through the groves, he saw a lost child, sleeping under a tree. No one was near—the brother uncoiled his whip. The child had no space to scream; its throat was severed at the first blow—again fate was as clement as it could be, having written such a stern sentence. The brother's own scream he bit back, strangling on delight, tumbling into a temporary death of pangs and whirlings, like great wheels.

This time, when he came to himself, he vomited. Not pausing to effect a burial, he fled the spot, concealing his bloody hands in his cloak.

He could not bear it. He must excuse his irresistible fault. Thus: *A god visited me, and ordered me to do these things. Not my will but his.* So, weeping and afraid, but under heavenly orders, the young man hid himself in his brothers' tent.

The venerable philosopher, he who had debated with Azhrarn on the nature of the gods, sat brooding through the hours of darkness.

From somewhere, some compartment of his brain, or of the night itself, a reverie had taken him. For though he did not suppose the gods to be stone, as in the stranger's malign parable, yet was it not conceivable for the gods to be *present* in a stone, indeed, in all the stones which littered the landscape?

Now, the old man fancied himself walking across a plain under the moon, and here and there the stones glowed with a supernatural light, but here and there they did not glow, and he turned his foot on them. Then a dreadful fear of sacrilege came over him, and it seemed he heard a voice crying from the stones: *Who treads on the gods shall know everlasting misery.* After this had occurred more times than he could number, the philosopher, realizing his error, attempted to walk always between the stones of the plain. But try as he would, always some flint or shard came eventually under his foot, and the voice clamored.

At last the philosopher resolved to cease moving altogether, and there he stood, in the midst of the plain, fixed, as he supposed, for eternity.

Waking from this reverie, the philosopher heard a baleful noise and rose, and trod uneasily across the floor of his tent. Outside, the moon hung, a lamp, pendant from the ceiling of the sky. By her illumination, the old philosopher beheld a neighboring stone-grinder sharpening knives out of the hours of his trade from the goodness of his heart. The philosopher, seeing the sparks bursting off the stone, was seized by a terrible rage. He flew at the grinder, beating him about the head.

"How dared you," cried the philosopher, "abuse this holy object in which the gods are resident!"

The grinder toppled from his stool, and the philosopher strode on, finding next a young woman baking cakes on a flat stone before her fire. The philosopher beat her also, and flung the food into the flames.

"Blasphemer! You must not cook cakes on the breast of heaven."

And stepping back from her, he turned his heel on a pebble, at which he knelt stiffly, and cupped the pebble in his gnarled old hands, all bruised from striking the faces of men and women, and he entreated the pebble's forgiveness.

As the moon was declining, a tan-haired girl lay in the back of a tent, her sister sleeping nearby, and she dreamed.

It was her wedding night, and her cousin-bridegroom, whom she had seen no more than three times, brought her inside their chamber, and shut and bolted the door.

A depression settled upon the girl, for though she did not mind the man's looks, she did not favor them either. And though she loved no other instead, she did not love him.

"Come, dear Zharet," said he, "let us lie down together."

So they lay down on the divan among the cushions, and he unknotted Zharet's girdle clumsily, and fumbled at the embroidery of her bodice, and drew the polished crystal pins from her tan hair.

As he was doing all this, and her vague sensations of aversion and mistrust intensified, her eyes strayed to the narrow window. There, beyond the iron lattice, sat a black velvet cat which gazed at her with eyes like pools of water. In these eyes like pools she read a message, clear as if painted there in symbols. *Only take up one of these sharp pins, with which the dolt has just scratched you, and thrust it through his skull. Do this, and you shall have another, better, lover.*

And Zharet recalled a dark man passing between the tents in the nights before the people had come to Bhelsheved.

Her bridegroom pinched and plucked at her breast, and lay astride her like a fallen mule, and the girl thought to herself: *Imagine if that stranger were a god, a dark god from the snow-pale city. And that he had selected me for his bride, but here is an impediment. To be rid of it is only an act of faith and worship.*

Just then the bridegroom put his unsubtle fingers to work on another part of her, and with a grimace, the bride snatched the nearest pin and thrust it through his head. He died without a sound, and his body rolled immediately away from her, and she forgot it entirely, for next second the black cat dropped, light as a velvet glove, upon her breast.

A moment only did the creature remain feline. Then it changed into a man, or into the form of a man. Only a glimpse she caught of the face, which was transcendently beautiful, and framed by the long black curlings of its hair, and lit by two black pools of eyes. Even so, she knew it was not the face she had glimpsed among the tents, not the face of that amazing stranger, but another, a little less amazing. Yet he was beautiful enough, this other visitant, beautiful of form and body, and like a pale shadow he covered her, and even his breath was marvelous, drugging her . . . and she tipsily reasoned the god has assumed this mortal aspect in order not to smite her with the energies of the divine one.

Then the demon of Zharet's dream (demon indeed, one of the Eshva, those that were the servants of the Vazdru princes of Underearth, at whose caress even the locks of doors would melt and open) began to caress her, and all her flesh seemed melting and the locks of her womb pulsed. Her body was altered as he touched it, strands of a fiery weakness coursed down her arms beneath his fingers, her breasts budded, her belly, receiving the impress of the silvery musculature of his, became a stream of lights. When he pierced her, though she was a virgin, she felt no pain, only a shaft of exquisite rightness, as if two portions of a severed whole had come together in wondrous healing. He moved upon her first as slowly as a river, but, like a river, gained momentum. His body was all she knew, his eyes all she could see. The river bore her on toward these eyes, these depthless pools, as if finally she would be dashed into them and drowned there, and how she yearned for her drowning, and herself began to swim toward them, and plead for them and for their waters to close over her head.

Almost in another moment, she felt the land, the very world give way, and cleaved the cleft itself to find the vortex of ecstasy. But this ecstasy was of a specialized kind.

The first moments of the ecstasy were searing green and sapphire, and in them she struggled, blinded and sobbing. But this was the first stage, and after these moments, she broke through into a second ecstasy.

The second ecstasy within the first was the color of wine, and here all her senses became one, and that one shot through her like the spindle of some revolving star, so that all about herself she spun. But this spinning drove her, thrust her, again into a third stage.

The third ecstasy was white, far whiter than any city. And

here she was transfixed, and her frantic writhings, her gasps, her cries, even her breathing, stopped. Here on this summit she became a silent shriek. She could neither change further nor return to what she had been. She could not move. Her spasms were one single master spasm, frozen in molten whiteness, without beginning or end.

In this third ecstasy she was suspended for a thousand years.

And then her demon lover let her go, and she fell back through a violet cloud and into her body, or so it seemed, as if her soul had known orgasmic rapture rather than her flesh.

Opening her eyes, Zharet saw the tent in the desert, and that in darkness. She was alone, save for her sister sleeping not far off, and all was quiet, even her own heart beat softly. Then, in the gloom, she savored the fading taste of her dream, trembling. And in her fingers, she turned a quite illusory, and quite murderous, pin.


The people continued to pour into the holy city, to experience sacred joys, to sacrifice, to pray, to confess sin, to come out again, with unfocused eyes.

In the camps all over Bhelsheved, the songs went on, and the feastings began, and the contests with bow and spear, the racing for prizes.

Days passed like flames, and nights like black leopards, running from world's edge to world's edge.

Something was not as it should be. What? An uncanny influence lay over the region, a cloud, a smoke. There was dissent. There was quarrelling. There were accusations. . . .

"Someone stole my little singing bird from its wicker cage. Was it you?"

"Someone blighted my rose in its pot. Was it *you*?"

"Who spilled my wine?"

"Who let out my sheep from their pen?"

"Who spied on me as I bathed?"

"Who told lies about me in my absence?"

"Was it you, or you, or *you*?"

And at the contests, there was cheating, and when the cheating was brought to light, blows. There was adultery, too, and rape. There was theft.

The storytellers forgot their myths and legends, losing the thread of a tale between one word and the next.

Lamps would not light. Fires lit and exploded, and tents went up like scarlet trees in blossom.

Animals pined and died, as if for some master they had loved.

The corpses from a series of gruesome murders were discovered, the victims both male and female, both adult and child, horribly mutilated by a whip. One was suspected, a kinless carpenter, and he was stoned. A mad old philosopher, about whom a wild mad sect was gathering, screamed curses at the mob, declaring the bloodstained stones were deities.

Girls who were soon to be married were come on, at odd times, playing menacingly with little clay images of their bridegrooms. In some of these images, long pins had been decisively stuck.

All this occurred about Bhelsheved, the holy city. All this which day by day, and—more definitely—night by night, grew stronger and more fearsome, like a contagion, getting a hold, like plague.

Vague reports filtered into the city, into the sacrosanct precincts, were whispered by nervous worshippers, through the filigree screens to the priests or the priestesses, who would bend limpidly and attentively to listen. But if the Servants of Heaven paid any heed, drew any inference, was hard to tell. Seldom, if ever, did these chosen ones speak directly to the people. Hearing of murder, arson, thuggery and upheaval of all sorts, their translucent faces never altered. They made the sign of a blessing or a protection through the screen over whomever had related the events, and then drifted away like gauze scarves.

A new malaise fastened on the people ringed about no less than a hundred paces from the moon city. A malaise of doubt, too faint, too inchoate as yet to overwhelm them, but which, given sufficient space for brooding, would undoubtedly do so. At some juncture they must come to consider that their elected priests ignored, or were incapable of sympathizing with their trouble. And since these persons were said to resemble the gods, could it be that the gods, also, were indifferent to the plight of mankind—just as a particular stranger had recounted?

No doubt, this fault in the priests was due only to their ordered and protected lives. They had lost, or never even known, a valid conception of human beastliness and despair. Told over to them, it must have sounded like the story of some other world. Perhaps they thought they were being jested with.

# CHAPTER 3

## Night Works

It was the last night at Bhelsheved. In the shining afternoon, the sublime priests and priestesses had emerged from sanctuary, and moved about the camps, scattering aromatics, sequins and blossoms, blessing the crowds. But the hymns which were sung had a limping quality to them now. Once a man spat, explaining hastily that the sacred flames had caused him to choke. Once a girl averted her eyes, tearing the holy flower, which had fallen into her hand, in shreds.

Did the priesthood notice? It seemed not. They floated by in their filmy garments, their filmy hair like sorcerous metalwork of the Drin, those lowest, almost obscene but cunning artisans of the Demon City. . . . But who would dare compare the tresses of heaven's servants to such stuff? Here and there, a few were doing so.

When the priests retreated back into their fortress, their isolated cold virgin of a shrine, where common men, being gross and vile, were not permitted to live but only humbly to visit, the sun also abandoned the scene.

Day's golden eye closed its black lid, and it was night.

Presently an awful commotion broke out. News spread like locusts across the campments.

"A band of robbers has stolen the Magic Relic which was to have been awarded to the most worthy among us, the winner having been chosen by popular vote."

"Sacrilege! In which direction did the devils flee?"

"Eastward. Let us pursue."

Strange indeed. Each year this wondrous trifle had been

awarded. It was nothing less than a gold-encased bone, said to have belonged to the skeleton of Nemdur's virtuous queen, she who had implored the gods' pardon and been saved from Baybhelu. Just as the last spilled drop of the sun had been wiped away in the west, two or three shade-like figures had been seen, darting light as air from the vicinity of the Relic-containing pavilion. Reliable witnesses deduced they had perceived the gold bone glintingly passing back and forth between the thieves' pale slender hands. A curious notion had come to the witnesses—that the robbers laughed at them, even mocked and insulted them, though they made no vocal sound. Whatever else, the fiends had sped eastward, and somehow they left a clear trail on the sands behind them—not of footprints, more like the track of a single huge serpent. Possibly, the marks' long cloaks might have formed as their owners ran.

The pursuit, which began in trickles, mounted into a flood of people pouring from the camps, with lamps and torches in their hands. Something like the joyous arrival at Bhelsheved. Not quite.

And over the twilight sands, all blue from the sky's deepening blueness, the crowds, thousands upon thousands, hurried, almost all who had come to Bhelsheved, cursing and yelling, toward the east. An unfortunate direction, conceivably, for in the east Nemdur's Tower had been blasphemously raised, when Sheve had been only a city.

Which may have occurred to them, for as they rushed on, it began to seem to the people that they could see the terrible blasphemy of the Tower, rising up again from the desert plain.

Seven miles east of Sheve that Tower had stood, and of yellow brick had that Tower been made. Seven miles east of Bhelsheved, the second tower, (if it were more than some bizarre configuration of cloud), was black. A shadow, then, of Baybhelu. Maybe a ghost? For if there might be ghosts of men let loose on occasion to walk the world, why not the ghost of a building revived to stand up there?

Nearer and nearer the mass loomed, cloud, or mountain, or ghost or tower. For an hour, or rather more or rather less, the people came on, stumbling now, holding their sides, breath and torches panting. And every eye staring. And if one said to another: "What is that I see?" the other might not reply. Or might answer: "I cannot say for sure." Or: "Do you behold it, too?"

But when they were three miles from the place where Baybhelu had been razed, full dark had filled the interstices of sky and land, and whatever had risen from the earth, or not, was hidden by that dark. Only in spots did certain familiar patterns of stars seem absent, as if some bulk had come in front of them.

Yet the mysterious, snakelike track wove on. The forefront of the crowd, staggering with fatigue, fists loosening, mouths slack, peered at it with hatred, and pressed onward too.

Two miles farther, with no warning, the track vanished.

They searched about, swinging their lamps, finding no clue.

"The thieves have flown up in the air," said one.

"Or sunk into the ground," another.

At both fancies, the spines of many shivered.

Then a lamp caught a gleam across the dunes. A man ran forward, stooped, arose, cried out gladly, waving something aloft.

"They have dropped the Relic! We have recovered the sacred bone!"

The cry ran through the throng and new uproar ensued.

In the midst of the uproar, a light flashed in the sky, bright yet pale as sunrise, or so it looked, as if an enormous flint had been struck, and hovering, applied itself to some gigantic pitch-black candle.

And the candle flared up—

Screams flared from the crowd, prayers, imprecations, the acrid breath of terror.

There had been a tower, no doubting it now, and still there was a tower. Baybhelu of the multitudinous tiers, a stepway ascending up into heaven, out of sight in the high roof of the sky. But Baybhelu jet black, and on this jet blackness ten million lights. As if its head had pierced the gardens of the stars and shaken them down to cover it. Garlands and skeins and nets and necklaces of stars, all glittering and blazing, sheens and glows, the cold green of limes, the tropic pallor of aquamarines, galvanic primroses and incandescent purples, and drops of the purest hottest blood.

The vast crowd fell on its knees, or made to run away, and faltered. Gradually, voice by voice, its clamor ceased. The

weird beauty of the black tower of colored stars laid its
hand upon them, and held them still.

Then they began to hear the soft alluring sounds that came
to them across the mile of distance.

Bhelsheved sang to its pilgrims as they approached along
the paths of shining stone, a hum of silver wasps. The black
tower sang a swarm of musics that mingled and were one and
blew like a gentle wind over the dunes.

And then, with the music, the aromas and the perfumes
began to come. They were like spices, like flowers, like
wines, they were like drugs and delicious forbidden things.

The melody and the scent of the tower, and the glory of its
lamps, were all one glamorous beckoning.

In groups, in battalions, the crowd rose, and began to wander with great eyes toward this sorcery.

And where some would have hung back, the onward motion of the crowd pushed them unroughly but irresistibly forward, until they too could no longer resist. And where some
would have argued with the spectacle, the delicacy of the
music made nonsense of their words, the balm drenched
their lips and tongues, and their heads reeled, and they
moved after the others.

As they came nearer, fresh marvels greeted them.

From half a mile away, the being of the sand was altered.
It had become a field of plants, thick upon the ground, as if
each grain of sand had changed into a thing of leaves and petals. Jasmine and hyacinths bloomed by night, lilies twined
with roses, myrtle and clematis coiled between. Treading on
them, they were not crushed. They exuded their fragrances at
every footfall, and sprang straight again. Moths with fluttering wings like panes of thin crystal soared over these meadows.
Tinselly chimings and harmonics came from their horned
eyes, like stamens, which gave you to believe they were nothing but flying musical boxes.

From a quarter of a mile away, you became aware that
there was much activity on the levels of the tower, much
coming and going, and wide-pinioned creatures flew round it.
Also, at this point on the ground, a forest had sprung up, and
as they went on, magnetized toward the tower, the people
passed into the forest. The trees were tall, but not of bark or
leaves. The stems were of crimson glass and magenta glass
and glass the tint of an emerald, and all lit within. And the

foliage of the trees was in each case cluster on cluster of phosphorescent birds whose mauve eyes blinked and dazzled, and whose leafy wings stirred the strings of silver harps that lay between the boughs, causing strange whirring glissandi.

Coming from the forest, the tower lay only a hundred paces away, and automatically the crowd, trained to observe such a margin, hesitated, piling up on itself like water behind a dam.

As they paused, they saw the uncountable windows and the countless doorways of the edifice dripping out their glows. They saw fountains of colored liquids which arced down the tiers. They saw the nature of the traffic which flew about the tower. There were horses black as ink with manes and wings of milky blue, there were lions black as coal with manes like chrysanthemums and wings like furnace blasts. There were slender dragons with scales of bronze. And nearer the earth, perhaps some twelve or fourteen feet in the air, there was suspended a broad carpet of crimson and silver weave, and on the carpet white shapes flickered, as though the wind blew them.

The tower, which was like Baybhelu, which was also like Bhelsheved, which was unlike and surpassing both, continued to compel. Presently, the crowd spilled over the invisible dam, and poured to the foot of the tower, to the area where the first gargantuan tier sheered up. There they stood gaping, conscious of sin or bewitchment, unable to go away or even to repent.

The first carpet sailed by, and after this carpet, others. Tassels cascaded, silks flowed. White women danced slowly to the beat of the many musics. Their bodies were now masked, and now revealed, through curtains of beads like rain. They lifted their arms, which were swans' necks, which were serpents. Their burnished limbs rubbed and brushed and stroked together. The black grape-curls of their hair were wound with sinuous silver ornaments. Their long nails were like crescent moons. The tips of their breasts were like rosebuds.

While the thousands of mortals gazed, a sudden tremor raced over the ground.

The people found that the world was rising up into the atmosphere. There was again some shouting, some collapsing on the knees, but by now they were mesmerized. These protestations of terror were no longer genuine, but mere habit, for to be afraid in such a situation was surely human etiquette, the done thing.

As they had abruptly come to understand, the fields of flowers, the forest of stained glass, that entire half mile of land which made the radius about the tower, and on which the mass of the people were now standing, was nothing except one more flying carpet. A carpet with a hole at its center, through which the tower protruded. And now the carpet ascended smoothly and quite leisurely up the tower, as a ring is drawn up a finger.

As the carpet caught up to them, the dancing women—who were, of course, not women, but demonesses—alighted on it. Similarly, the flying beasts settled among the flowers with claps of their wings. They browsed the jasmine and the asphodel. They stalked among the people, who drew aside with anguished sighings, mechanical creatures, or else illusions, those demon dream artifacts which the sun's rays could destroy.

The man who had retrieved the golden bone relic from the sand still clutched it, when one of the beasts, a lion, came to him, and stared in his face with topaz eyes. Perhaps this lion at least was one of the Vazdru themselves, in other form, because the lion spoke to the man in hypnotic accents.

"That bone," said the beast, "is neither from the skeleton of Nemdur's black queen nor from the skeleton of anyone of importance. Give it therefore to me. It amuses me to collect trivia."

And the man, shivering, extended the sacred relic he had gone such a distance to recover, and the lion took it in its jaws. There was a terrible crunch; pieces of fine gold and brown ivory were spat on the hyacinth's under paw. The lion then departed, its eyes shut as if in revulsion. Probably it *was* a demon, for the touch of gold, reminiscent to Vazdru and Eshva alike, of the sun, filled them with allergy. Only the Drin would sometimes work it, being less sensitive than the aristocrats of Druhim Vanashta. (Revulsion, no doubt, was the cause of the Eshva who stole the relic being seen continually passing the bone from hand to hand, each taking a fair share of the golden discomfort to spare his fellows.)

Upward, the ring of the carpet flew. As once Nemdur's court had careered up the long flights of steps, the people were borne toward the topmost tier.

For sure, they went on with their polite, habitual expressions of alarm. If this work of night, this tower, were tall as Baybhelu, might it, too, anger the gods, who would then cast it down? Yet something in them comprehended, a dim memory carried in their racial cells, that even the gods could not cast down the power of Azhrarn, or if they thought they could, they had never thought to try it.

Did the people then realize they were on their way into his presence, into the presence of an Azhrarn without disguise, an Azhrarn in the full aura of his princedom? That one who, they had always been told, was hideous, shambling, evil in his looks as in his deeds.

Perhaps already the vistas and the harmonies and the drug-smokes had taught them that wickedness did not always have an ugly shape.

The carpet continued upward. Through the fountains which seemed not to be of fluid but of heatless combustion. Past windows of sumptuous colors, behind which exotic jigsaws of activity went on, never completely viewed or explicable. By black-haired revelers who danced or embraced, or leaned out over balconies, languidly.

The topmost tier was suddenly reached. It was a lightless box, with doorways all around, each one of black lacquer. The stars seemed close enough to wound with a spear-cast, yet their silken glare did not alleviate this midnight peak, and the moon was old.

Now, the topmost tier, like that of Nemdur's original model, was the smallest of all the tiers, as it had to be. True, it was a massive structure, but even so, not huge enough to accommodate some several thousands of persons all at once. Accordingly, what next came about was perhaps an illusion. Or else Azhrarn, Master of Night and of so much more besides, had made a way into some second dimension, into that place, maybe, sometimes known as Otherearth. And here (or there) it was that he then entertained the multitude.

But whatever he did, this is how it seemed and how later it was recounted by each man, each woman and each child that had been raised that night into the sky about the black tower.

The glamorous music ended all at once, and only the winds that played about the tower-top were heard. Then, all the lacquer doors slapped open, and one by one, as if they had been instructed beforehand, the thousands proceeded in through these doors.

Inside the topmost tier was only night sky. A limitless sphere of black, scattered with stars and the dusts of stars, over which, now and then, a comet or a meteorite would unravel its ribbons, or through which some cosmic body might drop like a great coin. Indeed, certain children reached out and caught hold of products of this astral hail. One child told after of snatching and retaining a moment a star large as a cartwheel, which weighed no more than a small rock. But the star was burning, and holding it, the child saw the red wine in its own hands against the light, and then, though it felt no pain, its hands blistered a little, and it prudently let go of the star, which fell away, and under its feet, down and down, until it was no longer visible. A girl also spoke of catching a star by its trailing roots, the point at which it had snapped off the parent tree or vine on which it had been growing. But she too discarded it, when she felt her face grow tight as if with too much sun. All were later agreed that they had balanced on nothing at all, for all this heavenly debris passed them and away below them. Yet somehow they were not in fear, and the air they stood on felt solid as a floor. Whatever else, they knew they were much higher in the ether than the top of the tower had been, and therefore nearer to the gods. Yet, the gods they did not see, nor even their lesser cousins, the elementals of the uppermost sky.

Strangest of all, maybe, was that, as each entered this realm of savage space, he discovered himself alone, or seemed to. Even at that, they felt no panic.

Then, they were no longer alone. One other was with them.

Initially, it appeared to be the figure of a man who came walking toward them across the floorless floor of night. Almost all recognized the rogue storyteller, he of the eagle-winged cloak, for almost everyone had seen that man on the journey to Bhelsheved.

When he was three or four feet from them, the man halted, muffled in the cloak. For the interim of a heartbeat he stayed so.

And then—

An inky wind swirled, hiding the stars, swirled and became

a pillar of smoke, whirling, devilish; condensed and became a stormcloud, heavy blue and shot with spangles, split by a tremendous lightning flash. And out of the lightning flew a black gull on blade-like wings, and flying, the gull became an eagle with two of the stars seemingly in the sockets of its eyes, and the eagle grasped the night in its talons, its pinions shrilled and it was a dragon, dwarfing the dark, black as burned fire, mouth full of fire, of magma, a volcano. And then the flames sank and a black wolf with fiery eyes became instead a black dog, which reared upward and became that dog of cats, the panther, and after the panther, a jaguar, which in turn reared up, standing on its hind limbs, grew the slim waist and rounded hips of an amphora, the full breasts of a courtesan, a woman's face lovely beyond reckoning, with smiling lips, and an ocean of black hair. And then she too transmuted, and each one who stood, or kneeled or cowered before the metamorphosing force, beheld someone familiar to himself, a wife, a brother, a neighbor or a child. So exact the likeness, some few were moved to speak to the apparition, to call it by name in amazement. But then this shape was also gone.

And now he evolved before them in his masculine shape, after which, it was sometimes said, all other men were shadows of a shadow, all other men, and all women, too, as if they were unfinished statues, and he the only perfect creation, but if so, who could have created him?

They saw him as a Lord. A Lord of Darkness. A Prince. As his own people saw him.

The black mail which clung to his body ran with blue dynamics. And even as it was mail and metal, so his armoring was also of velvet. His cloak was not any kind of material, but a waterfall of jewels, blacks and blackest greens and brazen, too, as if washed in a stream of molten stuff. A collar of improbable weight, of dragons' skull-plates, rested on his breast, lanterned with rubies and intricately chased with a pure demonic silver, almost like pearl but hard as steel—Drin work, and no mistake. His boots were made of the skins of men, and no mistaking that, either, skins dyed black, for even the sombrous wholesome flesh of black men is not black as black really was, or is, and to demons, blackness was a sort of light. These boots were also chased with silver, but all the while the pictures on them changed, shimmering like snakes.

An actual snake was coiled about his left arm, a cobra, its hood spread, hissing. His face was like a fine carving, set amid curtains of black hair to which no other hair was comparable. His face burned and blinded, like the stars, and like them, without pain. His face may not be described, just as, then or now, it might not, may not, be represented. In the total truth of his form, he was so handsome that by the appearance of his face alone he could have injured or even, like Chuz, Prince Madness, have rendered insane those who looked on him. (Not only the sun could destroy.) And yet, how marvelous he was, how marvelous beyond all the marvel of man or woman or any earthly thing.

His fingers were ringed with jasper, jade and jet. His eyes were jewels more brilliant and more black than sun or sunlessness.

Tall, vital, breathtaking and immobile, so he stood over them, each one of them. Azhrarn, most rightly, and most inadequately, called The Beautiful.

Each felt a terror then that was not exactly terror, a pleasure that was not at all pleasure. Each shrank. Each, in his way, did homage. But homage was not precisely what he had wished from them. Besides, it was too late.

Finally, he smiled. His smile was cruel, and therefore full of a wonderful tenderness. Vazdru as he was, he was an artist in his vengeance, an aristocrat in his modes of irony.

"You may ask," he said to them, to each and every one, "a single boon of me, since I am here."

"Lord," they stammered, "master—" They were uncertain who he was, and like others before them, decided him to be a god. They fell flat at his manskin boots. And then each asked in a whisper for some cherished thing. And each thing, though different in each, was a wicked thing, or at best, a selfish thoughtless thing. Maidens asked him for the enslavement of men they wished to love them, and young men for girls to be put where they might come at and lie with them, whether willing or no. Others, young and old, required the demises or crippling of rich relations or enemies. Some asked for wealth, some for power, and many, very many, asked for their own revenges. Even the children requested bad things. Some of their requests were the nastiest of all.

In that entire crowd, who might have asked in several cases for a renewal of strength or health, or of youth, or of the knack of loving those that loved them, or of help for those they loved, not one was prompted to ask for such a thing. He had brought their worst qualities into instant flower, as leaven inspires bread.

And having heard them, to each one he said: "I will put the opportunity into your own hands. Do with it as you desire."

And so he did, later. And in some glass of Underearth presumably he watched them then, seize these opportunities to force and to enslave, to utilize the smothering pillow or the poisoned meat, or the unguarded confidence or somebody's ill-luck. But that was to come.

Having reduced them to the vilest part of themselves, he wrapped his cloak of armored jewels about him, and as he did so, the whole of that night sky in the tier was wrapped about him, and he and it were folded from sight, and black nothing engulfed the humans who had worshipped him.

When they roused, they were in the camp again, that camp outside Bhelsheved. Everyone supposed then he had dreamed, and that only he had gone after the Eshva thieves, trodden on lilies and through stained glass trees, scaled up the black ghost tower and met there a god of the dark, and gained a gift from him.

And only some who went out early saw the peculiar upheaval of the sands, as if an army had tramped eastward and then tramped back. And they refrained from comment. The tower itself, naturally, disappeared before dawn could wither it.

It was only years after, when the results of death and mayhem had come home to roost on this unhappy people, that they admitted to each other their dreams of that night, and compared them, and grew cold. By then their religion was corrupt, and their faith a sham, and when they went to Bhelsheved it was habit and greed and holiday and nothing else. The sweet fruit of religion and faith had soured, had rotted. The sweet fruit was no more.

There were, naturally, a handful who did not travel to the phantom tower that night. Of these, one was a young murderer, later found by his two brothers, hanged from a tree in the groves by the length of a whip. And one was a tan-haired girl, turning a pin in her fingers, who, deep in the reverie of a demon lover, missed the demons who had stolen the Relic, and so had not cared to run after the robbers. And thirdly were a philosopher and his followers, who were busy worshipping stones.

As for the Relic itself, like the three dark gems formed from the blood of Azhrarn when the whip cut open his palm, they lay hidden under the robe of the desert. Unlike the three gems of blood, the shards of the Relic were never located.

# PART TWO

## *Soul-of-the-Moon*

# CHAPTER 1

## A Sacrifice

He had demoralized the pilgrims. He had yet to deal with Bhelsheved's priesthood. Eradication, the sigil of demonkind in matters of requital. Not one brick to be left whole. Not one lamp alight.

The people had gone in their thousands, plague-carriers of disillusion and gray mischief, away from the white shrine in the desert. Gone with their burned-out torches, treading heavily, dreaming harsh dreams. And the holy city closed its four gates of ivory and steel and polished stones. Thus shut up, its water held within, it could have withstood an interminable siege. As well. Though none had yet attempted to sack this treasure house, there might now come a time when some would attempt it. But that was for the darkening future. For this while, serene, unearthly, the snow-hill of Bhelsheved slept under a dying moon.

And, under that wisp of moon, a panther prowled around the walls. Around and around. Passing the gleaming gates, the mountain sides of glazed blocks, passing under the veil of trees and through the groves, where petals were dashed on its pelt. Around and around Bhelsheved the panther circled, seven times seven times.

He was considering, Night's Master, the interesting flavor of retribution. And considering too, perhaps, the smart of that strange wound they had given him. For it is worth repeating that they must, astonishingly, have hurt him a great deal, and that in oblique fashion he was vulnerable to humankind. His involved acts of vengeance, his complex acts of

evil—could it be possible?—were like those elegant flourishes
and underlinings with which insecure men bolstered up their
signatures on parchment.

After the forty-ninth circuit, the night swallowed the great
cat.

Three seconds after, Azhrarn stood on the pastel shore of
the heart-lake at the core of Bhelsheved.

In the moonlight, the golden temple was silver, the
turquoise water was a sheet of tumbled black sky, reflecting
the four curving bridges in its mirror. A garden ran down
here, to the mosaic rim above the lake, and the trees exuded
their scent and had sprinkled the sugar of their blossoms everywhere. Somewhere a nocturnal bird was singing. It did not
guess who listened, or it might have fallen quiet.

An hour or more he stood there, brooding. A mortal hour,
which to him might have been only a moment. As he mused,
occasional images formed in the water near his feet, the
representations of what his brain devised, altering as his
musings altered. And some of these depictions were not good
to see.

The deadly moon rested on her elbow overhead.

A strand of whiteness moving in the water, brighter than
the moon, might have seemed at first the passage of a swan,
then of a flame. Yet, tracing its origin to the farther shore,
you saw it was neither of these.

A female figure walked about the lake, following the winding of its bank, the pallor of her garments and her hair
copied faithfully in the water. In her right hand she carried
a little lamp, the greenish color of a firefly.

Azhrarn waited in the shadow under the trees. Perhaps he
smiled. Perhaps he recalled the innocent beast which, going
after him into the desert, had met a lion.

Certainly, she would not guess that anyone was here, save
her own kindred of the temples, chaste and modest and sim-
pleminded creatures she might accost without misgiving.

Like these, too, she would be comely. The priests were
selected for their charms.

Slender as a wand she was, her waist looked narrow
enough to be snapped in the hands, yet supple as willow. Her
feet picked their way like small white birds. Her walk was
music. Her hair which, in most of her calling, by the temple
law, was bleached and tinted to enhance its pallid glisten,

seemed altogether too fine, too pale, too starry to be anything but natural. And very long her hair was; in repose it would robe her, the tips of it touching the ground. But as she moved, so featherlike and sheer it was, it lifted, blowing behind her like white wings.

Her dress was a gown of the temple, gauzy stuff with iridescent fringes. Tiny blue scintillants, which in the moonlight flashed like igniting flints, were embroidered on her bodice. Each breast, the cup of a flower, stirred softly beneath.

He had discerned her beauty from across the lake. Yet her beauty drew nearer to him as she did, like an approaching song.

She walked through the broadcast blossoms, her white wings at her back, the green gem of light in her hand. The loveliness of her face opened before him as a door opens.

Demons were beautiful. Rarely did mortals rival such beauty as was the commonplace of Druhim Vanashta. Azhrarn had known and toyed with and corrupted and broken most of the mortal beauty that there was. One woman he had himself made beautiful, who had been thereafter, in her time, a wonder of the earth.

But this white beauty was new to Azhrarn. He could not fathom it, nor find its floor, could not measure or dismiss it, could not deduce of what order it had come. Be sure then, it intrigued him.

So utterly motionless he had grown, she would, by no means available to men, have seen him or told that any was there. Yet, unerringly she came forward, and when she was within ten paces of him, she stopped. She looked between the trees at the area of ground he occupied. Her eyes were wide, and slanted a fraction upward at their outer corners. In color they were the turquoise of the lake, and like the lake by night they had turned dark and held reflections.

"Lord," she said, looking into the trees, "Lord, I knew you were here and have come out to seek you."

Her voice was beautiful, too.

Azhrarn remained, scarcely visible if at all, and watched her, and listened to her. Like a melody, she went on playing for him.

"Lord," she said, "I do not guess who you are, but I understand your essence and your purpose. I know you are here to work us ill, and to exact some due from us, because we have angered you."

At that, he spoke to her, out of the shadows, with some irony.

"How is it that you know so much?"

She did not start, either at his voice's suddenness, or its inherent sorcery. She was not afraid, not boastful. She answered simply,

"All this I know, yet do not know how I know it."

"Riddle-maker, then."

She said: "As a man may scent a fire burning in a neighboring house, just so I felt your presence in this garden. And as a man may know the nature of fire without seeing it, thus I know yours."

"Tell me then my nature."

"Cruel, so cruel, so cruel," she said. "Relentless, terrible. Your wish to cause pain like pain itself. Deeper than night, colder than winter, no more to be turned aside than the moon's rising."

"Why seek me then?" he said.

She lifted her lamp. She said: "The rigors and disciplines of Bhelsheved's priesthood have made me enduring, and I am far stronger than I appear. Yet also I may be easily hurt. For a great while I might be tortured before death overcame me. These are my recommendations, for I offer myself as a sacrifice to you. Work out your rage on me, Lord of Darkness, and spare the people."

"A sacrifice," he said. Was there bitter amusement in his tone? "Men do not respect those who undergo agony for their sake."

"Respect is not my aim."

"Tell me your aim."

"I have told. To avert your wrath."

"Can your little death do so much?"

"Perhaps, if you make me suffer very much."

"Are you not afraid?"

"Yes, Lord. There would be no satisfaction for you in harming me, did I not fear you."

"You suppose me pitiless."

"I suppose you are in need of recompense."

"You are young," he said, "to go out of this world like a candle flame."

"There is another world I shall go to," she said, "or maybe I shall return to this one."

In the black tower they had crouched to him, thousands on thousands, and asked him for wickedness and greed. Now one came to him and asked that he kill her in order that his anger and his need be solaced. And she more lovely than the stars in the sky.

"Look at me," he said, and he stepped from the shade, and she saw him. Long and long she gazed, and equally as long, let it be said, Azhrarn the Prince of Demons gazed at her. "And now," he said at length, "recite again what I am, and how you will appease me."

Her hand shook, and she lowered the lamp, but she laughed very low.

"Forgive me," said she. "I knew also your appearance would be godlike, and that you would be handsome. But now I see your beauty is like the heartbeat of the earth. To the beauty I imagined, yours is as the sea is to a little drop of water. And how can such beauty be the wickedness I comprehend you are, Lord of Lords? Oh you, who would lead us into evil, what a waste it is, for could you not lead the whole of mankind to joy and goodness by one look of your eyes? Yet, no matter. You are worth dying for, Lord. The world would die for you herself, I think, did she know you as truly you are."

There was silence then. In all his centuries, who had ever said such things to him? Who would have thought to, indeed, he being who he was?

Eventually, he said to her,

"I surmise, white maiden, you mistake what truly I am."

At which she lifted her gaze, as she had lifted her lamp.

"Or do you mistake yourself?" she said.

His anger came back to him then. His anger like a blowing out of all the lights of heaven.

"Woman," he said, "you are a fool."

Then he was gone, and there before her, a black wolf, whose lean head was on fire with eyes. And the wolf trotted to her and seized in its mouth her hand, and gnawed to the bone, in a terrible bite, her forefinger. (It is a fact, she must have discomposed him. He was not generally so crude.)

The girl cried out, and tears ran from under her lids. The wolf let go of her as soon as it had torn her, however. Slowly then, and still weeping, she held out to it again her mutilated hand, urging it silently to resume its ghastly labour.

Azhrarn, long, long ago, had submitted himself to agony, in that single unswerving sacrifice which had been his, and by this action he had defeated Hatred in one of its most mighty forms. Now the hatred of Azhrarn was what this priestess offered her sacrifice to curtail.

Those who share a similarity of adventures, are in some ways brother and sister.

The man, not the wolf, caught up her hand again—the wolf had vanished.

At his touch either her pain left her, or mingled with the exquisite sensation which the touch of Azhrarn could induce. He held her in one arm. With the long squared nail of his middle finger, he slit his own demon's skin, from the first joint of the thumb to the last. It was the second time he had spilled his blood through Bhelsheved, save now it did not spill. He pressed that nigrescently glowing ichor against her own humanly bleeding hand. In an instant, her flesh began to heal. In seven instants she was whole and without a scar.

Still he held her, and presently he said to her, more quietly even than the noise of the leaves all about: "My blood is now mixed with yours. Will that burnish you with my wickedness, moon girl, I wonder."

"Fire and water do not mix," she whispered, "one extinguishes the other." Her pain was gone, but as if she felt it still, she leaned on him, all her light weight, and billows of her pale hair streamed over the blackness of his garments.

"You will not do as a sacrifice," he said to her. "You are, after all, too fair to spoil."

"But you will spare Bhelsheved?"

"I have already fashioned a sword that will smite this Gods' Jar. In a year, or ten, or twenty. Even now, the foundations of your religion decay. And do you still think me other than I am, my child? Other than a Prince of Demons?"

But she, stunned by his embrace, as mortals tended to be, had sunk into a sort of sleeping faint or trance, lying against him, her head on his breast, her hair splashed over him like a river out of the moon.

Yet Azhrarn knew well enough that something had passed away from him with his blood, and that though the blood of the Vazdru might transmute, it did not fade, nor would it extinguish hers.

He picked her up in his arms, and the little lamp dropped from her grasp—somehow, all this time, she had kept a grip on it. Then he spoke a cunning word, and they were gone from the lakeside, he and she together.

He took her to a region of the desert of which nothing is known, though many an area, in later days, was pointed out as the place.

Maybe palms towered up there, and water glimmered. Or maybe there was no tree, no water, only the tides of the sands, coming in and going out like breath at the will of the wind.

He laid her down then, on the carpets of moss or grass or dust, and he himself lay upon her. But though he lay with her, he did not do so in the carnal sense. He stared into her eyes with a demon's stare that never blinked, and her eyes, meeting his, chained by his, ceased also to blink, only reflecting his. And in this way, they were through the night, unmoving, like stones laid one on another, in a bizarre ecstasy of utter stasis. And it seemed to the young priestess that his blood actually ran through both their bodies, and that their flesh came to be no longer separate, nor their minds, nor their souls—her soul, and what in him passed for a soul, his immortality.

Only when a vague half-note of color soaked through the east did he draw away from her, but still it seemed to her, even then, she felt the pressure of him yet, and the caress of his hair which had brushed her cheeks.

"I must leave you," he said, "for dawn is near. Where would you have me take you?"

"To Bhelsheved, since it is my home."

"Come then," he said. And he drew her up, and by his magic returned her to the blossom garden by the lake. Where, arriving, she found herself alone, and the broken lamp guttered out on the soil, as the sun split the horizon.

Her name was Dunizel, which, in that language, was Moon's Soul. Seven languages there were in the Underearth, and seven master languages upstairs on the earth. But of these latter seven each possessed a subdivision of ten, so that there were in reality seventy languages spoken by men. But the demons knew all of them, and so Azhrarn knew her name and its meaning. Perhaps he read it from her brain; she had not mentioned it aloud. He knew, doubtless, her history, also, though it would scarcely have mattered to him. His lovers had been as various as their beauty, the children of kings, of slaves; even once the child of one who was a corpse.

But Dunizel's mother had been an imbecile, drooling and incoherent, an idiot-girl who would stagger about the streets of her village, tearing out her filthy hair, scratching the house walls with her ragged nails.

# CHAPTER 2

## The Magical Engine

The idiot girl, certainly, had never made the journey to holy Bhelsheved. Otherwise, usually she was let roam as she wished, or when she grew rough, she might be trapped in a net and tied up to a post like a dog until her passion abated. Most of her violence was directed at herself; she never assaulted another, only sometimes she would rip washing where it hung to dry on bushes, or steal fruit from the trees. The village was piously forbearing with her, even throwing her the scraps of food which kept her alive. And there was a tradition, when there should be a wedding or a funeral, of putting out on the street by the tethering post—if she was tied there that day or no—a mug of beer or thin wine. But, though it did these things, the village felt itself befouled by her, considered her a curse the gods had visited on it for some wrongdoing in the past. When they treated her, as they reckoned, well, they hoped thereby to win the favor of heaven, which would then remove her, or strike her dead.

But she did not die, the idiot girl. And none dared kill her, though sometimes they threw pebbles or struck her.

One year, a few months before the harvest, a magus came to dwell in an old mansion on the hill above the village. He announced he had retreated from the cities in order to study his arts in peace, and he was besides a devout and god-fearing man. The village accepted him as a blessing, just as they accepted the idiot as a curse. However, he had little to do with them, being occupied with his experiments. Now and

then a roar would rise from the roof of the mansion, but
these sounds were not in themselves apparently injurious.
Once or twice, a villager knocked on the brass-bound door
which had been affixed to the mansion's portals, but received
no reply. And once only, a shepherd, seeing the magus out
walking with his servant on the hillside, hurried up and
begged the wiseman to alleviate an ache he had in one of his
teeth. But the magus seemed not to hear, and passed on, his
long robes, sewn with extraordinary symbols, brushing the
grass. The servant, however, turned about, and when the
mage was some way off addressed the shepherd.

"Which tooth is that?" inquired the servant.

The shepherd, agog, opened his lips and pointed at the offending canine.

"Oh, I shall see to that for you," declared the magician's
servant, and swinging up his staff, he knocked the tooth out
of the shepherd's mouth, and two good fellows with it.

Leaving the shepherd howling, the servant, howling also,
with uncouth mirth, lolloped after his oblivious master.

Now at this time this servant began to prove himself as
much a curse to the village as any other they had had. Repulsive in appearance, and unclean of person, he was kept by
the magician for his prodigious strength as a guard, and also
out of some perverse wish the intellectual had conceived to
observe such a type about his work. His mind being on
higher matters and himself protected from the servant's hor-
ridness, the magician failed to notice what went on elsewhere.

Firstly, the servant was given to playing obscure jokes
upon the villagers. He would tie the genitals of the billy goats
together, for example, and when the goatherd came running
at their bawling, the servant pounced on him and tied him up
with them too, in a similar manner. On one occasion, the
wretch crawled down through a chimney, having previously
put out the fire beneath by urinating on it, and fell out into
an old woman's house and terrified her almost into a fit. Next
he surprised a woman bathing in a pool. There would have
been small doubt as to the outcome of that, save she was the
reed-cutter's wife, and had intended to cut reeds herself, and
was therefore able to pull a knife from among her clothes,
which item she struck in the servant's thigh. At this reception
he hobbled away yelling. That night, as the woman cooked

her husband's supper, a tarnished copper bird flew through her window and said sternly to her: "I speak for the magician, and he asks, Why did you stab my servant?" The woman was alarmed, but her man came up and put her behind him, and he said to the bird: "Let your master consider this. When a woman as pretty as mine is able to come close enough to stick a knife in such a part of a man as ugly and noisome as that servant of his, then she must have some reason for her act, and he must have some reason for being so close." At these words, the bird put its head under its wing as if embarrassed, and the husband added, "Suggest to your master that he keep the oaf in check. Though we are in awe of a magus, the scum that serves him shall have his throat sliced presently."

As the moon rose that night, the magician set sprites on the servant to lash him, and the fellow ran about wailing. Strong threats were also added, and thereafter no further tricks were played on the villagers.

But the servant was not content. His phallus would trouble him a vast amount, rising up in the hours of the darkness to chide him. Sporadically, the magician might supply him with illusions that had the appearance and fleshliness of delectable and amorous youths and maidens, but only rarely did the mage, himself above such things, remember that his servant was not. A long while in the city, the servant had subsisted quite heartily on a secret diet of rapes and terrorisms—which also fulfilled his appetites. Now, in this parochial spot, his crimes had come swiftly to light, and all his pleasures were forbidden him.

Then one day, spying (it was all he had left) upon two lovers in a meadow, he beheld the idiot girl wander by. And soon the lovers, arising from the grass, beheld her too. From their words the servant found out that they considered her a bane, and longed that she should vanish.

At this news, the servant took to following the girl, and soon enough he learned how the whole village loved her. Shortly a plan occurred to him.

Under the mansion, in whose upper rooms the magus practised his sorceries, was a system of cellars, which in turn led into the stone chamber of an underground stream. Here the servant had frequently wandered, gathering funguses and occult plants at his master's direction, and also incising lewd graffiti in the walls, and doing harm to the harmless creeping things that lived there.

The resemblance of this subterrain to a prison had not escaped him, either.

Having by now tracked the idiot quite frequently, the servant had some idea of her possible wandering and resting places. Waiting until the night of a full red moon, when the mage was on the mansion's eastern roof, making lunar calculations, the servant roved about the countryside, until he came on the girl in one of her haunts, which was a ruinous hut without roof or door. Slinking in, the servant eyed her as she crouched beneath her matted hair, and she in turn, poor witless thing, stared vacantly back at him.

Being himself foul, her foul condition did not lessen the servant's eagerness. Wasting no time, he struck her to the ground, jumped upon her and violently forced her. Fortunately, his excitement was so imperative that she did not have to endure his activities for very long.

For her part, her cries of pain were very nearly abstract, and she did not struggle. She was so used to the casual illtreatments of men, and of nature itself, she found this new brutalization indistinguishable.

When he was done, the servant shook himself like some large animal emerging from mud, dragged up his skinny haphazard mistress, and loaded her over his shoulder. In this way he conducted her to the magician's house, and without his master's knowledge, conveyed her down through the cellars to the rock-cut where the stream ran. Here, he tied her—she had so often been tied, she made no protest even at this—to a handy stalagmite. He then raped her a couple more times, (for, sad fellow, he had been deprived a long while,) after which he serenely repaired aloft, and presented himself to the magician. He was just in time to get to work on the heavy machinery the mage inclined to have operated on the roof. It was an engine of enormous wheels and mechanical pistons, that was driven both by the brawn of the servant and by an uncanny power derived from certain radiations of the stars and other ethereal bodies.

As the servant lugged the levers into position and the engine bellowed, the mage shouted: "In only another one hundred and nine days and nights, as I judge by the aura of the moon and the rhythms of the stars, the comet I am expecting will certainly appear."

"Yes, master," shouted back the servant dutifully. His own mind was on lower things, and most happily engaged there.

The mage, however, had reached that peak of pale and shining elevation the intellectual achieves when some long awaited mental irradiation is in the offing. And so indeed it was. In point of fact, the magician's whole purpose in coming to this out-of-the-way spot, had been to confront the comet. He had learned, from his studies a few months earlier, that the apparition was due to manifest in that portion of sky to which the village was adjacent. He had abandoned therefore all his other projects and hurried to the vicinity. Here, having ordered the servant to construct the strange machine, the magus was now priming it, for he planned by its use to attract and trap a fragment of the comet's emissions.

The servant, however, had scant care for the mage's lust, being merry with his own. He pounded the levers of the machine and cranked it. When his task was done, he stole once more into the underground cavern, where he pushed stale bread and vinegary wine into the idiot's mouth, before bestriding her again with a master's pleasure in possession. For he had never owned anything before.

For some ninety days, then, things went on much in this sort. The servant would go down to the cellars and so into the chamber below, and there he would satisfy his desires. Intermittently, he would nourish the idiot girl on remnants of food. For drink, he graciously awarded her the length of the stream, or what part of it she could come at, being permanently tethered as she was.

However, after ninety days, something impinged on the servant's murky insensibilities. It came to him that a monthly rite, usual to women, was consistently absent in his doxy. At first, he hoped her imbecility had affected her womb, but shortly it seemed to him he could detect the changes about her that attended conception.

The servant fell then into a dreadful distress. Not, to be sure, for the lady's sake, but for his own. Feeble, half-starved and stupid as she was, she would most certainly not survive the birth of a child, and so he would lose her almost as soon as he had made her his. Accordingly, he debated with himself on various methods, and at length he brought wine and made her drink, and then beat her and kicked her soundly, trusting she might abort the infant, and still live. Alas, alas, the girl only recovered, and she remained filled.

So desperate did the servant become that he contemplated inquiring of the magician a method of curtailment, but by now the one hundred and nine days were almost done, and the mage had withdrawn into his private cell to fast and meditate, purifying himself for the mighty spell he intended to work. He emerged only now and then to examine the engine on the roof, and at such moments was preoccupied.

"Master," wheedled the servant, "a poor village maiden was at the door yesterday begging that you might remedy an unwanted pregnancy for her mother, already blessed with forty-three children—"

"No, no," murmured the mage, "your addition is quite wrong. Forty-*seven* are the number of syllables of the astral mantra I must recite on the comet's dissolution."

"Master," whined the servant, "if I confess to you I allowed a wicked woman, maddened with her desire to enjoy me, to lead me from the path of virtuous abstinence, and that now she threatens me with her father's wrath if I do not alleviate her condition—"

"What is this nonsense? The mechanism's condition is perfect. But you must oil this cog."

Eventually, the servant desisted. He began, instead, to take better food to the girl in the rock-cut, fruit and meat. Even he took her warm rugs to sleep on. Even he sometimes untethered her from the stalagmite, and led her up and down to exercise her. If she was aware of his novel kindness, she did not show it. Nor did she seem aware of her pregnancy. When the servant periodically flung her down and rode her frantically, (desperate not to miss an opportunity, since so probably he would soon lose her) she gazed at the ceiling of stone, frowning slightly through her filthy tangled mane.

On the one hundred and eighth day of the magician's vigil, the first foreshape of the comet emerged from a twilight sky.

Now the comets of the flat earth were of different origins and inclination from those which visit the rounded world.

Some evolved in the mass of chaos beyond the corners of the earth as then it was, and passing by error, or through some cosmic or seismic upheaval, into the uplands of the world's air, were hastily coated by the instinctive elements of that air with protective particles—for pure chaos and the standardized atoms of the world could not coexist without some compromising admixture forming between, to insulate one from the other. These comets came and went, and seldom revisited the sky, for once they regained the outer limits, chaos reclaimed them. A second form of comet was that created solely by tumbling stars, which, each trailing the struck flame of its descent, for some reason failed to hit the earth, and was thereafter carried back and forth—by random currents of the atmosphere, or the exquisite sorceries of sky elementals (who might ride such beacons over the ether). These second sort of comets might recur in appearance at regular or irregular intervals, circling the dome above the earth for centuries, until they were utterly burned out. But there was, too, a third variety, and it was to this group that the magician's comet belonged.

In those days, the sun, which always remained a precise distance above in its journeys over the earth, moonlike, waxed and waned, thereby creating summer and winter. Every night, also, the sun, having set, was plunged into the hardly explicable limbos which underlay the lower regions of earth—those nether depths that were beyond and below even the Innerearth, Death's kingdom. This psychic "death" during every period of darkness, would mysteriously revitalize the sun's disc, so that every dawn it was able to hurl itself up in the east again and refresh the world with its light. (The moon underwent a similar process.) However, it would sometimes happen—perhaps once in a thousand years—that, during its waxing stage, the sun would rise clad in more vitality than was necessary, or healthful. This overcharge would then stream off, like steam from boiling water, sometimes visible as clouds, or else quite invisible, to a mortal eye. The solar vapor would presently drift up beyond the apex of the sun's daily route. Here, in the colder environs of the higher sky, it would alternately ferment and condense, heat and cool, until at length it grew to be a flamingly gaseous sphere.

Once fully formed, the magnetism of the earth would begin to summon this ghostly fireball, and it would commence slowly falling through months, or even years, downwards, its hair spreading out behind it to mark its road through the atmosphere. Without exception, at a point far above the earth's actual surface, the fiery gas would once more unravel. The radiation, which at these moments would be released, was startling but beneficial. The gases themselves would be absorbed by the earth's tissue, or else dissipated into nothing.

Such occurrences were rare enough; the magician had believed himself very lucky in mathematically and astrologically chancing on one, for there was small visual forewarning. Only the flung-forward image of the comet might be seen the night before its arrival, an effect similar to that of a lamp reflecting on a wall.

At the sight of its preview, the magician was overjoyed.

Not so, the village. Ignorant of the character of such a phenomenon, they observed the new weird and bulbous star in the sky without celebration. When, as the night progressed, it grew larger, their nervousness increased in proportion. When day dawned, and still the thing was visible, indeed bigger and brighter, and with its diamond-lit tail in evidence behind it, horror filled every heart.

Some rushed to bang on the brass-bound door of the mage's mansion. There was, as ever, no answer, but after a while the servant appeared coming up the hill. He had been sent to collect special herbs, and was not best pleased to see the crowd barring his way, for he had found crowds were seldom personally auspicious.

Yet the village, in its panic, chose to forget its dislike of him.

"We beg you to beg your master to come out and tell us," cried the crowd, "what awful fate it is that hangs burning over us in the air."

The servant yawned with boredom. He knew how the comet would look, and was not afraid of it.

"Oh, that thing. It is nothing but some gob of flatulence belched from the sun. It will be gone by tomorrow, and good riddance."

The crowd conferred, partly reassured but indecisive. As they did so, the servant sidled by and got to the door, which a seal, given him by the mage, swiftly unlocked.

"But wait," said a man. "Will you not ask your master to speak to us? Despite your words, some of us are convinced the object is a terrible force and of malign intent. Already, from the shock of beholding it, three women have miscarried."

The servant, getting in through the doorway, hesitated. His obnoxious countenance convulsed in profound thought.

"Wait one moment," said the servant to the people, and slammed the door in their faces.

After three or four hours without any further sign from within, the villagers abandoned the door and rushed home. Here they and their women set about packing their furniture and clothing and getting their herds together. By midafternoon, the village was all but deserted.

To his first inspiration, the servant had now added subtlety. Once it was dark, the magician would require his servant's presence at the magic engine, but also, once it was dark, the full majesty of the comet would be revealed. The climax of its dissipation would follow. Now it seemed to the servant that if he could only bring the idiot-girl to the top of the mansion, tying her up, perhaps, on the western roof, well away from the locality of the engine and the mage, she must see the utmost activity of the comet and be duly appalled by it. The noise of the supernatural engine would cover her shrieks. If fortune were with the servant, she, like the other woman, would be delivered of her burden before the night was over. As for the mage, in the aftermath of the spell, he would be as one drugged and drunk, and would totter to his chamber, noticing little if anything of extraneous events.

Night came. The sky was quite black, all its stars blinded. Even the moon, when she floated up in the east, was opaque. But there was light, and to spare. Like a golden medallion on a silver chain, the comet poised above the earth, and radiance unfolded from it like wings, each moment more lucent than the last. All the tintings of the stonework were apparent, and the colors of the flowers on the hillside below, as if caught in the rays of a young morning.

The engine stood in silhouette like a toy some giant child had made itself from bits and pieces of metal, save that here and there a small flickering aurora would eddy up and down its tubes and pipes and wheels. The mage, at his ultimate preparations, had not yet emerged on the roof. The servant came by a back way, out of a trap door, shoveling the idiot-girl before him. Her wrists were tied, and a black cloth had been swathed about her head to keep the sight of the comet a surprise for her.

The servant let down the trap door again, and fastened the cord, which trailed from the girl's hands, into the iron ring. He did this leaving so little slack she must crouch down beside the ring. In such a position, the absorbed mage would be unlikely to see her. Actually, as the servant had long known, the mage scarcely saw or heard or noted anything that did not have to do with science.

When the dull pebble of the moon was a handspan up the sky, and the glow of the comet had grown like that of full morning, the magus stepped out on to the roof and walked straight to the machine, glancing at nothing, save the thing above.

This time, the levers had been set ready, and the mage had only to put his hand on a master coil to set the process off. As he did so, he called for the servant.

"Coming, O master," cried the servant, in his most fawning tone.

As the noise of the engine started up, the servant whipped the cloth from his lady's head, and ran to aid the magician, leaving her—as he opined—to mindless terror and its abortive consequences.

What went on in the deranged mind of the girl?

Contrary to the servant's hope, at first, not much. In her existence, all had been confusion, nothing made sense. One confusion more would barely overwhelm her. Also, as the clod-hopping rapist had failed to reason, since she had been kept timelessly in the dark, without benefit of sun or moon, for rather more than one hundred days and nights, she might only have concluded that the comet was merely day coming, and find nothing abnormal in it.

Of course, her eyes, weakened by the gloom underground, were hurt by the light, and so she covered them with her hands, whimpering. But this was not fear, simply another pain to add to the catalogs of pain she had already known. She took most pain as a matter of no moment.

But then, as the comet grew brilliant as a summer noon, something extraordinary began to occur.

Men, as logic and reason swelled in them, had lost most of their instinctual talents, which talents, in the case of magicians, generally had to be relearned. By this training, the mage had taught himself to understand that the rays of the comet, far from maleficent, were a tonic, even a panacea. Had he been a truly devout man, and less wrapped up in his own head, he might have said to the village—"Stay and benefit from this marvelous event. Put your sick ones out where they may receive the motes and beams to best effect." Instead, he had kept the whole thing secret, fearing to be pestered. He had, too, the plan to capture some of these benefits in his machine for future use in the arts of healing and beautifying. Also, let it be said, the mage was interested in what effect the radiations would have on the ghastly servant—but that was by way of individual experiment. Whatever else, the mage understood the comet was to be welcomed not dreaded, and the servant was so far indifferent to it, having been told it was incapable of harming him, and being too unimaginative to think up doubts for himself.

Conversely, the people of the village, having lost their animal awareness, and knowing no better, had run away.

The animals themselves, and the creatures all about, knowing nothing in particular, yet instinctively wise, rather than run away, had *gathered*.

As the comet burned brighter and more bright, all the birds of the region began to sing, their most melodious and lush dawn chorus, to welcome the great light. And as they sang, they flew and swirled about like leaves in a whirlpool, delirious with delight. Bees and butterflies and beetles also filled the air like flying jewelry. Lizards and serpents unfolded from the earth, basking. Cats and hares and foxes came, sheep which had been left behind, goats, an ocelot, all oblivious of each other, fell to rolling and purring on the grass. Monkeys and marmosets chittered in the tree tops, throwing gourds at each other in good humor. Flowers fanned into bloom. Fruits ripened and exploded from ripeness, filling the air with the scents of perfume and wine. Even the stones of the mansion, and those of the village below the hill, seemed to raise themselves, opening their cracks like thirsty mouths to drink the golden light.

The roaring sorcerous machine drowned out the sounds of most of these happenings, all save the noisy rapturous birdsong, which seemed to pierce through like chiming bells. For sure, it could have drowned the idiot-girl's screaming. Had she screamed.

Being witless, she had never learned a single thing, except, perhaps, that life was cruel and that her brother and sister humans hated her. Being witless, she had had no reason with which to drive her instincts out.

After maybe a minute of hiding her eyes from the hurt of the light, the girl's instinct had prompted her not to hide them. So, with water streaming down her dirty face, she had looked up into the heart of the light. And, being something of a cure-all, the blinding rays presently cured the weakness in her sight, and she was able to see, and rejoice in the seeing.

How beautiful everything appeared to her, suddenly, even tied up as she was. The emerald crickets dancing together on the stones at the roof's edge, the birds writing songs across heaven, the whole glory of this day-in-night. And abruptly, for the first time in many years, maybe for the first time ever, the idiot-girl laughed for sheer happiness.

A tawny rat was sitting on the roof nearby. Attracted, like the rest, by the comet, he had been interrupted in finishing the mage's supper. Now he mused on the juicy rope which bound the girl's hands to the iron ring. In his own way, the rat was also accustomed to abuse, and he did not venture near for some while. Then, seeing the girl did not pay heed to him, he slipped forward and began to nibble the hemp, rich in tallow spillings and grease, which, steeped in the comet's glow, were fit for a gourmet.

Finding her hands free all at once, the girl did not question. She had never questioned anything.

In that very instant, the comet began to diversify.

The sky, which had been black behind the gold, changed to a sumptuous rosy blue, a blushing blue, warm and lovely. And across this sheet of color, a golden rain began to stream in all directions, like the sparkles erupting from a colorful firework. And then these sparkles started to fall, in glittering chains, onto the earth.

"Stand well clear now, my dear," said the magician to his servant—even the mage had been affected. But the servant was already a safe distance from the roaring machine, gawping at heaven with his mouth open. The machine pulsed and whirred, and gemlike convulsions came and went around its wheels. Swiftly and surely, and well-practiced, the magician began to intone his forty-seven-syllable mantra. As he spoke the last words, a golden zigzag snaked down from the shining air and speared into the upper section of the machine, and so remained. The machine cried aloud in a wild register. Galvanic waves throbbed into it from the transfixing, still visible solar levin bolt, and all the shades of the spectrum sluiced over the machine.

"See!" feebly cried the mage, almost beside himself.

Then he saw another thing.

Drawn—without logic, naturally, rather as an insect is drawn to a bright-hued flower—the idiot-girl ran across the roofs of the mansion straight toward the machine and its sky tower of rainbows.

"Stop her!" cried the mage to his servant, but the servant had toppled down, still with his mouth open. The mage tried to summon a spell, but exertions had lessened his abilities. Before he could assert his power, the girl had reached the machine. Moths fly against the scalding cores of candles, and die. She flew against the scalding core of the comet fragment trapped by the quivering engine. But she did not die. No indeed.

She clung to the machine's framework, her cheek against its knot of pipes. Her face was blissful—was transparent. The mage groaned with chagrin as he perceived how the rainbow lights ran now, out of the sky, through the sonorous machine—and so into her body.

It had been his intention to build a conductor and a cistern. Never an instrument of direct transmission.

Despite the comfort of the solar rain, he was filled with frustration and rage. As air rushes to fill a void, so the power was magnetized from the machine into the girl's vacancy. He dared not detach the girl. Such a detachment might be dangerous to the engine—like pulling a leech from the flesh. A concussion might be caused besides, that would shake down the mansion. Or he himself might receive that concentration of the rays of the comet direct. He knew himself too crowded with cleverness and civilized thought to be able to survive such a raw contact. Only an idiot could survive it—an empty vessel. Ah! Only she.

And so he was compelled to watch as all that exceptional energy he had travailed for so long to capture, was dispersed into her thin, unwholesome, female body.

# CHAPTER 3

## Sunfire

When dawn returned over the psychically washed sky, the golden shower was finished, the magical gases dispersed, absorbed, and to be seen no more. The magician had also vanished—gone to his bed most sulkily to lament.

Far beyond the village, in an outcropping of hills, the villagers had taken shelter in caves and crevices—and so successfully missed all the miraculous outpouring of the comet's rays.

On the east roof of the mansion, a man was seated, playing with a tawny rat, letting it run up and down him, and now and then stroking its back and ears. Both man and rat seemed happy with this exercise.

The man was heavily built, and apparently very strong. His skin was clear, clean and a bronze appearance. His eyes were large, intent and sympathetic. In repose, his face was curiously attractive, almost beautiful, though it was only the beauty of peace and quietness.

Not the sky alone had been bathed. This was none other than the magician's servant. Probably, if he had suspected what the comet was likely to do to him, he too would have run. It had scaled his body of its dirt, and his mind also. Physically and spiritually it had enhanced him, and rinsed his ego of unknowingness. Like a chest full of drawers, each had been thrown open, dusted out, and heaped with valuables. Never again would he play tricks, brutalize or rape. The lusts of this flesh would be wholesome, nor would many refuse

103

him now. By his kindness and his understanding, hereafter, this man would win the love of others.

This then, had been done to the servant, under the parasol of rays.

To the idiot-girl who had embraced the machine and thereby the power source itself—what had been done to her?

At the other end of the eastern roof, an apparition was slowly dancing with its shadows. A young girl, with a sweet fey countenance, clean and white as a flower, her hair the gold of sun vapor, like the hair of the comet itself. Her movements were childish yet graceful. She looked at her shadow as she danced, and at her own arms and hands and feet, in pleasure and surprise.

Finally, she danced her way to the magician's servant, and she smiled at the rat now sitting on his knee.

"You must not overtax yourself," said the servant. "Do you understand you are with child, and I am the father?"

"Oh, yes," said the girl. "It is very wonderful."

"It might have been more wonderful if I had used you better," said he. "I am very sorry for it. But I will take good care of you now."

"No need," said the girl. "I believe I might have birthed a monster, or a deformed thing, but even my womb received that great fire from out of the sky. Inside me now is something most beautiful." Then she sat by the servant, and held his hand. She was very like a child herself, but an intelligent and trusting child, with wise thoughts beyond its years. "I was something witless and almost soulless, but I have been changed. I suspect I must change again, but not yet. Till then, shall we live here? Until this baby is born. I can barely wait to see her, she will be so rare. Begun by your body and by mine, but formed in the light of a star."

"How beautiful your hair is," said the servant. "It has the scent of lime trees and cinnamon trees. What is your name?"

"I never had one," said the girl.

"I will call you 'Sunfire,' because of the way your hair has become."

Presently, the tawny rat, seeing they had lost interest in him, ran off to his family. Having been exposed to the comet's rays, he had come to comprehend somewhat the speech of men. He boasted to his wives: "Two humans of exceptional good looks petted me. The man said he would call me Sunfire, for my hair."

"Oh," said the wives, and "Ooh," and they tactfully licked his whiskers to show they believed every word.

Later, when the day waned, they went up again to visit the magician, and ate the supper which had appeared for him, as usual, by sorcery, and which his dejection had precluded his eating himself. They were glad to help him out, and eventually upset the wine jar and fell to singing raucous rat songs of the centuries when their kind had ruled the world.

The magician, meanwhile, had returned to the roof.

As the open spaces of the twilight gave place to the closing vanes of night, he watched the couple talking softly and strangely to each other, as they walked about the hill below.

"Just as I thought," the mage muttered, observing the servant, courteous and gentle, take fruit from a tree and give it to the girl. "My despair confounds me!" the mage added, as he beheld the vague still glow that seemed to emanate from her skin and glorious hair.

Leaning over the roof's edge, the mage called to his servant: "I am going back to the city. Do you mean to come with me?"

"Dear master," said the servant, "if I can be of help, I will gladly accompany you. But then I would ask that you allow me to rejoin my wife."

It was spoken in a tone of such kindness, with such an obvious desire to be obliging, that the mage was filled with fury.

He turned and kicked the magic engine, one ringing blow, and stamped to his private chamber. Here he summoned some sort of flying conveyance, packed his books and instruments, and promptly vacated the premises.

The lovers did not see his departure. They were locked, for the first time, in love, amid the long grasses of the hill.

When the villagers came back from the caves, driving their herds bleating before them, they found the land was a little altered. And, as the days went by, the weeks, the months, greater alterations were come on, and greater yet. Men will fear almost anything changeable. It is part of the instinct of preservation and defense. But as these changes were of benefit, or else of charm or grace, gradually fear melted away.

In all the region where the comet's radiation had dispersed, there was not a dead tree or plant that had not put out leaves and blossoms, not a barren place that did not begin to mantle itself with seedlings. Fruits had ripened before season, and as they fell or were plucked, others ripened and burst out in their place. A mighty harvest overspilled from the earth, and as each stand of grain was scythed, so another began to grow, and after that, another yet. Three, four or five times the normal yield of the land was obtained, and for decades after, it would be so.

There was an old mine, long eviscerated of its minerals. Five months after the dispersal of the comet, the first traces of copper and gold were found there.

Blue roses, those prized flowers of the first earth, were found blooming under hedges, beside ditches. Orchids emerged from cracks in the walls.

Wild cats no longer attacked the flocks. Foxes no longer preyed on the chickens. Now and then, an animal would talk (though generally the substance of its conversation was unconscionable).

And, as time went on, unknown trees rose from the ground, with gilded leaves and heady perfumes. Fish with golden scales were discovered in the streams, the flesh of which creatures were inedible—though, when they died, they petrified into pure metal, and their eyes into sapphires.

A waterfall broke from the rock above the pool where the reeds grew. As the waterfall fell, it would make music, like the notes of a harp.

Men said to each other: "If so much excellence came to this place from that light in the sky, then surely it was not harmful after all."

The woman said: "If only we had not run away. If only we had looked for good instead of evil."

"If only we had received that flame from the sky also, we too might have flourished like the land."

They had noticed, additionally, that the idiot had gone at last. Heaven had removed the curse. Heaven had sent the light. They blessed the gods.

Scarcely observed, totally unrecognized, Sunfire dwelled by the musical waterfall in company with her husband. Their house was a bothy of stems and mud, the garden of which was the world beyond.

They passed their days and nights happily in this garden.

Animals ran to them and played with them. Food leapt out of the soil and from the trees to feed them. The water sang, and the man learned to sing from the songs of the water, and to make songs of his own. And Sunfire cut reeds and wove them into fantastic shapes—delicate boats, fragile birdcages, dainty figurines, and these she left on the edge of the pool. Women who came here to bathe would pick up these toys, marveling at the intricacy of their design, and bear them home. Coins and jars of honey and household articles were left in exchange.

Every morning, Sunfire would kiss the man as he lay asleep at her side. But as she wove the reeds, she would talk softly to the child in her womb, "Dear love, I shall never be as close to you as now I am."

And at night, sometimes, Sunfire would walk alone about the pool. She would gaze deeply into the eyes of the stars. The man would come to her, and ask her, "Are you troubled?"

"No, there is no trouble in me, or to come."

But her soul and her mind were far, far off, flowing up in the ether like two feathers bound to each other by a silken thread.

"I think," he said, "you will not be with me always. Even now, you are traveling to some other place."

She would put her arms about him, and her hair and skin would glow in the darkness. Moths would flutter to her as if to a lamp, and the nocturnal wasps who visited the water-flowers for nectar, would perch on the tips of her fingers. She grew big with the child, but in a neat and gainly way.

"How I long to look at you," she said to the child, the child of rape and horror, which had become the child of guilelessness and ethereal flame.

One day, when the man was from their house, gathering wild gourds, Sunfire's pains began. In her innocence, the girl was not afraid. The pains had a rightness to them, which encouraged her, nor were they beyond her capacity to endure. She knew their origin, besides, and her discomfort was mingled with eagerness. Very soon, the visitor she had been expecting would be before her. With the soundness of her animal instincts, she prepared. The light had made her strong. Her labor was short.

An hour or so after noon, when the man returned through

the young new trees that were coming up above the waterfall, he heard a baby crying, dropped the gourds he had collected, and ran for the bothy.

When he reached the house, all had been put to rights, and there sat Sunfire with her child, which was no longer weeping, but drinking from her breast.

When the child slept, they sat and looked at her. Though newborn, she was pale as a lily, and on her small skull, fine as morning mist, bloomed the palest, lilylike hair.

She had three parents, man, woman and comet. Yet, in her, the shine of the sun had become the sheen of the moon. She did not glow in the dark as her mother had come to glow. Only the beauty of the baby glowed. She wrapped her fists about the fingers of the woman and the man. A drop of milk spilled from Sunfire's breast upon the ground, and beamed for a moment like a filmy pearl, before the earth drank it gratefully down. Later, a flower grew in the spot.

"Soveh," crooned the woman. Soveh was the name she had chosen for her baby. The man did not argue, for Soveh meant flame.

In the darkness of the dwelling's corner, the man sat hidden and tears ran down his face, for he knew his wife would soon be leaving him, and he knew the child was not meant for him, and he knew that now he was enlightened enough to feel, he was to be gently and poignantly punished for his earlier wickedness.

But for almost a year, the parents and the child lived together. Sunfire made toys from the reeds for her infant. The man made a cradle of the stems. Sometimes they laughed and sang, and sometimes they were quiet. Sometimes the man and woman made love, and the child watched them benignly.

But often, in the pith and core of the darkness, the man who had been the magician's servant, would wake alone with the child. And going to the bothy entrance, he would see a candle flame gliding along the rim of the pool, and a second flame reflected in the water below. At first he took it for witch-fire or phosphorous, but as the flame moved about, he realized it was no elemental thing, but Sunfire, his wife.

There came a night then, when the year was almost done, and he beheld Sunfire walking by the water, and she was a doll of golden glass, lit within by a silver coal.

At length she came to him, with regret and with joy, and with a strange inevitable remoteness.

"You will be going, then," he said. He did not let her see his wretchedness, that it might not spoil her departure.

"It must be so," she said. "I shall not, I think, remain much longer in this form. How brief a time I have been a woman and known it, yet what sweetness I have shared with you and our daughter. I am sorry to leave you, yet not sorry, for this is my destiny. The fire of heaven which brought me to life is now reclaiming me."

"Do you have no fear?" he whispered, for he could see her bones through her skin like crystal rods, and blazing constellations had evolved in her eyes.

She said, "A child is not afraid to grow, nor a river afraid to return into the ocean."

They went together into the bothy, and looked at the baby that had been named Soveh.

"I do not suppose," said Sunfire, "that our child can live as other children do, or that her future will be commonplace. You must watch for portents. Events will demonstrate how you must bestow her."

"Could I not keep her, then?"

"No more than keep moonlight in a cage."

At that, he could not stay silent, and he said, "When I am alone I shall die."

"Do not waste yourself," she said. "Live, and learn."

In the morning, she was gone.

It is said that shepherds on the hills nearby caught sight of a woman walking the slopes, and one exclaimed that she was clad in gold, and another that her clothes were alight. But a third declared that as the sun came in over the shore of the earth, a topaz star flew up like a bird and spun away across the sky to meet the dawn. It was so bright, this starbird, he could scarcely glance at it, and yet it had, he said, the shape of a girl all of molten stuff, though she was also winged like a dove. . . .

There was a woman in the village, the reed-cutter's wife. A little more than two years before, she had gone to bathe and to cut reeds herself at the pool. There the mage's foul servant had sprung out on her and she had stabbed him in the thigh. Presently, as she cooked her man's supper, the magician's messenger-bird had come to chide her, and her husband had stood between her and the messenger and given back a stern reply to the magician. When the bird meekly withdrew, the woman had gone to her husband and embraced him. "How brave and clever you are!" she had extolled him, and they had let the supper she was cooking burn, and lain down together instead. When the comet appeared over the village, they, with all their neighbors, had fled. But though the woman was with child, she was not one of those who had miscarried. She took care, however, that none of the supernatural rays touched her, and later on, resumed her life in the village with the rest of the people. At the allotted time she bore a healthy girl-child, declared by everybody who saw it, to be of superlative attraction. As indeed, then and now, most new children are declared to be.

A morning came that the woman was at the pool once more, cutting reeds there, and her child nearby lying safe in a basket, or so she believed. The weather was hot, and the woman worked at her task slowly, singing to herself the while to match the harmonies of the waterfall. And her mind began to dwell on the wonder of that fall and how it made music, and on all the wonders that had accrued in the land, and the rhythm of her knife partly hypnotized her, cutting and cutting at the gray-green stems. . . . The child, meanwhile, had contrived to roll from its nest. In among the reeds, then, which to its unfocused gaze were a senseless jungle, it began to crawl. Up on their reed pillars, spiders like green marzipan stared down at it from many mulberry eyes which they wore like caps of jewels on their heads. Smart armored beetles scattered before its soft hands noisily, clattering their long horns.

The mother, pausing to rest a moment, glanced up, and caught her breath in horror. Some fifty feet away, her child was tottering drunkenly at the brink of the pool. Before she could prevent herself, the woman uttered a loud cry of alarm. The child started, and lost its balance. The water gave way like treacle to receive it. Then the surface knitted over, nor did it unravel to show the child again.

The reed-cutter's wife began to scream, and would have thrown herself directly into the pool, but in a moment more a man had dashed from among the reeds, and dived deep into the water. Without speech, in that mutual telepathy of human passion which will sometimes occur, the woman knew this stranger must have seen her child in the instant of its fall, and had rushed to help it. So she ran about on the bank, sobbing prayers of terror and frustration, and seeing how the black mud was stirred up to the surface by the man's activity. Once or twice his head emerged from the water, slick as an otter's, but only for a second was it visible before plunging down again.

Enough time had by now elapsed that anyone but the mother must have known her daughter to be dead. But she, of course, would not believe such a thing. At length, grim proof appeared. The man came forth from the pool once more, but now he carried something in his arms. It was a bundle, covered all over with water-murk. It might have been a great clod of mud he had dragged up, and incongruously offered the mother; save that the distraught expression on his face told another story.

But the reed-cutter's wife did not look at the man's face, only at the black and peculiar object he held out to her. And it seemed she did not recognize it, for she drew away, drew away from the edge of the pool, and suddenly she turned her back to the water, the man, the bundle, and began to scream again and beat her fists on the ground.

Just then the man, the magician's servant who lived by the pool, heard the bleating of a goat. There on the farther bank had arrived the little white she-goat, who gave his own child milk, and the child herself, who was called Flame. The man hurried to get to shore immediately, not wishing the tragedy repeated. Laying the dead and muddy infant in the reeds, he climbed onto the bank, and took up his own offspring in his arms. Soveh, disconcerted by the woman's screams, and made wet by this paternal encounter, sent up a howl of disapproval, penetrating as a thin gold wire.

It pierced the mother's ear, even through her own uproar. For it sounded in her head like a bell ringing out: Listen, listen! It is as you thought. No child of yours could ever die.

A heartbeat, and the woman was in the pool, swimming frantically for the area where the man stood, the girl-child in his arms. He, in surprise, merely stood and watched the woman, watched her till she too had dragged herself up the bank. And then she reached out, and snatched the child from his hands.

"You have revived her— Oh, a thousand blessings on you. And a thousand more from her father when he hears of it."

The man, who had come to live in serene naïveté, was lost for words, as this tune went on, but eventually he pointed at the reeds where he had set down the drowned child, and he cried, "Alas, it *my* daughter you have taken up. Your own child lies there."

At this, the reed-cutter's wife seemed to become quite mad. Her face shriveled on its frame, and blood engorged her eyes.

"Filthy trickster!" she shrieked. "Affecting pretense with an armful of mud to make believe my child was dead. Meaning to keep my child for purposes of your own. *My* baby, wet from the pool, as I can feel her to be."

There must have been some superficial likeness between the two small girls, or surely she could not so have deluded herself. No doubt both were fair, and of an age. Yet it seems an odd thing a mother should not know her own young, that which had budded from her body, which she had fed from her own breasts, and rocked to sleep, and carried about with her for two years, both in her womb and on her shoulders. But there is always this: her precipitate cry it was had pitched her baby in the water. A thoughtless, inadvertently murderous act. Guilt, in those days, was a wild dog, biting at its own tail. Perhaps this mother wished to be mistaken before she felt those teeth fasten in her heart.

"Vile robber," she shouted. "What evil did you plan? To kill and eat my daughter, maybe. Or to practice nastier deeds?"

And then, even as she ranted, she caught sight of a blueish scar upon his thigh. It was like a draught of strong liquor to her, that sight, for with it memory rushed back to her—of the rapist and her knife. She knew him in a flash of blood-red hate, and by that glare, she turned and fled, clutching her burden to her. Its stricken wails she translated to herself as fear of the devilish man who had seized it. Not as fear of its abduction by herself.

The man stood nonplused, staring at the mad woman. Yet, as she fled, he made to pursue, but the little goat got in his way. And, looking down at her, he remembered Sunfire who had played with the goat. And next Sunfire seemed to say in his brain: "Events will demonstrate how you must bestow our child." And he recollected, too, how he had guessed this was to be his punishment. Then he did not go after the woman, but began to cry, and the little goat nudged him, and he picked her up in his arms, and wept on her long white hair, his tears like a bitter song, to the music of the waterfall.

The woman, having convinced herself, convinced her husband, and next all the village. But when they went to look for the evil man finally to slay him, he had gone away. Only the bothy was found, and a few of the clever reed toys Sunfire had made, and an empty cradle. These, without compunction, the villagers burnt. And by the firelight, in the reeds at the water's edge, the spiders and beetles feasted.

And probably, for a month or so, some might remark to the woman: "How different your girl looks. It must be her ordeal has left its mark on her. Yet, if anything, she is the prettier."

And the woman smiled. (Though often in the ebb hours of night she would suffer a nightmare, seeing a tiny parcel of bones, with the green reeds growing through them.)

No longer was the child called Soveh, which is Flame. She was called the name the other child had had. That name is not remembered, but lovely she was, and lovelier she grew. Sunfire into moonflame. She, who might well have been born a monster, stumbling, ugly and mindless, transmuted by the comet's light.

But, being so wondrous, there began to be an apartness about her. Though she was demure and gentle, her very containment, her very sweetness, coupled to her extraordinary rarity, placed her inside a shell of crystal. She might be seen, and spoken to, she might answer and be heard, Yet who can touch through a shell of crystal? And who can love through one?

# CHAPTER 4

## Moonflame

The child grew. She was fifteen. She was beautiful. She was distant, perhaps unreachable.

The other young ones of the village reacted strangely to her. With the frequently valid instincts of childhood, they had known from the start she was not one of themselves. Yet, they had not feared her or disliked her. She was restful, peaceful in her beauty. If they were unhappy or troubled or hurt and no parent by, they would go to her, even when she was only three or four years, and somehow she would comfort and soothe them. They treated with her as if with an adult, an adult of their own height and age, but wiser than they. In some ways, as children, they were proud of her. When visitors came, they would be taken to see the reedcutter's daughter, she who had been drowned and revived. She was a sight-to-be-viewed in the village, almost a holy sight, though this they did not recognize as such, or would not, or could not.

But then she grew up, and the children of the village began to be obsessed with her. The girls would sit by her, and speak out their hearts to her, hanging on her calm replies. The boys would avoid her eyes that seemed suddenly bluer than heaven, look askance at her fluid slenderness, her platinum-colored veil of hair. They would think of her as they tended the flocks and herds, as they tilled the soil or cut the grain or hammered out pieces of metal on the anvil. They would think of her, too, when they lay over the bodies of other girls, or with the friendly whores in the tavern that had recently been

114

set up in the mansion on the hill. But, even as they thought
of bedding with the reed-cutter's daughter, some innate sense
of wrongness would overcome them. It was not that she was
undesirable. It was not that she was anything but filled to the
brim with the promises and forms of delight. Not even that
they had seen no passion in her, for there was a passion
about her quite beyond all expression, a passionate stillness,
like that of a closed and sleeping flower, the passion of that
which is waiting to break free, to blossom, to overspill the
margins of itself—and each must ask: Shall I be the one to
free her? Yet there was something else, beyond all this. The
shell of crystal, dimly, psychically perceived, in which this
flower lay.

However, human aspiration is often blind, its motto: I
want, therefore I will have. Which in some cases is an
excellent thing, but which, in this case, was mere folly.

The young men began to sue for the reed-cutter's daughter
in marriage.

The prideful parents were less aware of their child's un-
usual qualities, for they knew only that she was the best
daughter in the world, the loveliest, the most dutiful and virtuous—and all this they took for granted, since she was
theirs, and could not therefore be anything less than perfect.
But now their pleasure in her was doubled, for here was a
proposal for a wedding from the wealthy blacksmith's son,
and here another from the son of the landowner who
possessed more than two hundred olive trees, and more than
three hundred goats. And here a proposal from all three of
the baker's sons. And here from the vintner's young brother.
And here—oh, yes, best hide this one—a naughty offer from
the silk merchant's niece who lived in the town and, out on a
drive, had spied the reed-cutter's daughter through her carriage window.

"Is this not wonderful?" said the reed-cutter of his daughter. And very fairly he told her of each of the young men
who had asked for her, extolling their charms and good qualities. Nor, since he was an honest man, did he praise the
wealthiest ones most highly, but gave all equal measure.

The girl sat, quiet as a leaf, and her father was delighted at
her modesty. Strangely, it was the beaming mother who grew
uneasy and slowly ceased to beam. The mother thought of
the green pool and the dead child who had come back from

death, changed from a corpse or a mere lump of mud, into a
living baby. The mother seemed to see a faint sheen playing
over her miraculous offspring, but probably it was only the
summer sun through the doorway. The mother wished to put
her hand on her husband's arm, murmuring *Say nothing else*.
But probably it was only a mother's natural fear of losing her
daughter.

"Now," said the man, at the end of his recital, "you may
take as many days as you like to decide whom you will have.
It is a difficult choice, for many of them are fair, and several
are well-to-do. But remember, do not think only of coins.
Your mother and I have been poor, but we have also been
happy in each other."

The girl raised her head. She smiled on them like a bene-
diction, but she said: "There is no man I have met that I
would wish to live with."

The father was shocked. He was a man, and believed men
to be fine creatures.

"Come now," he said. "That is foolish talk. What better future can you gain than in the role of wife?"

She had always been obedient, and gentle. She had always
been loving, attentive and calm. She had been strong, too,
and oddly knowing, but they had missed that, confusing one
thing for another. Yet now she said to them, softly, carefully,
"I do not desire to marry. My answer to each and every one
is 'no.'"

Dumbfounded, the father. He was not a stern man, but anger began to brew in him. When he could not get another answer from her, he commenced to rant and rave. "You must,"
he said, "You shall." But, "No," she said, in a voice like a
water drop falling on a stone, the same drop splashing minute
by minute, year by year. "I will give you 'no'!" quoth he, and
he shut her in the house and would not let her out. He made
her sit among the clay pots by the hearth. And when she still
said "no" to him, he let the woman give her only bread to
eat, and water to drink. He became unlike himself, for he
could not understand. His wife wept nervously, and begged
her daughter to see reason. Sunlight stole through the door
and touched the girl on the foot, the ankle, the wrist, and
said: *Say yes, and be at liberty, and we will play together*. Or
the scent of flowers entered and said: *Say yes, and be at
liberty, and I will garland you*. Or birds sang to the girl, and

their song said: *Each of us is mated, and joyful in the mating. Say yes, say yes.* But still she said "no.' "

After a week, the father came to his senses. He walked into the house, and lifted his daughter in his arms. He put an orange into one of her hands, and a mug of wine into the other.

"I have been stupid," he said, "not to respect a young girl's temerity. You must forgive me." Then he slipped a thick gold ring on to her thumb. "I should not have left you to choose. I have realized my error and chosen for you. Here is the vow-ring of the landowner's son. In a month, you will go with him before the elder, and be wed."

Then he paused, observing his daughter as if he anticipated some tantrum or other. But she only raised her turquoise eyes, and looked full at him, a look without reproach or hysteria.

"You believe," she said, "that you have acted for the best. I regret you have not."

At her absolute authority, at the color of her eyes, the anger in the reed-cutter ignited. He flung up his fist to strike her across the head, but his wife caught his fist and hung on it.

"Only think," she cried, "how it would look. Our girl unveiled at her wedding, with a gold ring round her finger and a black ring round her eye!"

She could not know her curious birth, this moonflame of a girl. How could she? Who had there been to tell her of it, once she was old enough to reason? And surely she did *not* know, for the stars did not call to her, or the sun, as these cosmic things had called to her true mother. She had lived among men, had the Comet's child, grown among them. She had never protested or eschewed her fortune. Until now, she had never refused a single proper thing.

What then motivated her? Some secret intuitive grasp of her nature? She was the flower within the crystal. Of what were her mind and spirit fashioned?

It is perhaps a fact, that to the truly good, life, and the ways of men, and goodness itself, are very simple things. What to others appeared as her virtuousness, was to her merely her state of being. She did not set out to be good. She was good naturally, as another breathed. Hate and bitterness and envy and despair, those four envenomed serpents gnawing the livers of mankind, could not get in at her. But to herself she was nothing special; only herself to herself. And her sense of unexplained waiting, which was total, of inexplicable purpose, which was utter, these were as much a part of her as all else. She did not protest to the reed-cutter, though she never once agreed with his plan. Nor did she protest to the women who came to make her wedding garments, or to the neighbors who brought her gifts. When one or two of the young men who had lost out on the bargain hung about the house with wild looks, she went to them, and, as in the past, was able, curiously and obliquely, to console them. And when the landowner's son arrived, his handsome face pale with romance, she was courteous to him, nor did she refuse his token kiss. Only when he swaggered and said to her: "I think you will not mourn, being wed to me. You wish it too," did she quietly reply, "I do not wish it."

At this a small scene ensued. The reed-cutter pacified the prospective bridegroom. The prospective bridegroom's haughty servant was heard to remark that the landowner did not wish the marriage, either, and had only given in for fear the young man would otherwise slay himself.

When the guests were gone, the reed-cutter stormed about the countryside, convinced he would beat his daughter if he remained indoors.

But, unimpeded, the day of the wedding presented itself.

The women came with songs and flowers, and escorted the girl to the elder's house. And here, clad in her embroidered raiment, she was married to the landowner's son, who then lifted her veil and tore it in two pieces, as a symbol of the breaking of her maidenhead.

In a carriage drawn by dove-white mares, the bride and groom were carried to the landowner's estate, and here, with all the village, they feasted, amid the tamarisk trees, the olives and the tame peacocks.

Afternoon expired, the sun politely took its leave, and dusk wandered reluctantly after. But the eating and drinking and dancing went on, and soon the stars came out to see. They missed the bride, for she had just gone in, led by her new attendants, who took her to a chamber lit with scented lamps and hung with silken drapes. Here they unclothed her, perfuming her as the lamps were perfumed, dressing her in draperies of silk as the bed and the walls were dressed. And as they did this, so the handmaidens marveled aloud at her extreme pulchritude, for it was etiquette to do so. Thus, so intent were they on the protocol of these compliments, that they missed the evidence that everything they said was correct. She was indeed slender and supple as a lotus stem, her breasts, truly, were like the bells of honeyflowers. Her loins and her limbs were, for sure, a delight to eye and hand and every sense; her hair a fountain of starshine, her eyes like the holy lake of Bhelsheved. For once, all they said was no more than factual, but the women scarcely noticed. If you had asked them afterwards, was the girl fair, they would have answered: "Pretty enough." Yet she was like the new moon gleaming upon the sea. She was like the morning of the morning.

It was possibly this look of her, burning softly through her robe of silk, the glistering fall of her hair, that checked the young man when he came in to her. He was hot with drink and desire, yet maybe he was not entirely certain, either.

"My father at last agrees," he announced, however, "your lack of dowry is amply compensated by your loveliness."

Then he went to her, and embraced her. He did this with artistry. Love was an occupation in which he was well-versed, and he had learned the trade diligently. He caressed and kissed his bride, seeking out in her those responses to which he had become accustomed. But gradually there stole in on him one awesome new knowledge.

It was not that she was cold to him, for she was now, as in all else, tender and gentle. But she neither fired at his touch nor shrank in timidity. She seemed cognisant of all he could do, yet indifferent, or rather, removed from it. It was the crystal shell he made love to, then, not the flower. He could not come at *her*. Finding this, a terrific fury might have overtaken him. He might have forced her, lust not to be denied. But he felt no fury, and soon he felt no lust. The urge sank, and slept within him, and he was neither discomforted nor distressed. He found himself to be only puzzled.

"Is this some spell you weave?" he said at length. "A spell to make me impotent?" But he did not really believe such a thing, had suffered no foreboding.

"Your manhood is assured with others," she said. "But I am not for you, nor for any man, I think."

At this he paled, and he whispered, "Is it the gods them-selves who have kept you from this?"

"I do not know."

Then he sat a long time drinking wine, and finally he laughed and told her they were foolish, and he would lie with her after all. She stretched out with him, without demur, but things went as before, painlessly and nonproductively. And even now the impulse to rape or wrath or fear did not enter the young man's head, though a deep sadness came into his heart.

Eventually he fell asleep in her arms, which were a virgin's still, and that was their wedding night.

In the morning he was ashamed, but she reasoned with him with great care, untangling the strands of his anxiety till his self-esteem was in order again.

When at last the rich father came in to congratulate and tease them, and the women to mark the evidence of the wedding sheet, (or, if necessary, to falsify the drops of initial blood), they discovered the couple composedly seated at a board game.

Disconcerted, but seeing his son to be the tutor, the girl the pupil, in this activity, the father assumed that here was a cy-pher for the night's love-ritual.

"And does your wife take your instruction well, my son?"

The young man raised his sad, calm face and answered: "Alas, she is not my wife. Nor may she be."

The women had by now discovered the pristine bed, empty of all proper stainings of any sort, and stood about twisting their hands.

"Is there some impediment?" the father demanded, al-though, looking at the girl, he could fathom none—only some horrible concealed thing could be the cause. But again his son spoke softly to him.

"The impediment is the will of the gods. It is they who will have her. She can belong to no other than heaven."

The altercation which then broke out is easy to imagine and repetitious to set down, since it was thereafter repeated both in the house of the village's elder, and in the houses of most of the villagers, especially the home of the reed-cutter. Nor did this occur one or two times, but many. The land-owner's son, a young man of great character, stood beside his wife through all these displays of amazement and abuse, himself receiving, on the whole, more insult than she, and that of a very obvious nature. But he did not shift from his assertion that not he, but the gods, must have her. After some months of celibacy and debate, he began to be credited.

Now every twenty years, or thereabouts, certain elders of certain of the villages, and rich men, and others in positions of authority, would be drawn by lot. And they would make a journey through all the lands that held Bhelsheved as their religious center, and they would select from the children, and very occasionally from the youths and maidens, those that they thought fit to serve the gods in the white moon city in the desert. These young persons were then conducted to a separate establishment quite close to Bhelsheved. Here they were subjected to tests and particular trials, to determine which of them the gods preferred. Some consequently returned home, having been judged unworthy. Some remained and became the gracious and unworldly priesthood of the holy city.

The season for such another choosing was yet six or seven years off, but the problem of the reed-cutter's daughter gave evidence that a unique case had arisen. As anger and argument fell away, some new format was required to take their place. Religion flooded like water into a hollow. Then, at last, they looked at the girl with fresh eyes, and saw her, with astonishment, for the first time. How glowingly pale she was, how silver her hair, and such a lake-blue gaze. . . . Yes, in her form, she was fashioned for Bhelsheved.

Important men visited the village. An air of self-importance visited the village in their wake. Even the reed-cutter began to smile again. One pride was to be salvaged by another. Anyone's daughter could make a decent marriage. But to be chosen by the gods themselves. . . . Had he not always expressed doubts about her wedding, even shutting her in the house to make sure she considered properly whether she really wanted to wed?

She was examined, Moonflame Soveh, who was no longer known by such names. She was questioned. She had stayed serene through all the trouble, and serene she still was as cold-eyed women probed her body to ascertain its chastity, as frowning officious men probed her brain for promiscuity of thought, promiscuity sexual or intellectual, for evil meditation, or one solitary impure dream.

But she was like a flower to these also. Turned inside out, she was wholesome, delicious, and much more. For as their interrogation went on, they found they could not scathe her, or smear her, even by their words. So, and only so, they perceived she was within the crystal. And they interpreted that crystal as a thing of holy device, a glass jar the gods had put her in, and which they had stoppered by divine will.

The village wept when she was borne away to the desert, to the penultimate building a mile from the gates of Bhelsheved. But as they wept, they rejoiced in her. Her father rejoiced. Her mother. Those who had loved her as children and as adults. All of them. All save the landowner's son, who did not weep or rejoice. He lay instead with a girl, real, imperfect and marvelous as a rose, lay with her in love amid the pastel shade of the olive trees. And only when their bliss was achieved and ended, did he experience, once more, that empty cell within his heart, no larger than a drop of rain, or a single tear. Such a small emptiness. Such a tiny room in the palace of his emotions and his appetites. It would never again cause him any great grief. And never, never would it be filled.

The place of testing and preparation, one mile from Bhelsheved. It was none other than that earlier tower of Sheve, Jasrin's tower, where she had played with the bone of her child; where Chuz, Prince Madness, that master of delusion and dismay, had come to call. But centuries had gone by. The old tower was bolstered by new brickwork, and by a cluster of courts and attendant buildings. The pool, where a torch had burned under the water, was now rimmed by a cistern, and partly veiled by twining plants. The palms were taller, though one had died and its great trunk had been made into a wooden column which stood at the centre of the interviewing chamber.

Seated or kneeling, or on her feet, in company, or alone, the village girl, whose name had once been Soveh, endured many ordeals, verbal, and of the spirit, beneath this column.

But sometimes she must go elsewhere. To be shut up in isolation for many hours or days, or in a room where venomous snakes, golden and green, slid up and down, or within a wall of mirrors where she might see nothing but herself, or inside walls of darkness where she might see nothing at all.

At such tests, one other always attended, hidden but in ear-shot. Whoever underwent such a test and could not bear it had only to cry aloud three times to be set free. But after these compassionate freedoms came the kindest of all dismissals. Priests must be of stronger stuff. Or, of *stranger* stuff. For none of these tests were to gauge force or physical power, but the inner wells, the elasticity of psychic things. For the testing asked, in substance: Who can make equilibrium in himself, from dreams and faith alone? With this in mind, all the trials were just, and accurate.

And the girl endured. Did not even endure, as such. Strangeness seemed as natural to her as normalcy had been; perhaps more natural. She approached nothing with trepidation. Even certain ordeals that had to do with elements of pain—such as fasting in the guise of starvation—she showed no aversion to. She went to meet each thing alertly, without hesitation, her eyes wide, her heart open.

The final stages of the testing were the most obscure. They had to do with perception and sensitivity. For example, an apple might be brought and set down before the novice. "What do you see?" would be the question. Some would study the apple and reply: "This is life. Food in the flesh of it, future food in its pips, which may be planted in the ground." Or some would say: "Here is the emblem of a man—the skin—the flesh; the seeds—which in man are the seeds of his soul." The girl took the apple and she smiled. She threw it in the air and caught it in her hands. Surprising her earnest questioners into consternation, she lightly said, "Like a ball that children play with." Surprising her questioners into profound silence, she said, "Round, as one day the world may be, which now is flat."

Late in the day, they took her to the roof of the tower. They left her by the parapet: "Keep vigil until the dark has come."

The desert was softer in that era than it had been long ago. The day faded behind leaves and fronds, and the air turned to a sea of blue. Clusters of stars appeared. In the dusk, the girl heard faint music below her, and a woman's voice murmured, "Soon he will return to me." It was the voice of Jasrin, out of time, which was heard.

The girl was not alarmed—never so. All her life, she had been aware of supernatural essences about her. That she now beheld and heard them more clearly, fined by her training in this place, was inevitable.

Turning, she saw, against the sequined sea-sky, a black woman, young, slender and beautiful, and with her a woman with pale skin and yellow hair. The girl would have recognized them from the stories, as the two queens of Nemdur. But she knew them also by that infallible recognition which attended a mystic sight. The two women spoke together softly, and walked about the roof. The girl did not catch their words, (or conceivably the language of the area was greatly altered), and when they came to her, they walked through her. She felt their passage like a low summer breeze blowing btween her bones and across her blood.

Not all persons left on the roof witnessed the dark woman and the pale pass by. Only the most responsive did so, and this was all they saw, this brief scene, for some reason indelibly impressed upon the bricks and the aura of the tower— possibly because it was a scene of harmony, out of all those scenes the tower had been party to, of suffering and insanity, of evil and lament. As one happy day will stand out in the memory of a year of sadness.

But after the ghost women had gone away, the girl who was the comet's child, saw a third figure come walking across the roof.

To be sure, she did not see him well. There was, in the purpling intensity of the twilight, something cloudy about him. His purple cloak, also, blended with the rising water of night, and curious scintillants on the cloak might have been confused with far, dull stars.

She did not know this apparition, not even from legend, for hereabouts legends of such as he had grown corrupt and unrepresentative—as Azhrarn himself would learn. Yet, not knowing, still she *knew*, and at once she lowered her head and shielded her eyes.

"Ah," said he, in a most musical voice, "so you guess?"

"I do not guess your name, lord," said the girl. "But the air ripples like a stream before you."

"I will tell you who I am. I am your lunacy," said Chuz, Delusion's Master, Prince Madness, one of the five Lords of Darkness. "For you *are* mad, my dear, in following this vocation. Even your goodness is a craziness. But then, all the very good are mad, just as the very wicked are mad. In fact, there is hardly any difference between the holy and the profane, save in their ideals and their deeds. Both are fanatics. Both are ruthless. Tomorrow you will be sent to your temple. Before long, your fate will find you out. Do you wonder what it might be? No," added Chuz suddenly, "do not look at me. You have glanced, inspect no further. I understand the temptation is strong, but I would not have you any more than a fraction my subject. I will accordingly muffle my face."

"For that I thank you," said the girl. "Sensing your power, I comprehend you are generous."

"It is not my motive to enslave you. Another will come to you in due course. Which may be *his* madness, I believe, a delusion beyond all others he, though not I, have achieved in the world. Would you have his name? Best not. My third cousin, three times removed through the black dynasties of night. Less kin to me than a lizard is, but nearer to me than one grain of sand to another. And you will know him, too. I think you are mad enough, my darling, to pity him a little. And how he will stare at that!"

The edge of the cloak, damson-colored as the sky now was, brushed like a long wing over the dusty roof before her. She saw the stars of it were bits of broken glass. And she heard the rattle of dice in the moment that he vanished.

Those who questioned her after were perplexed.

"It was perhaps the temptation of a demon, which failed," they said. "Or can it have been an occult proclamation, some messenger of the gods?"

Whatever it was, next day they conducted her to salt-white Bhelsheved, to the hibiscus towers, the lake of turquoise mirror that matched her eyes. She was a priestess. They named her Dunizel, Soul-of-the-Moon.

In her bubble of crystal, now she floated by others in similar bubbles, (yet not the same, not at all), everyone magically adrift in the currents of the heavenly city, that Upperearth-on-Earth.

Friendships were rarely made here. Inner joys were woven, introvert candles kindled, divine eccentricities. Religion was the flower, and they the bees which visited and revisited, their sole purpose to make spiritual honey with which to sweeten the sourness of the outer world. Bhelsheved the beehive.

So, in her calm, waiting loveliness, her iridescent steely innocence, she dwelled for three years. Until the scent of somber fire came to her in the night, and she knew the wicked thing burning there like a lamp of black flame. And coming out, she found him, Azhrarn, whom Chuz had named her fate.

# CHAPTER 5

## An Image of Light and Shadow

The sun had come up over the world, and Dunizel, Moon's Soul, had been returned to the blossom garden by the sacred lake of Bhelsheved. And he who had lain over her, yet not with her, the marvelous weight of him, not in the least heavy or oppressive, yet of a substance that had seemed to combine with her own flesh, he had gone back to his city of Druhim Vanashta, underground.

That demon metropolis, lit eternally by the light of the Underearth, which was neither sun nor moon nor stars, yet most like starlight—though brighter—bright as a sun composed of shadow—and yet milder—more like the moon, yet not the moon, for colors palely glowed and swarthily smoked there. . . Did Druhim Vanashta seem fair to him, when he reentered there, into its lambency and its altered time?

The towers were still as tall and slender, still as fantastically ornamented, the lacelike parapets still holding their arrow shafts of burning jewels, the windows their multi-hues of glass and crystal and corundum. The walls still rose like blades, or curved like half-closed wings. The brass and silver, jade and porcelain and platinum were still purely wonderful to behold. The gardens and the parks of spangled black, where fish sang in the filigree trees and birds swam in the pools and flowers chimed like bells, had not altered, would never alter, never could. And the glamorous citizens passed up and down there, bowing, obeising themselves to Azhrarn, each one fabulous, his subjects, all of them in love with him, for demons seldom served anything they did not worship, and

Azhrarn they worshipped and to spare. It is pleasant to be loved.

But to love—

Demons did little in the paltry way of men. Their passions, as they themselves, were like the sheerness of great lights. They had probably invented sexuality, physical love. They could not have invented such a thing if love itself had not been to them some sort of key to the world's heart. But fire consumes, eating itself with what it feeds on.

Once, he had taken another, as a child, even into the demon city, had watched him grow there like a plant, like a young tree, and, at the first Azhrarn had said to him: "I do not give my love lightly, but once given it is sure." Which was not quite exact. Inventories of the liaisons of Azhrarn might be drawn up, some of them very light, very casual, the stuff of a mortal year, a day in Druhim Vanashta. But love has many houses, many countries. All exist, then and now, and for as long as what lives can see and feel and think. For love is, too, a product of thought. While it seems to destroy reason, yet nothing that *cannot* in some mode reason, can ever love.

Azhrarn went about his city and about its gardens and outer environs, in the changeless morning-evening, dawn-dusk of Underearth's sublumination.

Those who saw him, responding to his moods, as always, sensed in him an obsession with everything, and with nothing, or with something other than that underground place. They had been aware formerly of his cold anger. They had been primed to serve him in this anger, and had already done so when the sorcerous tower of blackness and lights had risen in the desert. Yet now the princely caste of the demons, the Vazdru, said one to another: "Our lord no longer requires our service. He has happened upon something which he will engage alone." And knowing, by a sort of empathy, what that something must be, they knew also the sharp gorgeous jealousy of their kind.

Even in attainment, to love may encompass pain. Beyond the moment of fulfilment, who can ignore other moments that lie in wait, moments of doubt, of unlucky possibility? Truly, most of Azhrarn's lovers, (mortals), had betrayed him—not, it is sure, by cleaving to another in his stead, since such was virtually inconceivable—but rather by disappointing

him, failing him, ceasing to surprise or entrance him. Or by
hankering after some other thing and wishing for it as
mightily as they wished to keep his liking. And as love's su-
preme law is that nothing must be of such value as itself, that
hankering of theirs each time lost them his regard, and, usually, their lives. For demons tended to kill those who failed
them, less from vengeance than a desire to tidy up the
trailing loose ends of an affair. (Rotten food is not cherished,
but burnt or thrown away.)

At the center of the garden of Azhrarn's palace, a fountain
played, a fountain of red fire that was neither hot nor illumi-
nating, yet most beautiful for all that.

He seated himself on the sable lawn by the fountain,
Azhrarn the Prince of Demons. The jet and topaz wasps
played about the transparent flowers, and sometimes he
watched them. His people did not directly approach him, but
once an Eshva woman went by, one of the handmaidens of
his palace, feeding the gentle winged fish in the trees from a
silver basket. Azhrarn observed the woman, who, like all of
demonkind, was superlatively lovely. He examined her loveliness with pleasure, but it seemed he equated her with the
flowers and shrubs of the garden. It became clear from his
glances at this Eshva, that if he visualized a woman, it was
Dunizel he saw.

How strange it was. The sun could sear him to ashes;
Dunizel was the child of a solar comet. Perhaps, not strange
at all.

But days and nights were passing on the earth. Seven days,
and twice seven days. A month passed. Two months, and a
third month began.

He had not gone back to her. He had sent her no sign.
Though the time of his lower world was unlike that of her
world above, yet he could measure both, and match them to
a second. He knew how long ago he had left her. Thus, he
thought of her, but did not seek her out. Could it have been
he was reluctant, thinking she would disappoint him, her attraction less, waning like the moon? Could it have been some
other thing he doubted, some aspect of himself? No easy matter to interpret such a heart and brain as his. But he did not
go back to her until the midst of the third month.

That night there was a full moon over the earth.

The blossoms were long finished in Bhelsheved, and the

leaves of the garden hung heavily as bronze. White pillars in
the walks were like the teeth of bone combs tangled in the
hair of the darkness.

There was no sound anywhere. No wind to stir the trees,
or the water, or to blow the husks of flowers or the little
drifts of dust along the colonnades like whispers.

In their bare blanched cells, the priests and priestesses
dreamed, waking or sleeping, of religious ecstasy, and the
gods, their fair hair washing around them like some silver
overflow from their brains. Here and there in a fane, a sacred
lamp was burning, some priest or other standing tranced
beneath. In the heart temple of Bhelsheved, poised above its
lake, vague glimmers came and went, the leftovers of magic
and reverence, lingering after the fact, like footprints in sand.
Till another sorcery quenched them.

At the heart of the heart of Bhelsheved, a black fire
burned and went out.

Azhrarn looked about him silently. There was nothing
readable in his face or manner. Only he himself was apparent.

He walked the length of the temple, past its stupendous altar mounted on the backs of the two gigantic beasts of gold.
He did not, demon that he was, care for the gold of the
temple. (He had manifested upward, from beneath the lake,
rather than through the golden walls of this building.) Yet he
paused by the beasts, for seated between the paws of one of
them was Dunizel.

Before her on the ground was a sheet of parchment, and
sometimes she would trace particular symbols over it with her
fingers. But she too was tranced, far off within or without
herself, in some esthetic kingdom of the mind.

Azhrarn walked closer, but he kept his shadow at his back
so it should not fall on her. His step was noiseless. He was
visible—yet invisible. Only the glamour of what he was might
have been detected, like a sound just beyond the level of human hearing.

He stood near to her, and he gazed into her brain.

She might have imagined herself abandoned by him. She
might have turned her reveries, therefore, to other things, to
her gods, indeed, as was expected of her. That would have
been pardonable, though he would never have pardoned her

for putting him aside more than a moment, even in her dreams.

So he stared through white hair, and whiter skin, and whitest bone, through the metaphysical casings of thought, and saw with her inner eye.

A great stillness came upon Azhrarn then, almost a quiescence.

It was for him like looking into a mirror, looking into the mind of Dunizel, for there he was, drawn in the colors of darkness, on the panels of her dream.

For though she saw the gods—each of them was Azhrarn. Some were female and some male, some exquisite children, some exotic animals, but each was Azhrarn, each and all. And if she saw a sky it, also, was Azhrarn. And the seas were Azhrarn, and the earth.

He himself, looking at other things, had suspended his belief in them. But she believed and saw, clearly and merely through the medium of Azhrarn. He had made all things real for her, by imbuing the nature of all things. He had become for her all things, the life, the essence of the world.

Perhaps, if her meditation had been apart from him, or simply anguished, or—worse—trivial, he might after all have avoided her, punishing her for failing him. She had not failed him. She had made him God.

So he put out his hand and laid it softly on her beautiful head which had become his temple.

When the pilgrims came to Bhelsheved, and walked the gleaming, sorcerously sandless roads that led into it out of the desert, the city sang to them. This was because hollow chambers lay under the roads, which the reverberations of so many footfalls above stirred up into echoes, a silver thunder. Only at the perimeter of the city did these chambers end, and coming onto the last stretch, the echo-sound ceased, adding to the amazement of the crowd. But the touch of Azhrarn sent its resonance through the body of the girl, a note which did not die, but woke new echoes, echo upon echo, song upon song.

She came from her trance gently, as if from summer water to a summer lawn. Her eyes fixed on Azhrarn, and she smiled at him.

He took his hand from her head, but looked at her still a long while, unspeaking.

At last she said to him: "Do you wish me to bow down to

you? Or do you understand my homage goes beyond obeisance?"

"Do not," he said, "bow down to me." And then he said, "I have been from you some time, by mortal reckoning. Did you suppose I would not return?"

"But," she said, "you never left me."

He knew it was as she said, both for Dunizel, since she had retained his image in her soul, and for himself. When in the Underearth, yet truly, he had been with her.

He leaned and lifted her to her feet. All humankind responded to his caress, but he was attentive, seeing her response to it, as if he beheld his own influence for the first.

"There is something I shall say to you," he said, "but not yet. I will take you traveling tonight. Do not be afraid."

"If I am with you," she said, "I shall fear nothing."

"Like all your priesthood, you are a magician. Yet you are more than that. Shall I show you what you are?" (He had always known, or he had swiftly discovered, her genesis.)

"Will this fresh knowledge alter me?"

"Perhaps."

"Do you wish me altered?"

"No."

"Do not tell me, then, or show me. Show me only what will keep me as you desire me to be."

Azhrarn was amused, disturbed, maybe, at this abjection which was not abject. Demons relished flattery and service, and knew their weakness.

"You will negate and deny yourself," he said, "if you seek only to please me."

"I am more than my body and brain and ego and spirit," she said. "I am my love for you. Nor will I negate and deny my love."

Azhrarn did not reply to this, but he wrapped her, as if it were in a swirling of the starry night, and they were drawn down into the lake under the floor of the temple—and he was a black fish with meteor eyes, and she a silver scale upon his forehead. And then the fish leapt upward. He was a black eagle, that familiar shape of his. And she was a light upon his breast—no white feather, but a white flame.

She saw, even as a burning flame, even knowing what he had become and what he had made her, and she felt joy at his power, and her joy made her brilliancy more brilliant, a fire that seemed to have flowered from his heart. Possibly it even hurt him, this sun-related moon-ember held fast against his flesh.

The night sky burst about them, as the water of the lake had burst. Currents and streamers of starlight, wind, and the intangible ether, parted and poured by. The moon had gained the peak of heaven. The world shone below like a heap of somber crystals.

Mile on mile he carried Dunizel as a white fire. She saw lands and waters come and go beneath them, living cities in their spider webs of light, ruined cities that slept in their draperies of shadow. In a forest built of the night, he came briefly to rest above a bending and ancient tree. And in this tree, a rose-colored bird, luminous as an afterglow, perched quietly on a bough, and now and then it raised its head, and uttered a single note of song that was like the striking of a beautiful clock. And later, as the moon began to descend, the black eagle carried Dunizel over the quilted surface of a sea, and settled on the mast of a phantom ship. Two hundred oars churned the water, and the sails of fine membranous fabric turned themselves to the wind, and the wheel also carefully turned this way and that, as if some hand guided it, but no one was aboard, no man, no ghost even that was discernible. He took her also to a remote sarcophagus, and flying in through a high-up opening, dropped down to where there stood a wonderful jewel, between five and six feet in height, and in color blue-purple. At first there seemed no form to this jewel, but gradually you might discover it was a statue which depicted a young man and woman embracing. Their long hair mingled, and their garments, and their arms were wrapped fast about each other with a wild fierce tenderness. Underneath the statue was a tablet of marble, engraved with two names, and beneath, the words:

*These lovers, due to die at the hands of enemies, and being both magicians, transmuted themselves, by the arts of magic, and of love, into this jewel, which is the shade of love. Pity them. Or be envious.*

And when the moon was setting, the eagle glided to a vast meadow where night-blooming flowers grew taller than a tall man. In the dark the flowers were gray, but their scent was like the sweetest and most costly incense.

Here, Azhrarn put on again his masculine shape and

restored Dunziel to her human form. And here they walked together, not speaking, between the slender stems.

At last the stars lowered the wicks in their lamps, the tides of night began to ebb away along the beaches of the morning. It was that hour before the dawn when each thing seemed to hold its breath. And overhead the gray flowers closed their wings like sleeping birds, and even their scent grew silent.

Azhrarn spoke, at length, in that silence.

"At our first meeting, I wounded you, and healed you with my own blood. Do you remember this?"

Smiling, she said, "Did you think I should forget?"

"I have never lain with you in love, Dunizel. Do you understand that, for demonkind, carnal love requires no excuse? It is our pleasure, skill, recreation, nothing less, or more. We quicken no living thing from congress. Procreation, with us, necessitates more thought, and greater intent."

She gazed at him, and she said, "How, then, are your kind begun?"

"By several means," he said. "But among the Vazdru, it is a device of blood. My blood," he said, "has mingled with yours. I lay one night upon you, and thereby fixed my image within you as surely as the seal-ring leaves its impression in wax. If I willed it now, but only if I willed it, you might carry my child, and bear my child. But if I leave the last sorcery unmade, what I have prepared in you remains dormant. It will neither harm nor benefit you. You will only know of it because I have told you it is so."

"And do you tell me," she said, "because you do not will that I bear your child?"

"I tell you that you yourself may decide whether or not you would carry and bring forth a procreation of mine. Let me inform you of the whole of the matter. The child will be female, for you are the mold in which she is cast, since you possess a womb, as mortal women do. But though she will resemble you, in herself she will be the feminine principle of Azhrarn, Prince of Demons, Night's Master, one of the Lords of Darkness. And what I am, in great measure must she be. Consider this. For though you will render her your light, her genetic substance will be darkness. Can you house such an image in your body, Dunizel? And bring it forth? And rock the creature in your arms? I did not and do not choose you randomly for this act. But neither will I impose it on you."

"Why," she said, "would you father a child at this time?"

"To father also mischief in the world. And pain, no doubt, and misery."

His face was cold and cruel.

"My beloved," she said to him, "you are mighty beyond mightiness. You must not listen to what fractious small men say of you, and believe it."

"Do not," he said, "anger me again. I would not wish to be angry with you."

"I do not credit your wickedness," she said. "You have millennia before you. It is the malice of your infancy on you now. Your infancy that is wiser than any wisdom of the earth. But you will come to other things. While they live, all trees must grow."

"Be silent," he said to her, and the flowing away of night seemed halted, foundered, and the shut wings of the flowers sizzled inaudibly, as if before lightning. And the grass beneath the feet of Azhrarn curled about itself, shrinking from him. Azhrarn lowered his eyes that were like black suns, to look at the grass that curled and shrank from him, and his lashes, that were long and straight like splinters of the night, hid the thought behind the eyes. As he watched the grass, or appeared to watch the grass, and as the air flickered in terror about him, he said to her, "You do not comprehend the stasis of immortality. Only men, who die, foretell their future."

And perhaps, or perhaps not, she saw in him then, faint and far away, some glint of a curious fear. All creation, now and then, had feared Azhrarn. Why should he not, once in twenty centuries, fear himself?

And because she saw his fear, maybe, she went to him, and kneeled to him, as if it were she herself who was afraid. But in truth, if he had killed her in that instant, she could not have feared him; love had left her no room for fear.

Presently he raised her to her feet and held her before him.

"You have not told me," he said, "if you consent."

"I have told you," she said. "You do not need to ask."

"If the sun became the moon," he said, "that is you."

And then he spoke a phrase to the sky, in one of the magic tongues of Underearth, and the sky, already fading from darkness, paled further, but only in one place that seemed, from below, about the size and structure the round moon had been. And this loosened piece of the night fell slowly down toward the meadow, revolving a little as it came. Yet, as it fell, it grew neither larger nor smaller. Into Azhrarn's outstretched palm it fell. It was no bigger than a plate, and of a thin, translucent blackness. The night, in itself, was not and could not be palpable—yet Azhrarn, by his sorcery, had somehow made it so. And now he fashioned it, deftly, delicately, until a figurine composed only of shadow stood in his hands. It had a female shape, a woman's shape, full-grown and perfect, but all tiny as a doll.

He said no word to her, but as if inadvertently, Dunizel lifted her hands to take the shadow shape from his. As her fingers touched the shape, a soft light began to come from it. It was like moonlight, yet unlike. Like starlight, yet unlike. It was like the light of the Underearth itself, the subluminescence of Druhim Vanashta, city of Demons.

The figurine then enlarged. It soared to cover Dunizel from head to heel, next shimmering and drawing in, conforming to her every contour, her every bone and strand of hair. Even the lashes of her eyes it seemed to approximate. For a few seconds, Dunizel was held within a second skin, like black water. And then the water sank inwards, in through her flesh, and she in turn was the skin which held the shadow. And dimly, through her skin that was so diaphanously white, you almost saw the twilight glimmer of that shadow, like pale black fire behind alabaster.

In the east there was a blueish sheen, evoking that of a polished knife.

The meadow of flowers was empty.

In Bhelsheved, among the trees that overlooked the lake, night returned unexpectedly: Azhrarn. And Dunizel a star caught up in that night.

There were only minutes before dawn would slit the horizon with her gilded nails. Time enough, perhaps, to say some secretive, profound thing. Yet even as he and she evolved on the edge of the darkness, Azhrarn beheld another was before them, a figure which poised on the water of the lake itself. It seemed most like an insect, a mantis, possibly, compactly yet vaguely folded in the cloudy mauve vanes of its wing-like cloak.

Dunizel turned to gaze at this apparition, but Azhrarn guided her head against him, away from sight of the creature.

Yet he himself stared across the water straight at it, and now the wing-tissue cloak stirred a fraction, and a head was lifted, and half a face came visible in a cowl.

"Why, good morning, handsome un-brother," called a melodious voice over the lake. "You are out late, are you not? The sun is almost up. Whatever can you be thinking of?"

"That need not concern you. For yourself, I assume it is Bhelsheved's madness which has brought you here."

"Hardly Bhelsheved's madness. That is a dull item indeed. But there is something much more delectable."

"Perhaps you are in error," said Azhrarn. "Let me suggest that you are."

Prince Madness, Delusion's Master, laughed. It was a noise reminiscent of rusty pots scraped together. He shook out his damson cloak. He smiled, or that half of the face which was visible smiled, its eye downcast.

"Azhrarn the Beautiful," said Chuz lovingly, "it is your beautiful madness I have come to see."

Azhrarn, shielding Dunizel both by his body and by his magic from this visitation of Chuz—unaware, or unwilling to recall she had already met with him on a previous occasion—shot a blasting glare of cold rage at the insectile being balanced on the lake. The Lords of Darkness seldom, if ever, went to war with one another. Such a notion was alarming maybe even to themselves. The warlike games they played against each other, therefore, adhered to certain rules. What rule was here in operation is difficult to conjecture. Nevertheless, Chuz stayed in the lake and did not advance or unveil his double aspect. Nevertheless also, the eastern sky was warming, the sun burning through—Azhrarn's limitations were more definite, and not of his own devising.

"Say what you want," Azhrarn said to Chuz. He spoke contemptuously, politely. He gave no hint of his agitation, but it was self-evident. He could not face the sun. In a minute or less, he must abandon the girl—or take her with him underground, an act not without complexity, seeing she was adult and psychically unprepared for such a descent.

"I have said what I want," said Chuz, "I am deliriously content."

"This maiden is mine," said Azhrarn. "You knew that?"

"Oh, trust me, my dear. I do indeed know. I have overheard your whisperings, I have watched you lying in each other's arms, still as the blue-purple jewel in the tomb. The madness of love. I have been entertained, since I am partly responsible. I brought about Nemdur's madness. His madness brought about Baybhelu. And Baybhelu brought about Bhelsheved. And Bhelsheved enticed you from the cellar. And now here you are, and here is a mortal woman who will bear you a daughter. A madness of extreme and magnificent proportions. Actually, un-brother," said Chuz, swaying a little, like a poisonous water-plant over the lake, "I came to stand uncle to your unborn child. And to offer her a gift."

In the east a gate began to open. Birds sang frenziedly in the trees—it might have been a cry of fright as much as of gladness. A freckle of palest yellow started in the lake—but it was only a fish, leaping.

"My lord," Dunizel said to Azhrarn, "I do not fear him. He means me no ill, for once he told me so and was courteous to me. The sun is near. Leave me, I shall be safe."

"He may be courteous," said Azhrarn in an acid tone, "but he has two sides to him. What gift?" he inquired of Chuz off-handedly.

"What else but something dear to me? Let me approach," wheedled Chuz, smiling and smiling over his writhing mauve reflection in the water.

"You," said Azhrarn, "can render nothing I may not render. In certain lands, your title and mine are mingled. I too am a master of delusions."

"And I," said Chuz, sweetly, musically, "have sometimes been called, as you are called: The Beautiful. Though only by those who saw me from the *right* side."

Suddenly he raised his left hand—black palm, red nails—and flung something over the water to the land. It fell with a brief bright sound at the feet of Dunizel. It was a single die, and seemed made of amethyst, strangely marked in black.

Azhrarn bent swiftly and took up this thing. No sooner had he taken hold of it than he hurled it back into the lake. But Chuz reached out and caught it just before it broke the water. Smiling still, he kissed the die Azhrarn had momentarily held.

"I have also," said Chuz, "three drops of rare Vazdru ichor, hard as adamant, which I discovered among the dunes about Bhelsheved. They say these drops are the blood of Azhrarn. Do you remember the young man with the whip? Do you remember grasping the tongue of the whip and how the blood spilled? The price of telling parables is high. You will not be the last to find that out."

Chuz turned suavely, and began to walk away over the lake, under the arched bridges which supported the temple. As he did so, a small horrid thing happened: scores of fish, brushed by insanity, flopped out upon the shore, convinced they might live in the air, and drowned in it at the margins of the colonnades and gardens.

As Chuz vanished, the east opened like a fan.

Azhrarn drew his black cloak over and about himself. Looking after Chuz, his eyes shone malevolently, but the foretaste of the sun, like fear of fire to one already burned, drove him down into the earth. He was storm, then smoke, and thereafter gone, without the space to say to her one commonplace word.

Dunizel stood alone. On her hand she found he had set, she did not know when, a ring of silver lit by a gray-green gem. On her wrist was a bracelet like a silver snake with eyes of sapphire, and from her ears hung silver filigrees that softly chimed to her as she moved—demon jewelry, Drin work, of surpassing fineness, and wondrous, too, in the unobtrusive manner of the giving.

But as the sun filled the east, in her womb Dunizel felt a slight but unmistakable twisting.

She wept then.

The sun made her tears golden. It combed her hair with gold. It clothed her and shone through her. She was perhaps even lovelier by daylight, and Azhrarn, save in some blurred mage-glass, could never see her as now she was.

Her tears ended quickly. She walked under the shade of the trees and the columns, mindful of what grew within her.

# PART THREE

## *The Bitterness of Joy*

# CHAPTER 1

## Seventeen Murderesses

It was winter in the desert. By day terrible winds blew back and forth, the shrunken sun was netted in sand. At night, rime armored inches thick along dunes. The reeds by the waters were brittle as green sugar. The palms took on a sulky iron hue. The trees in Bhelsheved had lost everything now, blossom, leaves and birds. The strewn dust grated over the mosaic tiles, before their tidal magics swept it away. The lake had a myopic look, like a beautiful eye which went blind. It was a harsh winter, dry, acrid, the old-age of seasons.

The priestly servants of Heaven walked dreamily about in the dust and frost, bound in their contemplation of the gods. They had been trained to ignore bodily discomfort, indeed to incorporate it as a part of their religious pleasure. With this tunnel vision of the senses they missed a lot. They almost missed the dire miracle which was occurring in their midst.

She had carried his child now into the seventh month. Truth to tell, she had not grown big, her supernatural pregnancy was barely obvious: she resembled, in that seventh month, a woman in the third month. Nor was there any heaviness to her, any laxity or sluggishness. Dunizel glided, her swan-white hair drifting about her. The bright shadow of Azhrarn's child shone from within her—but none of them might have noticed. She did not speak. She moved as ever about the shrines. Some nights she wandered in the gardens of the holy city. Once or twice or three times, some priest, mooning in the twilight over the gods, glanced up and saw a black cloud rush from the sky on black wings. At midnight, certain of the groves seemed haunted by strange intensities, perfumes, and hints of melody. At noon, Dunizel walked in the shade. Where the winter sun fell in stringy bars, she turned aside. When alone, she did not seem alone. When she worshipped in company with many others, she seemed quite alone. But they did not really see. They were in love with heaven. What else could she be in love with? The watchful yet mindless sorceries of the place confirmed her a virgin still. Her celibacy, her innocence, her loveliness, were all unchanged, or enhanced.

They almost missed the marvel Dunizel had to show them.

Or maybe, such a marvel could not, by the laws of the miraculous, ultimately be missed.

One day, an hour after sunrise, there came a susurration, as if feet passed over the echo chambers beneath the desert roads leading to Bhelsheved. When the susurration ended, there came a furious knocking on the western gate, as if hands smote there.

It was not the time of year for any to visit, certainly not the time for any to be admitted. The priesthood gazed uncomprehendingly at each other, the rocking gate, the silent fanes. Soon they flitted away, paying no heed to the external uproar.

Voices began to cry on the far side of the gate, over the howl of the winds: "Let us come in. We demand judgment and justice. We demand an answer of heaven."

To those priests who heard the cry, it must have seemed gibberish. Nothing was ever *demanded* of the gods.

The gates were not opened.

The knocking grew quiet.

Wind-driven skeletons of hag-like leaves hurried down the city walks after the priests.

Outside the walls of Bhelsheved, the crowd straggled, disconsolate and sullen, aside from the gate. There were in all some ninety-eight persons, and of these, seven were young women who walked or stood all together, and perforce, since each was roped to another by her left wrist. Their hair unbound, their eyes reddened from the winter winds, from lamenting and from rage, they murmured viciously to their neighbours, or to themselves.

The rest of the crowd conferred. Presently, as at times of

festival, they drew off and pitched a haphazard campment a hundred paces from Bhelsheved's walls.

Later in the day, another crowd appeared, from the south. Its aspect was not disimilar. Three girls were roped in its midst. Seeing the first crowd, the second crowd joined it. Voices again were raised, but now no one knocked at the gate.

In the height of the afternoon, two other bands arrived.

All told, there were now four hundred people bivouacked outside the city, and seventeen were young women in groups of seven, four, three and three, every one roped by the wrist.

It was a fact, it had been agreed to meet at this place on this day. Messengers had gone about through the lands. The burden of the message, in every case, had been this: That particular maidens, on their wedding night, had slain their bridegrooms. Some by use of a knife, or a botched-up nasty poison, most by the application of a long-stemmed hairpin driven through the skull at the doorway of an eye. And these murderesses, standing over their husbands' corpses, had violently proclaimed that the gods of Bhelsheved had told them to do it. That one of the gods himself had instructed them, promising that, as a reward for their faith, he would take them to wife instead. But the god had apparently not kept his promise. "It is *your* fault!" wailed the murderess-maidens, waving their bloodied weapons or their poison-vials at fathers, fathers-in-law, wedding guests. "You have interrupted. You have spoiled *everything*."

There was already a strange, gray doubt about the gods. About their care and their validity. Also an obscured and tantalizing dream, a shadowy magnificence, which had promised something to each and all—but this, as yet, was not discussed.

Some story had long ago circulated about a maiden in one of the villages who had refused marriage, and being wed, obstructed consummation, and that the gods had recognized her; Dunizel's history, somewhat tarnished. The outraged and horrified kindred of the murdering brides did not, therefore, seek temporal justice. They roped up their daughters, nieces, sisters, and drove them back to the holy city like little herds of goats for sacrifice. Even those whose sons and brothers had been killed at the slim fair hands of these women, made no complaint, simply prowled behind the new procession, their eyes narrowed against grit and hatred alike.

But the women were proud, stepping proudly, shaking their unbound hair.

Each supposed she was the chosen of the god, her fellow murderesses mistaken. But still each had sympathy for her fellows, understanding the motivation of a deed which she, too, (the positively chosen), had acted out.

Exalted and venomous, the seventeen murderesses stood among the leafless groves outside Bhelsheved, and the crowd of their accusors, unable to get a divine answer, muttered, at a loss. Their discontent swelled, and was not only connected to the closed western gate.

None of them had ever seen the area at this season. Early summer was the time of pilgrimage; during the winter they kept at home. Now they perceived Bhelsheved in its nakedness, pallor frigid, gardens bare, sand like mummy-dust creeping along the walls. It is not always pleasing to peer behind the facade of things.

The night came on in heavy, darkening breaths, and the biting, snapping cold of the frost descended. The moon appeared and gazed down at them from blue eye-sockets, until the very fires they lit seemed cold. Flames and faith withered together. They held council where once they had feasted.

"We shall get no help from Bhelsheved. We must decide this matter outselves."

"For sure, the gods would have spoken by now—if truly they had ordered our daughters to do such terrible things."

"Your daughters are wild cats. I have a dead son to prove it. Your daughters must be punished. Here and now. We need no gods to tell us how to tie a cord to a tree."

"The gods are, in any event, obviously indifferent. They do not wish to be bothered with us."

There were tears shed, wringing of hands, some altercation and many oaths. A few exchanged blows. Eventually, the decision, taken by some with fierce approval, by others with despairing regret. At first light, the seventeen maidens should be strung from the trees a hundred paces from the city, and hanged until dead. And that this might be a kind of profanation of a holy spot either did not suggest itself to them, or else it brought them bitter satisfaction.

The murderesses, crouching now by their own meager fire,

still tethered, lifted their heads as fire-eyed men strode up to them.

A girl with tan hair brighter than the flames, stared boldly back into the unloving stare of her slain husband's father.

"Well, now," said she, "what news?"

"Good news, Zharet," he said at once. "You are to die at sunrise."

Sixteen girls began to sob and bemoan their destiny.

Tan-haired Zharet smiled like a wolf.

"Kill us, and be accursed. Though I alone was chosen of the god, these others acted in the belief of his favor, and he will revenge us all upon you."

"You demented slut," cried the man, "you have gone mad with your filthy dreams. I see you now as I saw you last, your fingers painted with the blood of my son. And tomorrow I will see you dance from a tree."

Then she sprang up, and she shouted at him: "I will dance in paradise when you squirm and shriek on the blades of fiends."

At which he struck her, and as she lay on the ground she said to him, "And for that, the god will shear off both your hands."

The men turned and walked away. Their steps were quickened, as if they wished to run.


In the midst of the night, as the moon went down in the bare trees, Zharet woke because someone gently combed her hair.

The sensation was soothing, and at first she did not question it. But then she felt again the bruise of her father-in-law's fist. She remembered what she had done and what was to be done to her, and that none were likely to comb her hair. She started up.

"Hush, beloved," said a caressing voice. "It is only I."

Zharet's eyes widened, for an ass's jawbones rested by her face, cheek to cheek with her, and it seemed they had spoken. Then she turned a little, and saw Chuz, seated gracefully cross-legged on the frozen sand beside her.

The moon was obscured, and the pathetic fire had died. There was scarcely any light to see by, save for the weird luminescence of the frost itself. Nor did she know of Chuz, who, like others, was poorly chronicled in the region. For a moment she took him for her god, but only for a moment. The gleam of his hair was pale, his right profile, though unusually handsome, did not charm or reassure her. She had got the glimpse of a most unenchanting eye—

"Since you are to die at tomorrow's dawn," remarked Chuz conversationally, "why waste the night in slumber?"

The girl shivered. She noticed he had combed her hair with a broad ivory fish bone. A fish from the holy lake?

"Even though I die," she announced, "I shall proceed in spirit to the arms of my betrothed."

"And who is this fortunate one?"

"The dark god of Bhelsheved."

"Your faith is admirable. Your sisters do not appear to share it."

He indicated, with a white gloved hand, the tumbled sixteen girls who lay about on the ground. Even in exhausted sleep, their restlessness conveyed apprehension, and several groaned at their nightmares.

"He will comfort these, too, no doubt," said Zharet loftily. "Although they presumptuously mistook the summons he offered me as being also for themselves."

The jawbones of the ass laughed. Melodiously, for once.

Chuz tossed a pair of dice on the sand.

Gaunt with her ordeal, Zharet nevertheless took offense.

"It is not seemly that you dice here."

"Dice with me then."

"Less seemly still."

"Tomorrow you will dice with lord Death."

Zharet covered her face with her hands. In the dark of that self-embrace, she beheld her husband's body, with the crystal knob of the pin protruding neatly from his eye, and she giggled. Chuz seldom came where he was not wanted, where indeed his aspect had not come before him. When she reemerged from her hands, she could make out a little more of his face, or of his two faces. They did not alarm her.

"Very well," she said. "We will play at dice. And will you help me to evade hanging if I win?"

"More. I will let you walk in Bhelsheved, despite the shut gates. And you shall see a wonder there."

"Shall I?" she cried. He excited her. Madness recognizing itself, feeling itself at home. "But your dice have no markings."

At which she began to see markings on the dice.

"Call," said Chuz.

For a while they played then, and it seemed quite normal to her. But her luck was not good. The dice seldom fell as she wished.

"No matter," Chuz said at length. "I will allow you to win. Provided you kiss me."

The girl laughed scornfully, propriety forgotten, and leaned forward.

"Not," said Chuz, "on the lips. On my left cheek." And turning himself, he presented to her that cranky left side of his, husk-dry, the seamed skin like gray parchment, the rusty, bloody hair hanging down like worms. Zharet checked a moment, then she shrugged. She kissed him firmly and without reservation. While she did so, though she did not witness it, Chuz slipped off the glove from his right hand. A forefinger that was a writhing serpent gnawed through the length of rope that bound her to another captive not far off. As the rope fell between them, this second maiden, who up till now had not stirred, did so. But Chuz said two or three words to her, whose syllables remained unspecified, and she slumped back in a stupor.

All around, the camp was likewise vanquished. Two men who had formerly stood sentry, leaned upon a tree, snoring in unison. Only the noises of sleep came and went. She did not know, the murderess, elated by her rescue, if her companion had caused this unwakefulness to prevail. Surely the gods had sent him to her. She had half looked to be plucked from the noose itself, before the gaze of all, by stormy sprites, amid fanfares and lightnings. This method was less spectacular than she might have hoped, yet also less hypothetical.

"Come," said Chuz. He was standing ten paces away. A fire which still burned had caught the edge of his mantle. A perverse reaction was taking place, for the material seemed to be burning the fire to ashes, rather than the other way about.

Zharet walked dutifully forward, and Chuz moved ahead of her, between the empty stalks of the groves. But hearing a soft stumbling, Zharet glanced back. Her sixteen companions, their tethers still intact (groups now of three and three, and four and six), were fumbling after her, and after Chuz, their eyes barely open—tranced.

Chuz came to the great western gate of Bhelsheved, closed

and secured from within. Chuz murmured to the gate, tapping its panels with his re-gloved fingers.

"Who dared leave you ajar, mighty gate?" asked Chuz.

The gate did not speak, yet all who were near knew it replied. It said, though it did not say: "None left me ajar. I am bolted and barred from within."

"I regret you are mistaken," said Chuz. "I have only to press lightly against you to come in."

"It is not true," did-not-say-said the gate. "Not true. You lie."

"I shall push against you. You will fly open."

"Never."

"Without doubt."

"You are mad, thinking you can get in."

"You are madder than I, thinking you can keep me out."

"None can enter."

"One can and does."

"Who?"

"The moon comes and goes as she fancies."

"Yes," said-did-not the gate. "I have been concerned about that."

"I shall enter now," said Chuz.

"No, no. I will lock myself up against you." And there came the sound of large mechanisms and valves as the gate frantically moved its bolts the only way left to them to go— and unlocked itself in error.

Chuz pushed at the gate and it swung wide.

"Now I cannot get in," said Chuz.

"Ahhh," did-not-sigh-sighed the gate.

Chuz walked into Bhelsheved, and the seventeen murderesses went after him, sleepwalking, all but Zharet, who stalked at their head.

The fanes were like tombs in the cold darkness, though here and there a watch-fire blew, ghost-white. The lake was dull and opaque, its surface matted by the dissolving of leaves.

Clearly, the gods did not winter here. The gods had gone away, or did not exist.

Chuz halted.

"Listen."

Wake, or tranced, the seventeen murderesses listened.

They heard a noise like silver tinsel, like silver beads, and then a song like the path a snake makes through fine powder.

"Look," said Chuz.

Zharet beheld clearly, the others as if through soft smoke, a thing that was like a whirlpool of stars. There had been a garden, but the garden seemed to have become a part of space itself.

"Shall we go nearer?" inquired Chuz, politely.

They went nearer. Beyond an indefinable limit, they could not go. Something like a filmy curtain contained the garden. It was not that they were unable to force a way past this curtain, more as if, reaching it, they had no desire to pass beyond it. And yet they did desire to.

Inside, was the youth of the summer. Trees bloomed and had put out blossom, the grass was thick with flowers. Another sky, a sky of summer night, lambent with colossal starbursts, shone overhead. A few stars had fallen to earth and become flame-colored lamps. And though the filmy curtain held this summer inside, the winter out, yet gleams, and snatches of music, and elusive wafts of incense, penetrated the outer world.

The murderesses clung about the vision, flies trapped on a web.

They beheld figures moving like the lights. A maiden reminiscent of a pale taper, with silverwork in her cloud of ebony hair, stroked notes from an ivory frame and strings of crystal. A young man, pale and dark as she, poured a glittering drink into bowls of phantasmal jade.

There was another curtain beyond the curtain. It obscured, yet did not obscure. They perceived Azhrarn, prince and lord, and shining night creature, through this gauze, and at his side they perceived a woman white as the stars. Inside the second curtain was another earth. On this earth, which was the private universe of love's obsession, the two unique inhabitants dwelled, and knew only each other. Here he had woven her into the tapestry of his magic. Here he had set sorcerous protections on her, here, in all ways but one, he had made her a part of himself, and she had responded by becoming that part, their growing together like a marriage of vines, twined, indistinguishable.

All these things the maidens saw who stared through the two curtains which had separated love from the yearning for love. And each of them knew, in trance, or in waking, that here was the god, and here was his chosen. And not one of them was she.

Perhaps because sixteen were stupefied, it was Zharet who first turned away. She walked along the mosaic brim of the lake some twenty-odd paces before she stopped, her hands pressed hard against her side, as if she had been wounded.

Chuz, like a coil of mist, went after her.

She did not berate him for the unforgivable sin—that of revealing the truth to her. She only said, "How shall I bear it? To have everything taken from me, who was promised so much."

"And how *will* you bear it?" he asked her.

"I shall not. Let them hang me tomorrow. I do not mind it now."

"I offered you freedom," he said.

"I do not want freedom. I can never be free. Winter has touched me. I am tired as a dead leaf left on the tree. To-morrow they will cut me from the bough. I am glad to die. I could die without their help. I could close my eyes and die as the leaves fall. Winter has touched me."

Then Chuz took her in his arms, and she sobbed on his breast, as long, long ago mad Jasrin had sobbed, not many miles away.

Maybe he required her sorrow, a sort of food or wine. Or maybe he was compassionate and kind to those who became his subjects.

But desolation tended to follow in his wake.

At last, he said to her: "Other than to die, what is the wish of your heart?"

"To kill him," she said. She did not properly know what type of "god" Azhrarn might be, and might therefore be excused the foolishness of uttering threats against him. "Though, since he is an immortal, I suppose he is not to be slain."

"Less and more than an immortal, beloved," said Chuz. "But certainly you cannot thrust a pin through *his* remarkable skull, nor harm him at all. Save in one, not illogical, fashion."

The murderess nestled against the shoulder of Prince Madness.

"Tell it me."

"There is only a single thing more precious," said Chuz, thoughtfully, "than a drop of Vazdru ichor. That is a Vazdru tear. For they are very rare. To the Eshva, weeping is a song. But the Vazdru smile when their hearts break, knowing demon hearts are mended by human blood. Yet Azhrarn has sometimes commanded his whole country to weep."

"What is Azhrarn?" murmured Zharet. "Is he not a monstrous devil that lives in a sewer underground?"

Chuz kept his face straight, but the ass's jawbones guffawed. The girl shivered, and she plucked at Chuz's mantle.

"I have not forgotten you," said Chuz.

At that moment, the awful screaming began. Zharet turned, and saw her sixteen murderess companions had roused, and were running about. Truly demented—less interesting to Chuz for being so obviously and wholy his?—they tore their hair and skin. Their shrieks were of betrayal. Their shrieks were of a virgin mother of gods, who was not themselves, for, sorcerously sensitized, they had, of course, understood her condition. None know the color of the cloth better than those not permitted to wear it.

The glamour in the garden had already vanished. Not a trace remained, either of the Prince of Demons, or of his mortal lover. It is conceivable it may all, in any case, have been a delusion conjured by Chuz himself, though faithfully copied from an original.

"Come," said Chuz again to Zharet. "We will go into the desert. You must learn to wait for what you want. Being my subject, patience may come easily to you."

"I am cold," she said.

"I will warm you. Are you not warmed already?"

"Perhaps. . . ."

Alerted by the cries from within Bhelsheved, and by the probable retraction of Chuz's spell, the crowd outside the walls was coming to itself. Already some had found the murderesses escaped.

Others had noticed one of the gates stood open.

Chuz and the seventeenth murderess slipped out of the gate, two vague shadows, as three hundred and eighty-three persons began to shamble in at it.

An unsure glimmering was in the eastern sky. A sense of confusion was everywhere, and many looked at this light in fear, before recognising it as the preamble of the dawn.

"We will not leave the city," the men declared, "until this matter is settled."

They stood on the mosaic roads, about the lake, along the white bridges, at the doors of the heart temple. No, they would not move. This holy sanctuary, which had been denied to men save at one season, was now choked and blotted by them. It seemed they might never go away. They demanded information, and they demanded action. The unworldly priests, who had scattered out like frightened birds at the shouts beneath their windows, wheeled aimlessly in fluttering groups. Hysteria, for the first time, had quickened them. The proximity of these uninvited ones, over whom they now had no control, and whom the gods had failed to keep out, was like a violation, a rape.

Another handful of messengers had ridden off. Elders and important men had been sent for, those versed in religious ethic. For now neither side, priests or laity, knew what to do. And neither side would shift to aid or accommodate the other.

The sixteen murderesses—one had mysteriously disappeared, likely having wandered into the lion-mauled, winter-hungry desert—had not been hanged. They had been tied up to a leafless tree on the lake shore. They no longer screeched, having worn themselves out. Nor did they seek to evade death, which now, ironically, was refused them. Some had attempted to drown themselves in the lake, but the ropes would not reach far enough to facilitate submersion. In frustration, they gazed at the ground. "What have you seen?" they had been asked. They had told, in vast detail. Their loss and humiliation; a maiden with child; the god's wife.

No wonder the crowd refused to go away. No wonder elders and philosophers had been sent for.

# CHAPTER 2

## Mother and Daughter

Dunizel stood in a little temple on the north side of wintry Bhelsheved. She had not heard the shouting, or, if she had, had heard it in a psychic manner. She sensed the breath of human intention hot on her heels. She was not afraid. Yet she felt a familiar sadness. It was a portion of her love, as happiness was a portion of it.

By day the demon jewelry he had given her grew pale. It was wrapped with safeguards, and yet she guessed his protective magics attended her less strongly when the sun filled the sky. The pallor of metal and gems was an omen of this. The child within her, however, seemed stronger by day, as if it answered the light, challenged it, strove with it.

She loved his child, and as her own mother had spoken to Dunizel in the womb, so Dunizel would speak to her own unborn daughter.

In the center of Bhelsheved the crowd roared and confounded itself. In the small northern temple, seated quietly under a blue window, the memory of the touch of Azhrarn's mouth, which was half a world's craving, upon her own—still vital, always so—Dunizel told the embryonic child a story of its demon father.

"In the beginning, my dear, there were in the world all beasts but one."

So it had been, they said, a million years before the flood, that giant precursor of Baybhelu, had shown the gods' hand to be evident only when cruel.

"Swans swam," said Dunizel, "and fish in the waters. Deer

155

ran upon the plains and dogs barked at a moon so young she scarcely knew what she was. Birds ruled the air, and man made pretense that he ruled the land, though he fought for every inch of it, with the wild ox, the bear, and the dragon."

There were demons also. Always, perhaps, there had been such. Though it was related that at the commencement, they had had no lord. But, for the purposes of the story. . . .

The best loved beast of Underearth was nothing other than the serpent. Down below in the bright shadows, he was admired for his grace and elegance, and for his cool blood and wicked self-command. Presently the demons, innocent then, or merely extremely cynical, brought the snake up to the earth, supposing thereby to make men also fall in love with him. But men took against the snake, scenting his demoniacal origins, mistrusting his lack of legs and ears, his smart teeth and implacable garment. Indeed, they turned on the snake, threw him out of doors when he came in, brained him with mallets when they were able and cursed him and spat on him when they were not.

The Eshva mourned for the serpent, for they loved him best of all. The Vazdru said to each other: "Let us trick mankind into adoration of the snake." And this they did by various means, causing him here and there to be elected a god and worshipped, or venerated as useful in magic.

But one of the day-nights in Druhim Vanashta, certain Vazdru princes began to bet with each other that they could persuade men to like the snake for himself. And this they tried, and this they failed at.

At last the vexatious problem came to the notice of Azhrarn. And accordingly Azhrarn went by night to the world to listen to men's opinion of the snake. "How we abhor his cold scales," they complained. "And his teeth, which are sometimes venomous, and his forked tongue, which might be. And how allergic we are to his leglessness. He is all tail, and the sound of his hiss causes our hair to rise up like bristles."

Then Azhrarn smiled, and he went back to Druhim Vanashta. There he took up a snake and he inquired of it, "Would it be worth while to you, in order to win the affection of mankind, to be a little changed?"

"Of what good is mankind's affection?" asked the snake.

"Those they love," said Azhrarn, "fare well. And those they hate they harm."

The snake had heard reports from his cousins concerning mallets, and after some thought, he agreed.

Then Azhrarn conducted the snake to the Drin, and the Drin made for the snake particular extras, which had all to do with what men had said they disliked about him. First the Drin made him four muscular little legs with four round little paws on the ends of them. And then they made him two little pointed ears to stand up on top of his head. Then they bulked out his body with a cunning device, and straightened his tongue with another—but it remained in fact a thin tongue, and in fact a great deal of tail remained to him at the back. Next they made him an overcoat of long soft black grasses, and decorated his face—which was now very pretty—with ornaments of fine silver wire. His jewel-like eyes, which had always been quite wonderful, they had need to alter only a jot. Lastly, to compensate for removing his venom, (although they left the shape of his teeth alone), they presented him with some sharp slivers of steel to wear in his round feet for purposes of self-defense.

When Azhrarn beheld the result, he laughed, and ran his hand over the new animal's spine. At which all was transmuted into flesh and muscle, and the coat of grass into luxuriant, velvety hair. And at the touch of Azhrarn also, the new animal made a strange sound, not a hiss, but—

"My dear, you are purring," said Azhrarn, and again he laughed.

To this day, no cat can bear to be laughed at, even in love.

However, sure enough, the animal, legged, eared and furry, was an enormous success on the earth. Men were pleased by his grace and elegance, admired his cool blood and wicked self-command. And when he grew sometimes peeved, forgot himself, and hissed—they did not remember the snake, but remarked: "There is the cat, hissing." Nor did they notice how both the cat and the snake slew mice, or enjoyed milk, though both became the pets of sorcerers. And men never would credit that if you overlooked the fur and held flat the two pointed ears of the cat, then and now, you might and may see still the wedge-shaped demon head and the sharp teeth of the serpent, poised there, under your hand.

When Dunizel had told the story, she could sense the embryo's interest in it. It was a childish, satisfying legend, or maybe true. But it was inevitable Dunizel would think of her

lover in this way, while others spoke exclusively of the blood-
shed and viciousness of his deeds among men.

The story finished, Dunizel sank into a sort of dream, the
sky-blue window light drifting over her. She imagined she
and her baby rode on the back of a winged lion. Possibly,
probably, the unborn baby shared in this fantasy. She was not
like other unborn infants.

Several hours passed before Dunizel lifted her head at an
enormous shout that seemed to rock Bhelsheved.

It had happened that sages and philosophers had already
been traveling to the city, and had therefore been intercepted
by the messengers sent off to summon them. Some of these
wise men had intended to chastise the previous crowd for ir-
religiously going there at the wrong time. Some had been intrigued by abnormal portents. An astrologer or two had read
mysteries in the positions of various stars. One way or another, Bhelsheved had magnetized them. The messengers conducted them across the sands, over the echoing roads—which
did not echo for there were too few treading on them, on this
occasion, to produce more than the dullest of concussions. In
at the solitary open gate they went. Up to the priests and
priestesses they went. And the priests and priestesses fluttered
anxiously as pigeons.

"We beg your pardon and the pardon of heaven," said the
sages.

"Are you uncognisant of the miracle that has chanced here
by divine will?" grumbled a number of seers—added to the
testimony of the messengers, the portents had tumbled into
place. (Each seer was quick to claim he had predicted an
Event first.)

"Where?" howled the astrologer, a more basic fellow.
"Where? Where?"

The priesthood cowered. How frail and foolish they appeared.

No woman among them looked a candidate for heavenly
visitation, and not a single girdle on a single slender frame
had lifted by so much as a quarter inch.

"Where?" howled the astrologer once more. His fingers
plucked the atmosphere as if eager to pluck open robes and
bellies, and gaze within.

A reverend philosopher stepped hurriedly forward.

"My friend desires to know, as indeed do we all, where the favored maiden is to be found."

Some of the priesthood began to cry.

A voice spoke from somewhere in the throng. The throng made way. An old man leaning on a staff emerged. The priesthood glanced at him in new terror, obviously not recalling that here was one of their erstwhile teachers from the antique tower, the building in which they had proved themselves capable of undergoing all manner of ordeals—except, demonstrably, that of holding conversation with men save in the form of ritual.

The crowd, however, knew the old man.

He stared about with merciless eyes. The immaturity and silliness of his students clearly caused him acute disgust. Yet, had there not been one student, who, even as these now offended him, had once caused him to rejoice?

"Be still," said this old man, and the crowd fell quiet. "Attend to me. I will bring to your minds a girl of superlative beauty, of extraordinary holiness and occult vision. One, who for her demeanor and her looks, was named Soul-of-the-Moon. . . ."

Just as these words were spoken, Dunizel felt the grip of fate brutally fasten on her. No doubt she herself had foretold what must come, the unspoken wish behind Azhrarn's use of her. Yet to be used by one who loves you is infinitely forgivable.

Along the walls of this little temple where she had lingered, were writings, for the priests would often inscribe spiritual graffiti there about the gods. She might read such sentences as: *The law of heaven is eternity.* Or, *When I think of you, O Masters of the Firmament, my soul arises like the sun.*

Dunizel now took up a pen and dipped it in the silvery golden ink, and she wrote this:

*The bitterness of joy lies in the knowledge that it cannot last. Nor should joy last beyond a certain season, for, after that season, even joy would become merely habit.*

Then she laid her hand over her body, above the vessel in which her child waited out its term, as if she warmed her hand at that dark fire.

Next moment, she was aware of a vast, concerted tread, the feet of many people, moving toward her along the pastel roads. Still she was not afraid. She felt pity, for all of them, and for the child. Even for Azhrarn—Chuz had prophesied she would be mad enough to pity the Prince of Demons.

For herself she felt loss; the end of joy.

The multiple tread drew near, resembling an incoming tide, or a wind blowing through the city. At the door of the little temple, the noise ceased. And then the door was flung wide.

Winter sunlight streamed in, cold and very hard, like an edge of broken glass.

An old man walked slowly out of the light, leaning on a staff.

He, and those that pressed in after him, and those who could proceed no further than the door (for the entrance way was narrow), beheld the mirage of a girl, all whiteness, tinted by the blue sheen of a window at her back. Her beauty was supernal. Their quest being what it had become, she was the only acceptable thing for them to come in and find. (And how had they found her? Perhaps one of her order had noted her enter the temple, and relayed the information. Or had she left some sort of supernatural trail behind her?)

She faced them. If she had denied the truth, they would not have listened. The way she was, the way she appeared to be, only the gods would have recognized, in that second, that she was not one of themselves.

On the shore of the lake, unnoticed, the sixteenth murderess felt a piece of loose mosaic under her hand. She prised it up, and with it she cut the veins of her wrists. Dyed with her blood, courteously, she offered the shard to the fifteenth murderess.

They escorted Dunizel to the heart-temple. An apartment was made for her behind the opalescent altar and the two golden beasts. The priesthood were coerced into waiting on her, and their incompetent ministrations augmented by those of young women of good birth. The messengers came and went over the winter desert. Cavalcades and caravans sought Bhelsheved, through the smoke-colored days and the bladed nights. Gifts were brought, for mother and for child, rare and frequently obscure. All wished to touch the bride of the god—her forehead, her fingers. They kneeled, awaiting her blessing. The poor, who could not offer gifts, milled outside the city, sometimes venturing in, hoping for a glimpse of her. It was once more a festival of worship. A hushed celebration of self-congratulatory awe. Not only had a woman been chosen by a god, but in *their* era, at *this* time, which now would ascend into history and myth.

There had been a hasty burial outside the city: sixteen graves. This, too, had carried a sort of importance, and they had marked the spot with a stone, hastily scratched to read: *We who were deceived lie here, to entreat the forgiveness of heaven.*

When darkness came, the fires glittered about Bhelsheved on the frosty plains. Attendants drew the spangled curtains and closed the doors of Dunizel's invented apartment, leaving her alone, bathed, anointed and clothed in silk, as if prepared for a bridegroom. The god would visit her—nervously and with pride they scanned the deepening twilight over the city. Some claimed to have seen him arrive, astride a horse made of stars, his cloak billowing the moon.

Dunizel remained in her apartment, as was expected of her, though it was unlike either the cell she had occupied, or the gardens by the lake. It was a chamber of screens and draperies, built also of the beliefs of others.

It did not surprise her that Azhrarn did not come to her there. Gold dripped from every curtain, the metal hated of demons. A miasmic sense of watchfulness was equally present. How many, scattered in the colonnades or on the paths outside, held their breath, innocently, inadvertently, trying to catch the rustle of gigantic wings, or the muted gasp of etheral love? Love which pierced but did not despoil virginity.

The seventh month waned. She felt the child within her stirring, turning in its half-sleep.

By night, the magic jewels he had given her shone and glowed. Yet he had never given to her one of those tokens, for which, in certain tales, he was renowned—those articles which would draw him to a mortal's side. But on this night, experiencing the child's movement within her, Dunizel understood quite well that she had only to say his name to summon him, and this she did.

Between one moment and the next, he was there, a tall black shape like a furled leaf which is really a serpent, and in the blackness his eyes blazed.

"Do not reproach me," he said to her at once. "For I warned you how I am and how it would be."

She turned and saw him, and his face came gradually into the light, as if some invisible lamp were burning up.

"Do I reproach you?" she said. "I think, before sunrise, the child will be born."

"You will suffer no pain," he said to her instantly. His countenance was stony, as if he no longer cared anything for her, and by this she might have known it was not so, if she had ever doubted. "And when the child is free of you, I will take you from this trap. She shall be my legacy to them. I will make her strong and terrible, and then I am done with her. And you are done with her also, Dunizel."

"No," she said. "I will not leave your child alone in this, or any place."

"I intend," he said, "to put her callously to work. As I told you, I am the father of wickedness; do not think I will have regard for this creature I grew within your womb, not even for your sake. My plan is only this: Since these people so vehemently adore their gods, I will give them a god to adore at first hand, and let them discover what it is to be ruled by such. Nor will they enjoy the lesson."

"No," she said. "You may leave me, I could not prevent you. But the child shall not be abandoned here."

"We have never lain together," he said. "You do not know love as I can teach it to you. Not the world, as I can reveal the world. Even Druhim Vanashta will open its gates of steel and gem and fire to you, at my will."

She did not remonstrate with him further, only looked straight into his eyes with her eyes that the comet had helped to form. Some fragment of gold in the draperies reflected in her gaze, and abruptly her eyes, too, were golden. Perhaps he disliked that reminder of the sun, for he glanced aside from her.

"I will send the handmaidens of Underearth to you," he said.

And then he went about the chamber, tearing the gold from its moorings. Whether the touch of the metal offended him was not apparent, save that he performed the task somewhat too meticulously and unswiftly, as if each piece of metal were heavier and more awkward than it was. And when he flung these items away beyond the draperies, they fell without a sound, as if he had robbed them of their substance.

When this was done, he sank again immediately through the temple floor, his face once more in shadow. Yet, even as he vanished, she felt the brush of his lips upon her own.

Then the Eshva women began to evolve like slim dark ghosts. She had seen them often, and they had served her reverently, for what their lord cherished, they too would cherish utterly. And it is said that even the Eshva marveled at her beauty. Truly beautiful she must have been, and truly beautiful she was.

They had brought with them white flax gathered from the margins of Sleep River, that water which flowed by the borders of Azhrarn's kingdom. And this they stacked on the floor, where it began, of itself, to burn with a creamy flame.

Before, she had known no pain. The increasing restlessness of the child merely suggested coils of sparks were spinning in her womb. Now, at the igniting of the flax, a dreamy quality descended on her, and next a separateness, so she seemed to float upward from her body, and hover in the air. In this position, she saw what happened clearly, as she would observe the actions of another.

No effort of her own body was necessary, or so it seemed. The child was already eagerly seeking an exit from her. At first this may have puzzled Dunizel, yet intuitively she must soon have realized that the Eshva, who could charm a fox from its earth or rain from the clouds, were charming the child, hypnotically though speechlessly calling it forth.

Neither blood nor any other liquors attended the passage of the child. It had been altered in itself, becoming strangely amorphous and flowing, changing—yet unchanged. Had it been perceivable as it evicted itself from the chambers of the maiden's body, the process would have been revealed as quite unnormal. Narrow and sinuously flexible, the baby negotiated the way, causing no harm either to itself or to what had contained it. Presently, suddenly, it emerged, unnaturally legs first, which in its case was perfectly natural, rather as a cat will fall upon its feet. As the lower limbs came from the body of the mother, they assumed reality and acceptable contours. Next a torso, bland and unblemished. The arms were upheld, in the position of a swimmer poised to dive, the head thrown back. No stain disfigured the child. No natal cord connected it, just as no placenta had contained it in the womb—there would be no afterbirth. It dropped neatly into the hands of the Eshva women, who sighed over it, so that the perfume of their breath was the first—misleading—flavor it knew of the outer world.

The child was white of skin, and long-haired, the hair being the burnished black of midnight oceans and skies; the hair of Azhrarn. Nails, tiny and unflawed, were evident on its hands and feet. Teeth, whiter than salt, glinted between its parted lips. Not having employed the natal cord, it could acquire no navel, its belly was as smooth as a pane of alabaster. It would not, in any event, have looked exactly mortal, the child. The closed lids, heavily fringed, were an astounding molten blue from the eyes which waited beneath. It had turned out to have something, after all, of its mother.

Dunizel, as she hung in the air above herself, examined the child, unstartled but surprised by it, pleased by it, and ineffably sad. It was lovely; it was not human.

It had not cried, nor did it ask to be fed. Maternal milk was unessential to it, and Dunizel had known these fluids of nourishment had not gathered in her breasts. But now the child was to be offered its initial sustenance.

A silken rope, a snake, wound itself about the arm of one of the Eshva women. It lowered its head, kissing her, and where its head rose up, it left a printing in the flesh, the mark its two long teeth had made. Dark as ink, demon blood welled from the two little wounds.

The demon woman put the wounds against the lips of the child. Not opening its violet lids, silently, the child drank blood.

Oblique though she was, surely through the heart of Dunizel then, there might have shivered, like a falling leaf, some intimation of the alien, the unconscionable. Not lessening her emotion, becoming part of her emotion, as sadness itself had come to be. She the jar of her god, (as Bhelsheved was the jar of gods), the elected citadel for this ultimate magecraft, this witchery. But she herself as far from the core of it as now she seemed from her own fleshly frame. The jar does not need to credit or comprehend the wine which is stored in it.

But now the magic flax soothed even her detached soul asleep. She saw the child had been laid down in the midst of the flax's burning, illumined, at peace, her long hair, black as jet and loosely curling as a fleece, poured through the mysterious flames.

No longer the child of Dunizel, to which she had related stories. His child now, and only his, of whom he had said: "Do not think I will have regard for this creature. I will make her strong and terrible, and then I am done with her."

# CHAPTER 3

## The Aloe

It was a scene without compromise. The rocks fell sheerly from both sides into the gully of a long-dead watercourse. Sand ran in the gully, in tactless imitation of water. Once a pool had spread, which now was a dry cracked paving. In the paving, bitterly there grew a bitter aloe bush. Some moisture, or memory of moisture, had sustained it, and though the winter had stripped it of fruit and leaves, it huddled over itself and grimly lived.

The bush, the gully, the rocks, the desert beyond, all had their story to tell, quickly and totally and without words. It was possible to survive in such a place, but the price of survival was very high.

There was nothing gentle there. Even the wind scraped the face.

There was nothing gentle there, certainly not she who dwelled there now, in the lee of the rocks.

Her tan hair was whitened by dust, and her face, which was young, scored by dust and the winds, and other inner unkindnesses, looked old.

She had been in the region less than a month, but already she had become a part of the area. She might have been there centuries. Might have been born there.

In the morning, she would climb the rocks on the north side, and go up into the desert. A thin muddy spring persisted half a mile from the gully. Here she would drink, unless on that day the sands had choked the hole. If she could not clear the hole again with her fingers, as was sometimes the case, she did not drink. A miniature lizard might be sighted. She had grown skilled with a sling made from her girdle, and using the sharp flints she had found on the gully's bed, she would kill the lizard and afterward eat it. Such meals were unappetizing, and frequently she did not bother with them. The small deaths angered her, too, for she had killed a man with a crystal pin, and killing anything reminded her of that deed and its uselessness.

During the day, Zharet sat beside the aloe bush, or if strong winds blew, she crept among the broad cracks in the rocks. The days passed with speed, for she spent them in brooding on how things might have been if the promise had been fulfilled; on how things were since it had not. Occasionally she revisualized that glimpse of the dark garden, the woman who was not herself, the knowledge of choice and love and the bearing of a divine child. Or she would recall the dream of rapture when the god had possessed her. Then she would lift her head and scream at the sky, many, many times.

Now and then, she received a visitor.

"Good day," said Chuz. "Are you happy to be free?"

"Why do you mock me?" Zharet cried. "What do you want of me?"

"I am unsure. I think I have gone mad," said Prince Madness, and threw dice in the air like a delighted small boy.

The aloe definitely went mad, and began to put forth leaves, which the wind eradicated.

When Zharet slew one of the lizards, then Chuz might appear, seated like a piece of murky twilight on the ground, or walking over the horizon. He seemed to admire her aptitude with the sling.

"I explained," he said. "You must be patient."

"I am patient," she said, tearing her garments with her teeth.

"I will make music and you shall dance," said Chuz. He shook a brass rattle which sounded like a sistrum. Zharet danced, against her will yet frenziedly. And the graceless idiotic display made her feel better. At length she fell on the sand in the gully floor.

"What do you wish?" inquired Chuz.

Zharet did not speak, did not need to, for an ass's jawbones had now appeared and brayingly spoke for her, her innermost desires.

"I would wish to chain him and lash him with seven instruments each of which had tails of white-hot steel. I would bind him to a wheel which rolled across the sky and through the blazing emissions of the stars. I would rip out his heart and show it him."

"You shall," Chuz said.

At that, Zharet did speak.

"That cannot be, since he is a god."

"It is a fact, you may not harm his body. It is his psychic frame which shall be chained and lashed and bound to a wheel and scalded, and his psychic heart which shall be ripped out. But he is not a god," said Chuz. "Have you not yet fathomed who he is, that lord of tricks and lies?"

Zharet raised her head. She stared in the face of Chuz. Both sides of it were being shown to her, the ultimate mask of insanity, and she did not blink, her eyes like those of the lizards she killed.

"Who, then?"

"Azhrarn. Do you recall? The monster from the sewer under the earth."

Zharet was outraged. She would not have been misled by *that*, have suffered ecstasy at the urging of—*that*.

"No," she said.

"Come now," said Chuz, "all the lands of Bhelsheved have been deceived. He is a powerful demon. Do you suppose he cannot put on a handsome shape when he requires to? Only consider," said Chuz, stroking Zharet's hair tenderly, "would the true and actual god have chosen another than yourself?"

Zharet now stared through the face of Chuz. She pondered.

"All Bhelsheved is in error," said Chuz, "yet already there are doubts. The child has been born."

Zharet started.

"Is he fair?"

"Just so. But not a boy-child, a daughter."

Zharet frowned. It had seemed to her the child of a god would be a son, one who should be a hero and king of the earth. Among her people, women were taught to regard themselves as something less than men. How could a god choose to manifest his holy seed in female progeny?

"Bhelsheved," said Chuz, "is troubled as you are, by the

gender of the baby. Also troubled by other matters. A dream of the last festival of worship, of a dark tower jeweled with lights, a shadow-shape that granted certain aspirations. Strange goings-on," said Chuz. "Young women violated, unable to identify their attackers. Rich men dying abruptly and in quantities, leaving their fortunes to their heirs. Men bellowing their love of plain or ugly or repulsive but always simpering girls. Sicknesses and cripplings. These things, in and out of the white city. Azhrarn has been busy."

Zharet rose to her feet.

"Go to Bhelsheved," said Chuz. "Be a seeress. Tell them what you know. Warn them, the hapless dolts, squirming in his net. Recollect the story: How the Prince of Demons sought to destroy the world, but the gods sent him packing. Be a servant of the gods, my tan-haired dear. Send him packing also, this monstrosity who so beguiled you and made you wretched."

Zharet began to walk, steadily up the rocks, almost thoughtlessly forward, unerringly in the direction of the city.

Chuz laughed softly. His awful eyes were fixed on her back. The jawbones spoke to him.

"Azhrarn should not have refused the gift to his child. Azhrarn should not have set himself against me."

Chuz drew the mantle over the foul side of his face; he gazed at the sand, lowering his eyes. He was now beautiful. He himself murmured: "Sweet Azhrarn, who plays at usurping my title, I have no quarrel with you, I make exchange. Barter is not war. Be then yourself Delusion's Master. And Chuz shall be the Bringer of Anguish, the Jackal, the Evil One."

Enter Bhelsheved now. One might not have recognized it. There were crowds everywhere, within and without. Men in fine garments, wealthy women in litters, paraded up and down with their pets on gemmed leashes and their ungemmed slaves. It was no longer blasphemous but fashionable to be seen here at the proscribed time. Vendors had crept in surreptitiously and currently sold fruit and wine and sweetmeats, and sometimes little dolls of carved wood representing the holy mother and her child. (Most of these carvings had had to be altered. Prepared in advance, they had each depicted the child as male.) Fresh caravans constantly arrived. Trav-

elers from a long way off had come to see the miracle.
Camels bawled through the groves, donkeys vociferated. Such
animals were bought and sold. Bhelsheved had become a
marketplace. Papers, rinds and dried dung rattled over the
pastel streets where only sand or leaves or blossoms had
formerly wended. The sorcerous winds of the city failed to
blow these items away, perhaps not distinguishing them. The
smoke of roasting pastries and chickens had stained the white
walls of the fanes. Fish were being trapped in the lake and
put into transparent bladders full of water to carry home as
souvenirs. The poor gambled in the porches of temples. They
begged the gods' pardon at every throw. It gave them a
strange pleasure. Some asked the opulent ladies or philosophers for money: beggars.

The priesthood generally were seldom seen. They had gone
to ground, rather, to heaven, locking themselves in their cells,
pining and starving and sinking into long deathlike swoons of
disillusion. Only tradition had kept the city inviolate. Tradition was a chameleon. It had not needed an army of enemies
or thieves to destroy Bhelsheved. Or at least, not yet.

In the heart-temple above the lake, Dunizel would come to
sit in a tall golden chair that had been made for her, between
the golden beasts before the altar. She came there often, since
she was called for often. Whenever she was absent, a clamor
gradually went up. They yelled for her and for her child, a
passionate demand. When she and the child appeared, they
were worshipped. The child was very quiet, scarcely moving
on Dunizel's knees. A guard had been marshaled to keep
back the mob which strove always to touch her. These soldiers lost their footing on the heaps of gifts on the floor, skid-
ding in grapes, bangles, the broken eggs of rare birds.

In other areas of the temple, sages expounded the meaning
of what had happened. They were thought great men, and
most clever, for each one had a different explanation.

Dunizel must also pass up and down the broad streets of
Bhelsheved, carried aloft by her soldiery, the child in her
arms. Then the child was not so still. The child fretted, disturbed by the fierce noon sun.

When night came, the city was noisy, not the old noise of
reverential songs and storytelling, but a new noise of dispute
and coins. Commerce had come swiftly on sensation. A few
paces from the west gate (not a hundred, no, nor fifty, but

ten, some women and young men had set up a crimson pavilion, and here they sold their bodies to whoever wished for
congress. They, like the sages, had an explanation: No man
should pass into the holy enclosure with venal thoughts,
therefore best get rid of such desires before entering the city.

By night, they looked for the visit of the god, anxious to lie
with his virgin wife. A bough groaned in the wind: "It is the
sound of his wings!" A camel coughed: "It is the cough of
his starlike steed." A man cried out inside the crimson pavilion: "Ah, the god is satisfied."

Yet those who brooded deeply upon such matters were
aware the god had not positively evinced himself, nor come
publicly to own his offspring. The sages had no explanation
for this, nor for the child's fretfulness in the sun. A god's
creation, though only a female, should be capable of enduring sunlight. Was not the sun the ultimate symbol of all heavenly lusters?

In her chamber, amid new welters of new gold, unknown,
unseen by men, Azhrarn did come to Dunizel. He stood each
darkness like a slim black tree growing in the corner of the
room, and he said to her in an iron voice: "Have you re-
lented now? Have you grown aware now of our time together,
which you waste?"

And Dunizel replied: "My love, my lord, my life, I will
not leave your child alone here."

"You will," he said. "It is only a matter of my waiting.
Can you bear so easily to be parted from me?"

"I cannot bear to be parted from you."

"Then leave the brat and come with me. I will make her
more fearful than a dragoness. She will not be vulnerable, I
promise you."

"I cannot."

"I might take you with me, whether or not you wish it."

"Truly. And will you?"

"No. But nor will I continue entreating you like your servant."

But every night now he would return, and every night their
conversation was the same. They did not touch, though the
room grew drowsy, sweet, electric with the inner reaching out
of both of them toward the other. And neither would surrender the argument.

In its jewelwork cradle, the child turned its head upon its

luxuriant hair to watch them with eyes like the blue kernel of a twilight sky.

Zharet walked into Bhelsheved at the same open gate by which she had left it.

She looked about and saw alteration everywhere, saw it contemptuously and uncaringly. But she in turn was looked at.

Some power had come with her. Some power from Prince Chuz, most likely, which he had awarded her by virtue of their many physical contacts. Amid all the variegated persons filling the city, Zharet stood out. Young and old at once, emaciated, almost beautiful, her hair striped through with white and tan. An indefinable scent clung about her. It was the odor of the aloe bush, caught in her ragged clothes.

On the street, they made way for her. The beggars did not ask her for alms. The philosophers ruminated that here was a crazed mystic out of the desert. Even women might incline to mysticism, at which time they became wilder and less partial than males of that inclination.

Zharet walked, and segments of the crowd walked after her.

The rich ladies pointed, scornful and jealous.

Zharet climbed the steps of a modest fane, and stationed herself there, apparently gazing down at the crowd, in fact through them, to her bitterness. She was not self-conscious, or actually conscious only of self. Her pain was the center of the universe. She need not tremble at a crowd.

"Oh deluded ones!" She suddenly shouted, and her voice carried, flying like a bird, "Oh worshippers of false gods!"

The crowd stirred, muttered. Its interest had been caught. It is not always boring to be criticized.

"Fools!" cried Zharet. The wind, whining, blew her hair about her; she raised her skinny arms, and felt Chuz laughing at her back. "This *god* who has sown his seed in Bhelsheved is none other than that dark foulness, the Arch-Demon of the underground pit."

At this, cries answered her cry. Predictably they told her she was a blasphemer, a liar. They told her they would rend her.

"Rend me then. Your punishment will still come upon you."

They told her the gods would strike her down.

"Let them strike me," she shrilled, "if I say anything but the truth."

Then she described to them how Azhrarn, the ugliest and most abysmal fiend extant on earth or under it, had crawled up to the surface of the world, and obscenely fathered a similar fiend, although in innocuous infant form, on the vilest harlot who would accommodate him. The crowd was horrified at her apostasy. Zharet assured the crowd the apostasy was theirs not hers, for they credited a demon as a god. When she had said all she wished to, she came down the steps again, and went away through the crowd to find another portion of it to harangue.

The day swelled coldly, grew disappointed in itself, and began to dwindle. Zharet had spoken many times. Her voice was hoarse. Some had remembered her vaguely. But those who connected her to the seventeen murderesses supposed that, like the others, she had died, and was here in spirit form to alarm them. A provocative thought, for surely a spirit might know something they did not.

By the time the day had reached its edge, there were few who had not heard, or heard of, Zharet's wailing.

A well-heeled lord, who prided himself on the interesting specimens he could claim to have entertained at his table, sent his slave to ask Zharet to his tent. Zharet accepted the invitation with hauteur. She went in and sat down among diaphanous curtainings, a conflagration of lamps, some ten or eleven eminent rhetoreticians and wise men, and thirty eager guests. Whether she was daunted for so much as a moment was not obvious.

When they offered her food, she refused it.

"Shame and anxiety are my meat and drink."

When they offered her fruit and wine she declared in her roughened theatrical voice:

"The sweet grape has become for me the aloe, bringer of bitterness and purging."

The guests gorged themselves, listening in fascination to Zharet's depressing utterances. At length the host prevailed on her to recount her history. She did. She spoke fluently of the demon couching, the ecstasy beyond ecstasy, the murder to which she had been persuaded, her supernatural escape at the hands "Of a great Being, who pitied me." She did not mention Chuz by name. Chuz had done something to her tongue, most probably, to safeguard his reputation. By implication, however, she made him sound like a heavenly messenger.

"A wonderful divertissement," said the lords' guests, faintly uneasy.

Rumor ran out of the tent, carried on the evening wind, or by the mouths of those who listened and came away.

That night was like a seething cauldron. The ingenuous began to doubt. The sophisticates, already yawning over the sameness of Dunizel's child, roused to the hope of something new. The esthetes debated violently.

A fish was seen strolling on its fins along the lake shore: Madness was also about.

In the morning the sun and Zharet rose together and went together across the city. The waves of the crowd poured up and down. The temple emptied in preference for the more peculiar show outside. Zharet's diatribes were taken for preaching.

When day waned, a famous philosopher sent his slave to ask Zharet to his tent, that she and he and his fellows might discuss her teachings. She entered the tent and sternly admonished him: "I am only a woman, and you seek to elevate me to the intellectual status of a man. But small surprise, since you think a god may be born in female shape."

"How astute she is," said the men, deeply troubled and gratified.

Night's wings closed over Bhelsheved.

The temple was empty, sacred flames burning bright on its goldwork. On the mosaic floor, near to the golden throne where Dunizel would sit with the child, someone had scrawled the symbol which translates exactly as:?

And, in the shadow of that darkness, maybe Azhrarn said to her; "They will abuse you. Now surely you must leave the child and come with me."

But still she would not leave the child, nor he consent to take it. But neither would he force her from the place against her will.

In the morning, the shout was audible: "Zharet! Zharet the Seeress!"

Zharet answered the shout in a voice which was raucous now as the raven's. "I am the aloe," she croaked. "Let me be your medicine. I will purge you of your blindness." She believed everything she said, even when, as sometimes happened, she glimpsed a ghostly figure in the crowd, wrapped in a damson mantle, grinning at the ground like a death's head with brazen teeth.

But as Zharet's third day in the city merged into the third dusk, a third slave came to her. He was dressed with extraordinary richness and simplicity, yet a curious shifting, like the play of colored flames—perhaps from the fading afterglow—obscured his face.

He did not speak to her, this man, though all about other servitors clamored, begging her to come to this tent or that. He did not speak, yet his whole stance conveyed the meaning *You must come with me.*

"Very well," said Zharet.

She was not sure why she had deigned to choose him, he had not even announced his master's name. But she felt a quickening. It was stronger than the thirst for fame or vengeance. As the walls and the lights and the groves and the clusterings of people were left behind her, she said peremptorily, "Where is the tent of your lord situated?"

The slave half turned, and she caught an image of his face. He was handsome. She shivered. Before she could ask again, the tent was in front of them. It was coal-black, and like a coal seemed shot with incendiary effulgence. Was this some trick of Chuz's devising? She had never really detected who or what Chuz was, other than her guide, her spiritual aide, to whom, by right of her suffering, she was entitled. But also she hated Chuz, For he had shown her the uncharitable facts of her destiny. She glared at the black pavilion, but as she did so some of the drapery folded away.

*Enter*, said the slave, but still without speech.

Rosy and somnolent, the lamps in the pavilion, burnishing things of dark metal, pale marble, heavy silk. Richer than the rich man's tent, more inspiring than the tent of the philosopher.

Zharet found she had gone in. The instant she had done so a bemusement seemed to come on her. She was reminded of the vision of truth in the garden. A cup was set in her hand. Before she knew what she did, she had sipped—and choked. Thick gall was in the cup. No, not gall. The juice of an *aloe.*

She resolved, mindlessly, to fly the place, and saw one

stood before the entrance to the tent, slender and smiling and beautiful, with a sword of blue steel naked in his hands.

"But you are not to die by a sword," said a voice, gently, marvelously, in her ear. "You are to die more cruelly. More horribly. You are to die of what you hungered for. Upon a sword of a different kind, pierced to the soul and shrieking."

Zharet flung about again, seeking the owner of this voice. No one was near. It might have been the voice of Azhrarn. They say it was.

She had, besides, the space for no more than one swift terrified glance, before a multitude of hands fastened on her, invisibly. No longer was she the demented murderess, the haughty seer. She was a young woman, fearing torture. And, knowing none could hear her, or save her, for clearly she had been brought among demons, yet she screamed. Maybe she even screamed for Chuz, by whatever name she had come to know him, which undoubtedly was not the real one. Undoubtedly, too, the tent had been secreted by magic, or else removed into some other dimension. Chuz could not have located it, nor did he.

Thus at first she screamed, at the initial clutch of the torturers, but in a brace of seconds her screams became very small amazed whimperings, for the hands of the torturers were caressing her, and the caresses began to produce in her twisting shudders of irresistible pleasure. And then again she sensed, (thoughtless, by instinct alone, for the shreds of her reason were already driven away like dogs), that this pleasure was to *be* the torture. At that she would have screamed again, but cold voluptuous tricklings and boiling flinchings of feeling had already closed her throat.

Carnal love. It was their art, their genius. No coin but has two sides.

So the delicate tracery of fingers was, one moment, exquisite delirium, next the fine lines drawn by a razor; her internal pangs—a mounting euphoria, a ghastly quake within her flesh.

They pierced her, each of those who, unseen, attended on her. And the piercing was now a wonder, and now a blade, a spike. They tongued her, mouthed her—the epitome of delight, the gnawing of wolves.

Up the stairway of thrilling horror and disemboweling paroxysm they danced and dragged her.

At last, even though her mouth was stopped, once more she screamed.

She had formerly known three ecstasies. There were countless others. Ecstasies like knives, ecstasies like the volcano's heart. Through each orgasmic vortex they thrust her. She passed through the eyes of many needles, each one narrower than the last.

At the seventh gate, shrieking, she died.

In the cool gray light before the dawn, the corpse of Zharet, a cage from which a frantic soul had torn its way, lay on the sand. Her limbs pointed at the four corners of the earth, splayed and deformed. Her face was the representation of all mortifying spasms, petrifying to any human that might see it. Her body bore no other marks.

As the light waxed, a young man could be discerned, kneeling beside her, as if he mourned, his blond hair falling like a stream of smoke across his cheek.

"Ah, no, un-brother," said Chuz. "You do not play fairly with me at all. Ah, *no*, un-brother. Poor girl," said Chuz to Zharet's corpse. "Tell me, poor girl, what am I? Am I madness? Yes." Chuz sighed. "Your sinews have not stiffened yet," said Chuz to Zharet's corpse.

Chuz came to his feet. He turned his shoulder to Zharet, lying on the sand. He pondered. "Who, after all, is less sane than Lord Death?" And then over his shoulder, he snarled: "Get up, you slut, and obey me."

And Zharet's corpse, its limbs still rigidly splayed, its toes and fingers clenched, its eyes clenched shut, its mouth clenched wide, lumbered upright behind him.

"Ah, no, un-brother," repeated Chuz, so charmingly, so musically, that the wind lessened, trying to emulate his tones. "Ah *no*."

# CHAPTER 4

## Dice

The infant, divine or demon, being a month old, could walk, and as she did so her long curling hair swept the earth. As yet, she did not say anything. She was more Eshva than Vazdru at this season, telling things and asking them with her eyes. In the sun she grew white under her translucent pallor, drew her tresses over herself like a robe, occasionally seemed to weep—without tears. Patently only the genes Dunizel had imparted to her, the saving virtue of the solar comet, kept her from enormous harm. She did not like the sun, abhored high noon, but was not blasted.

She had none of the softness or pudginess of the baby. Already she resembled a very small child of two years.

There was slight privacy for the mother and her daughter now. The only decided privacy they had ever enjoyed had been when the child was still in the womb. However, in Dunizel's improvised lavish apartment, they would sometimes have leisure to sit, and Dunizel would still recount stories, or conspire in strange silent games with the child, involving colored beads, or the forms made by the curtaining. Now and then, on an overcast day, they might journey up to a secluded part of the temple roof, a shielded area set between two golden parapets. Here, in a golden alley, the blotted sky of a desert winter above, the child might run about, playing with a ball of silk like a cat, while Dunizel watched her. Unlike the sun, gold seemed not to offend the Demon's daughter. Once or twice, indeed, she would disappear, as if by sorcery, into some intimate interstice of the metal-scaled masonry. Dunizel would allow her to absent herself for lengthy periods of time, only eventually seeking her, quietly saying the name by which she had called the child: Soveh. Perhaps a coincidence, perhaps an unconscious or psychic memory that Dunizel also, at her genesis, had gone by such a name. Certainly, Azhrarn had not revealed this detail. Nor had he himself attempted to name the child, to which he gave no notable attention, and which he seemed to detest.

Neither mother nor daughter was properly human. What they thought, or the bond between them, is not easy to decipher. It appears that Dunizel, in her determination not to abandon, displayed a fundamental maternal reaction. The child, by her antics, displayed trust, also fundamental. And yet, the perfect prenatal liaison was no more. The child had been born, drunk Eshva blood, given evidence of her demoniac qualities. Azhrarn's daughter, despite his neglect.

Today was overcast by storm, the sun dim, but the strength of the winds themselves had not penetrated to Bhelsheved. The child was dancing, attractively and lunatically, in the gold alley on the roof of the temple. Dunizel reclined nearby. Observing her face, one could see an intense silence at the depth of its loveliness. She must have been thinking of Azhrarn, her parting from him, with which he constantly tantalized and attempted to overcome her resolve. She had not seen him in five nights. Knowing she had only to speak his name aloud in the darkness to bring him to her side, she knew, too, that to do so would be to acknowledge surrender to his wish that the child be unconsidered as anything save the tool of his wickedness. It is conceivable Dunizel had pictured the consequence, a tiny figure seated on the bright chair so much too big for it, casting homicidal lightnings from her fists. "I will make her more fearful than dragons," he had said. No, Dunizel would not resign her child (hers, also, hers) to such an advent. She could not call to him.

She examined the silver and the gems that ornamented her, his gifts, imbued with his protections of her. She wore no golden thing. Maybe she considered the demon city. Every night the sun sank into a limbo under the world, but could she, the comet's child, endure the sunless country underground?

Bhelsheved was unusually still all about, yet not peacefully so. This, too, Dunizel must have felt. She may have deduced

herself and the child as the source of some second storm
gathering beneath the sky. If she did, or if Azhrarn had
warned her, it had not diverted her intention of remaining.

In the leaden noon, the child Soveh came and sat down by
Dunizel, looking into her face. Soveh raised her hands and
caught at Dunizel's platinum hair. There was no clumsiness
in this gesture. Soveh was couth, coordinated beyond her
years. Dunizel leaned closer to facilitate the exploration. She
seldom talked to the child, respecting, save when she told stories, Soveh's Eshva element which had not yet attempted its
voice. For there is little doubt such an infant could have
talked a few hours after its birth, if it had had the mind.

Suddenly a door was opened onto the roof, and men appeared at the far end of the golden alley. They were important notaries of a new hierachy—that which had taken over
the management of temple affairs when the Servants of
Heaven wilted. Now, however, they had brought with them a
priest and priestess, fear-eyed and thin as sticks from their
spiritual anorexia.

"Dunizel, Favored Among Women," declared one of the
notaries, "some controversy has come about. Accusations
have been made. A woman emerged from the desert, of vast
learning and religious power, and she chastised us for holding
false beliefs. And despite her anger, she herself was loudly
praised for the clarity of her arguments. Now she has vanished. We are concerned, and request that you will come into
the temple, where the ablest among us will solicit answers of
you, on a number of points."

Dunizel rose, gathering the child with her. As in her village, so in Bhelsheved, she had never replied negatively to
any proper thing.

She went down with them into the body of the temple, and
the escort kept their distance, and avoided the uncannily and
totally focused eyes of the child.

There were over two hundred men present below, to inter-
rogate the woman who might be the mother of a goddess, but
most probably was the harlot of demons—so far and so assured and so unnerved had the doubt gone and become, the
sown seed of the aloe.

She had been interrogated long ago, in the ancient tower,
before she had become a priestess, before she had entered

Bhelsheved. She looked no different now, save for the child on her lap.

The child's face was quite unchildlike. She observed, she seemed to listen. She did not grow restless.

One spoke.

"Dunizel, Favored of Women. The god who fathered your infant, comes to you only by night, and in secret. Is this not so?"

"Yes," she answered. "But if you know it to be so, why do you ask me?"

Another spoke.

"The visitation has begun to trouble us, holy maiden. For if he comes only by night, is it then that he is a being of darkness?"

"Yes," she said. "And can you not have realized this?"

"But the darkness, holy maiden, is synonymous with all dark things. With deeds of mischief and hidden ill."

Dunizel did not speak.

It was difficult, after all, to exclaim out loud what had been whispered.

But yet another spoke.

"There was one who came among us once, and only by night, who brought unquiet thoughts, baseness, treachery and murder. If your lover is a god, Dunizel, what is his nature, other than the nature of night and of deceitful shadow?"

Again, Dunizel did not speak.

"You must reply!" They shouted, another and another of them.

The child looked at them, and Dunizel looked at them, both with their blue eyes like a turquoise lake or sky, until the shouting ceased.

But: "To be mute will not protect you," yet another stated eventually. "In this instance, dumbness implies guilt."

"Inform her," some cried, "of what her guilt is reckoned to be."

"Why, of lying with demons. Of bearing from her womb a perverse entity. Of the pretense thereafter that these things were sacred and wholesome, which were an offense to heaven."

"I have pretended nothing," she said then. "You have declared my lover was a god, you have told me what I have brought forth, and the essence of my child. You. Not I."

She was so calm. She accused them of nothing. Their accusations slid from her like water passing over glass. Though she must have known this day, this hour, might come, must come, with all its peril, she had not been able to renounce her fate, nor would she now. There was no cleverness, no cunning in her, for she had no use for such devices, and perhaps they could not have saved her from this.

"Tell us then," they said to her, a multitude of voices, dying away, making room for one voice, or two, that were the collective voices of all, "Tell us the title and the name of your unearthly husband."

There were many ways she might have evaded them. She was wise enough, she was cool and still. And yet, and yet, how could she deny his name? They had only to question her, which they had never done, to learn the truth.

"He is a Lord of Darkness," she said to them gravely. "He is named Azhrarn."

There followed a dreadful absence of all sound.

But after a long, long while there started up a last voice, which said quaveringly to her: "Can you be so poisonous, so damnable? Do you not loathe this thing you have consorted with to the shame of all humanity?"

And to that she might have said so very much. She might have recited the litany of love, she might have grown proud, or tragic, or even doubted herself, perhaps, with the face of her own kind turned against her utterly. It was also noon, night far away. He could in no way come to her. She might have implored their mercy. But Dunizel did none of these things. She looked upon the two hundred men, their aversion and their might. And gently she said to them: "The lord Azhrarn is the reason for my life."

It was as if she had flung fire into their midst.

The seventy men who had come from the desert, moving oddly over the dunes and along the ridges, were quite unlike those two hundred men within the heart-temple, those two hundred dressed in finery, oiled and combed and perfumed and ornamented, who now screeched prayers and imprecations, who beat their hands on the floor, who presently sent for servants, guards, slaves to bind the human demoness in their midst, bind her with cords of silk, and all the while in dread of night and he who might return to save her then.

No, truly, the seventy from the desert were unlike those.

For they wore humble garments. Some were clean and some stank, but none were oiled or perfumed. Most bizarre, too, was their mode of advance, which in each case was hesitant, although hesitant in a remarkably purposeful manner.

Now one would stop. He would circle round something. Now another would stop. He would make a sign, he would kneel down. He would kiss a thing upon the sand. What could it be? A stone. He had trodden on it, and now he kissed it, murmuring. And the murmur? This way: "Oh exalted one, forgive my vile heel, which has bruised you."

At the head of the straggling erratic band, walked an elderly leader with a sterner and yet more eccentric tread, for he had mastered, long before the followers of his sect, an almost empathic awareness of what pebbles might lie before him, and he was generally able to avoid them all. His face was savagely introspective, and vainglorious as that of a great king. It was the venerable philosopher, he who had debated with Azhrarn (unknown) on the nature of the gods, he who had later become convinced that the gods were in the stones. And they who mooched and circumnavigated behind were his converts.

"And why do you travel to Bhelsheved?" they had had demanded of them. "Is it to revere the supernal child and its mother?"

"There is no god save a stone," intoned the philosopher and his companions.

They were going to Bhelsheved to see if the supernal child was made of, or in any way related to, stone. If it was, then it was the child of heaven. If not, they would denounce it.

As they had slept, sprawled on the powder and debris of all those stones which, over centuries, had become the desert itself, the hour before dawn approached them, and with it a figure clad in a damson mantle, who had stolen about their recumbent forms. They would have been insulted to know Madness felt quite comfortable with them.

When the aged and venerable philosopher who led them woke, he found lying by his hand a most beautiful and uncommon stone. It was made of mauve quartz, and was four-sided. If he had not been obsessed by the idea of gods, he might have guessed it to be an abnormal die.

"See," the philosopher instructed his waking acolytes, "it is a sign from our celestial masters. Here is their representative, one of their more lovely messengers."

And everybody praised the die of Chuz, and adored it, and the philosopher placed it in a leather bag about his neck—in which previously he had stupidly carried a golden curio. They had already, all of them, a large collection of shards and quartzes.

That day, about noon, the band of fanatics advanced upon Bhelsheved, and in the groves at the foot of her walls they came on a young woman, who squatted in the dust under the leafless trees, and who, on their arrival, rose up and distressed them with her hideous appearance.

She held herself like a huge winged toad, her legs thrust out, and her arms. Her toes and her fingers, besides, were rigidly clawed, her eyes screwed up tightly as if she wished to see nothing of the world. Her mouth stretched wide in a ghastly rictus. A vague bitter scent came from her rags and from her ragged hair.

The philosopher halted in dismay. Even his faith and his narrow-mindedness were shaken by such a visitation. Behind him, sympathetic to his whims—for surely all he did was inspired and theological—the sixty-nine followers also came to a halt.

Each gazed at the hideous woman.

"By the protecting majesty of the gods everywhere about us on the ground," declared the philosopher at last, "why do you stand in our way?"

And then a voice burst from the throat of the woman, so incongruous and unpleasant that some were seized by panic. It was a voice indeed which gave the impression that if the woman's throat were being utilized, whatever used it was not herself, but some possession—a weird harsh shout without expression of any kind.

"I come to demonstrate," this awful voice howled, "how the gods punish those who worship falsely. Behold my condition, and be warned."

"And what is that to us?" the philosopher demanded, "who worship in perfect enlightenment."

"The gods brook no evasion," roared the frightful woman.

The philosopher, wishing to regain his sense of personal command, stepped forward and grasped the creature by her arm—it was as stiff as a board.

"The stones are gods."

The maniacal face let out another rush of noise.

"So they are, for gods can kill. A crystal god mounted on a pin, driven through the eye of a man, will kill him. A flint god, set in a sling, whirled about and thrown, will also kill."

"I will not countenance such blasphemous talk. The gods are not to be thought of in this way."

"Only veritable gods may dismiss the false god. Let fly the gods. Fling them against the harlot of Bhelsheved."

"I will not put up with this," said the philosopher.

He thrust the woman from his path. Rather to his distaste, she toppled to the earth and lay still as one dead, her stiff limbs pointing in four directions. She did not seem to breathe, nor had she all the while he had conversed with her.

The followers of the sect filed after him, and, as they passed the corpselike body, they caressed and patted those stones they bore about with them as talismans.

Presently, they passed into the city, and so into chaos. For such the city had become. And of the chaos, the philosopher and his sect inquired what had happened.

A great shock and horror was sweeping that spangled and commercial congregation, the reaction to Dunizel's confession, for the gist of it had spread quickly. Indubitably, mixed with the general sense of disaster, were feelings of nervous guilt for individual and particular crimes and impieties. Added to these, doubtless, the old prohibition was reviewed. They should not have ventured to invade the city at the wrong season. And some were actually soon in flight from the area, in their turn dragging out the dire news with them. The bride of the god was a slut who had birthed a beast with blue eyes and the shape of a small female child. But only recall, she had been born with teeth and hair and nails! Ah, was it *their* sins which had induced this event? How else could evil have entered Bhelsheved.

The soldiers who had been the guard of the chosen woman were now her jailors. They looked at her with loathing, and with caution at the silk cords, tight as wires, causing her wrists and ankles to bleed. Were these bonds tight enough? Could she break free by use of subterranean magic? No, for the Demon could only venture to her side by night.

She had been taken out, and the ends of her bonds secured to the ornate carving of the west-facing bridge leading from the golden temple. More than this they had not done. Nor had they done anything at all to the child, which Dunizel herself had put from her lap and settled quietly in the tall chair within the temple. From this position the child had not shifted, and none had laid a hand on her. For how were they to destroy the progeny of the Demon? And the woman herself, how might they chastise her? For if he could not come to her aid by day, night must return, and he with it.

Already they had attempted to find one who would lash her. No one would accept the task. Not the highest noble or the lowliest seller of confits.

So, the child was left in the temple; Dunizel was bound on the bridge, a white and gilt butterfly in the spider's web. That was how matters stood, with the crowd roiling and squealing on the four broad streets where animals had been permitted to foul the mosaic, and fringed robes had been pawed by beggars and pickpockets.

The overcast sun had crossed noon's threshold, and now, barely discernible, began to descend from the zenith. The lour of the distant storm was deepening, dyeing the air with tints of purple.

Some had hurried into the countless little fanes, regardless of their purpose, entreating for an omen, or merely for rescue. Most milled about the lake, staring at the enwebbed butterfly on the bridge. Their allergy intensified as they looked at her, she seemed so fragile, so far beyond them. They interpreted her marvel as damnation, and, more perversely, her patient silence as a leering arrogance.

Occasionally a priest or priestess wandered or poised transfixed in the body of the crowd. They were grabbed at, stroked, gripped, badgered for intervention. As ever, these ethereal ones scarcely understood. Where able, they retreated. But in their cells now, also, the crowd pursued them, hammering on the doors and mewling: "Save us!"

And some had seen the seeress Zharet, or her phantom, all twisted, her face held in the semblance of a fit, and she had told them that this was how the gods had punished her for her long belief that the Demon was a God. And how much worse, she said, their punishment must be when it came, since they had cherished the error longer than she, and still would not avenge it. These words were not conducive of comfort or good cheer, and like most such words were widely reported and leant credence.

This their dilemma, then: To be revenged on Dunizel would most probably draw down on them in turn the retribution of her atrocious lover. Not to be revenged on her would be to incite the retribution of heaven.

Yet surely the gods were more powerful than the disgusting one from the pit? Surely the gods would save their people if Dunizel were slain?

But no one could decide this weighty point. They wavered. Who dared take responsibility either way? None of them. Not sage, not fruit-seller, nor prince, nor whore. Let another move first. Let another show them the way. Let there be a portent, or a shepherd to step out at the head of the herd, or to drive them before him.

And Dunizel stood, butterfly-winged by her gemmed garments that the edges of the storm winds softly blew, and her hair, misted by the dull sun as it descended from the zenith. And the purple hints and tints of the storm fluttered like ravens back and forth over the city. They knew, if no other knew, and had gathered as ravens did, when death was imminent.

But Dunizel, so calm, clear as glass, did *she* know?

Her mother had been translated gradually into golden flame by the comet's touch. Dunizel, once called Flame, called afterward Moon's Soul, she too seemed turned into a fire, the pale blue-silver fire of stars, or of that particular queen-star of dawn, or of dusk. As she waited on the bridge, she appeared to be metamorphosing into pure light. As if, knowing she was near to death, she prepared for it by melting away her physical form, allowing her soul to burn through.

Azhrarn could not come to her, that she knew. Not while the sun, however tarnished, was in the sky. And his protections of her must be weaker under that sun. And the human hate about her was like a distant sound of breaking things, which grew steadily nearer. Oh yes, for sure she guessed she must die. And what had she had of life, to wait there in such uncomplaining peace? And what fulfilment had she had of love to wait there without weeping?

The old philosopher, his amethyst die-god hanging from his neck in its bag, his acolytes pushing to make the way for him, had reached the foot of the western-facing bridge, and now he glared at the maiden tied there.

"Is that she?" the acolytes asked of each other.

"Yes, it is the great harlot, the trull of the monster," replied voices from the crowd, with shiverings and sobs and curses.

"She does not to me," announced the philosopher, "suggest a trull, but rather a virgin."

"Oh," one muttered close by, "she remained virgin since the child was not got in the wholesome fashion. It was implanted via the adjacent entrance, and carried in her bowel, thereafter dislodged in the manner of excrement."

At these sentences, the elderly philosopher who had come to venerate stones, felt a stab of the utmost rage. Something in the maiden's beauty, which even from the foot of the bridge, and with his fading eyes, he yet saw adequately—as the light of a star is normally visible to all—caused him to feel disgust at the mood of the crowd, What did such fools, who trod on stones, comprehend of anything? The philosopher would have struck out at the man, but could not be certain who it was. So he said, partly to locate him, "I am convinced some marks of her defilement would besmirch her, and they do not. Even if she has committed sin inadvertantly, I think her blameless. She shines with her innocence."

"She is luminous as moonlight," agreed a subtle voice by the philosopher's ear—not the voice of the fellow who had previously spoken. The philosopher turned and found a charming young man, muffled in a mantel empurpled by the storm glow, at his side. The young man's eye—the philosopher saw only his right profile—was modestly cast down. The philosopher was roused, for here seemed a natural aristocrat, a youth of fine feeling and spiritual possibility.

"And do you think this girl has done as they say?" inquired the philosopher.

"I know she has," said the young man.

"Then you reveal your lack of judgment," said the philosopher. "My new faith has brought me to conclude there are no such things as demons, save in legend and story."

A bark of laughter, like the laugh of a fox, escaped the

young man. As if to smother it, he raised a white gloved hand to his lips, and still he kept his gaze lowered.

"I see you scan the earth," said the philosopher. "That is sensible. The gods manifest upon the ground. But tell me, is the child of this girl a stone? Of marble, say, or opal? Have you ever come close enough to tell?"

An eye came up at that. The philosopher started, he was not certain why. Was the eye bizarre . . . or was it ordinary?

"My dear," said Chuz, "you are under the curse of my beloved un-brother, who maddened you in simple childish spite. But there. You have, I am afraid, something of mine, which I should wish returned."

Taken aback, the philosopher avowed: "I am sure you are mistaken in that."

"Not so. This morning I chanced by your camp in the desert. Unfortunately a possession must have slipped from my cloak, by accident. I think that you picked up this thing, and have it now in that bag about your neck."

The philosopher touched the bag involuntarily.

"I have here a violet stone, a messenger of heaven, which I found beside my hand as I woke."

"Just so," said Chuz affably. "A die of mine, of which I am foolishly fond. Return it, if you would be so kind."

The philosopher instantly reviewed his earlier opinion of the young man. He was not charming, or spiritual. Also it almost seemed the left side of his face might be disfigured. . . .

"Do you imply that this elect being, resident in the violet stone, is nothing more than a gambler's toy?"

"How you enervate me," said Chuz. "Give me what belongs to me, or I will strike you, old man."

At this, within all the uproar of the crowd, a unique and separated pocket of uproar broke out. For the philosopher's sect had been listening to Chuz's discussion with their master, and now that Chuz resorted to insults and threats, these wild stone-worshippers spat at him and fell on him with their fists and feet. Was it not dreadful enough to learn of the holy city's confusion, without having their leader attacked on the premises?

Now Chuz, as a target for blows and projected saliva, proved unsatisfactory. Mostly, he seemed not to be there, so

that a sound kick landed on nothing, save perhaps the shin of
a brother acolyte, and a punch to the jaw resounded only
upon the material of the purple mantle—which stung like
wasp stings, being decorated with smashed vitreous. Then
again, as ass's skull sometimes appeared and brayed in their
faces, and one was almost brained by a brass rattle brought
down smartly upon his crown. Three or four acolytes
tumbled in the lake. All about, the rest of the crowd, having
nothing to do with this fight, became nevertheless very excited and disturbed by it, being unsure what went on, and
fearing it to be some evocation of gods or demons.

And then, quite suddenly, the insolent young man—who
had been getting much the better of them all—apparently attempted to flee. As he did so, his sting-sewn mantle seemed to
come to pieces, and out of it shot a myriad of small objects,
which whirled and bounced among the crowd, to the crowd's
further consternation. Most of these objects were beyond
analysis, though a quantity called up the idea of accessories
to astrology or calculus, though some it is true also put one
in mind of strange insects which had been petrified in the act
of changing from one thing to another—a beetle into a fish
for example. These latter were not very encouraging to gaze
upon. But a great many of the spilled items were dice, of all
colors, weights and markings.

"What is happening?" the crowd shrieked at itself.

The philosopher and his followers were looking for Chuz,
who had vanished. They began to cry out to their stone gods
in perturbation, and the people round about them caught
their cry.

"They are speaking of stones."

"It was stones, then, which were thrown at us?"

The final deduction was inevitable. None of them rendered
it aloud, but their heads, their faces, their eyes, reverted to
the bridge where the girl stood helplessly in her bindings.

While the objects from Chuz's cloak still rolled and skit-
tered over the mosaic, the notion took hold. The fight had
been no fight, the exploding of objects had been a series of
miscasts. Men were flinging stones at the harlot. She was
being stoned.

The shepherd. The leader. The one to walk before.

They dropped to their knees, scrabbling. They found flints,

scatterings of cracked pots; Chuz's dice they found, illusory
or real; they used their knives and their nails to pry up lumps
of the mosaic itself. And straightening, they hurled these mis-
siles up across the bridge. Then, seeing they were too far off,
rushed nearer, crammed on to the bridges over the lake, and
their hands flapped and opened like mouths. Pebbles and
stone chips plopped in the lake. Portions of tiles and fragments of wood hit the gold-scaled walls, the temple's four
faces.

The maiden's guard poured off the bridges. Some dived
into the lake and swam for shore.

The crowd could not see if its offerings struck her. She did
not stagger, did not fall. To some it seemed her garments
were torn, others saw a trace of blood, like a delicate scarlet
embroidery, sew itself down her throat. But it was not sufficient. They wanted to hurt her, wanted to hear her screams,
for they themselves might be made to scream for this deed.
So they scrabbled and cast, again and again.

The philosopher cried tears of anger. He denounced their
blasphemy in so polluting the stones. Sickening his very soul,
certain of his own band, waxing hysterical and recalling the
words of the ghastly woman-thing at the gate, were throwing
their own talismans at the girl. *Let fly the gods.* He cried also
for that, as for the death of innocence.

Yet, was she not unharmed, or scarcely harmed? (A faint
blue bruise on her shoulder, a flint caught in her hair like a
brackish jewel.) The safeguards Azhrarn had set on her, even
by day, must have protected her.

And yet.

Nothing scores the diamond save another diamond.

Azhrarn had safeguarded her, this girl he loved, and perhaps nothing could get by those safeguards. Only he, then,
could have negated them. Only Azhrarn. Or some thing
which was Azhrarn's. Was *of* Azhrarn.

The fragments, flints and pebbles hurtled through the air,
and Dunizel stood in the rain of them. Her lids were shut;
she could not lift her hands to cover her eyes or her face.
And now and then the rain slackened briefly as the people
dug about for more detritus to hurl, and squabbled over it.
And the dice and toys of Chuz, also picked up and thrown—
these were less lethal than anything else, since they tended to
dissolve in the air, to become petals, or resins or flakes of

charred snow. However. With those dice, out of the mantle
of Chuz had been dashed one other thing, a thing he had
come on and thereafter taken about with him, for it was rare.
Very small, it was, this keepsake, yet darkly lambent, and ex-
travagently hard. It was the black pearl of Vazdru ichor that
Chuz had disinterred from the dunes, along with two other
identical drops, currently hidden elsewhere. Each of them the
blood of Azhrarn.

It was simply a question of chance and time before someone, picking frenziedly at the ground, should snatch up this
appallingly significant commodity, snatch it up disregardingly
also, since it was so minute, seemed so ineffectual, and then,
with a fistful of weightier stuff, fling it at the witch-demoness,
at her pale radiance that was like a star.

Who, unwitting, cast her death? It is not recollected. Nor is
it fitting that it should be recollected. It was, in the end, like
lightning or the sea, a murderer without clemancy, or
knowledge.

The adamantine drop spun and flew. It pierced her just
beneath the breast and tore upward, lodging in her heart.
There was a kind of terrible rightness in that. She dropped
down at once, not crying out, not even changing her expression or opening her eyes. It was very swift, very complete. It has been said, it may not even have been pain for
her, to be pierced by his blood, but pleasure, like a sorcerous
kiss which kills. Or maybe the pain was unbearable, as if he
had himself come to her and slain her. But it was suddenly
done, suddenly over.

She lay on her wings of hair. She looked only asleep. No
blood of her own had spread from that awesome, tiny wound.
But the jewels and the silverwork he had given her, which
had shielded her from everything but that one thing they
could not keep out, some or any particle of himself, those
magical things grew murky, and their colors and their sheens
extinguished, and then they were no more than brittle papers
or dead leaves lying on her, and they shriveled, and the flickering wind blew them away.

The ardor of the mob came to an end in much the same
fashion. The yelling and the flying of hands and stones.

They were too afraid, too stunned at their own achieve-
ment, to go near and see how wonderful she remained, to see

the throwing away of this wonder, like a flower torn up by the roots.

Only the sun looked in her face as it slowly declined, and the sun drew the storm cloud over its head. Even the sun, it seemed, could not bear such waste.

# CHAPTER 5

## Love and Death and Time

One other beheld her, but not in the world, or from the sky. From beneath the earth's crust, from the hollows of the earth's inner lands. By staring in a sorcerous glass, smoky, troubled and faulted by the light of day.

They said the glass shattered in a million fragments, like grains of salt. They said that for aeons after such fragments, getting under the skins of men, drove them into otherwise unaccountable paroxysms of grief and rage, so they would slay others or themselves. They said that true despair had not been created until that instant of the mirror's shattering.

It was so quiet in Druhim Vanashta undergound that you might hear the faint chime of a leaf falling on the black grass, until all leaves failed to fall.

No demon prince or princess of the Vazdru stirred. They stood among their playthings, their music, their horses and hounds, struck as if to marble and jade. The Eshva froze like winter reeds. The crafty artisan Drin, having crawled beneath their work-benches or behind their braziers, gave up making anything. No fish flew, no bird swam, no dog barked or horse shook its head, and no snake danced. Not even the foliage of the dark trees whispered. Not even the flames of the fountain of red fire in the garden of his palace trembled. No breeze blew. The starless starlight of Underearth itself congealed, and for a moment lost its beauty, like a gorgeous face turning sallow with unimaginable fear.

Druhim Vanashta, which had always been, or which had become, the heart of Azhrarn, had ceased to beat.

It seems he had been awaiting calamity, for surely every time he attempted to persuade her to come away with him, the foreshadow of her danger must have prompted and goaded him. Yet he had not credited it, her death. She was a part of him, and he immortal. He would, no doubt, have wished to immortalize her, though the paths to human immortality were perilous. In his mind, perhaps, he thought of her as already immortal, invulnerable, eternal. And she being more of the soul than most of humankind, the illusion persisted. If truly he had reckoned on her death, he must have taken her from Bhelsheved, with her consent or without it. And yet again, to ignore her will, which in everything else had surrendered itself joyfully and supremely and with such dignity to his—that, too, would have been a sort of blow against her life. Maybe he could not do it.

Whatever the cause or the premonition or the disbelief, she had remained, and they had killed her. And he, powerless for once, had witnessed it.

A second of his time, far less. But time appeared to have stopped in Druhim Vanashta.

He stood above the last few grains of the shattered mirrow—the mass of them had swirled away. The ruby windows of his palace bled on him, and the emerald windows wept, and the windows of blackest sapphire bathed him in a shade that was not a color but a dirge.

As if one must not speak of him and how he was, it is only the silence of his city, the shattered mirror, the blood and mourning of the window glass that are mentioned. Those were the expressions, and he quite expressionless. (Where his fingers brushed the inlaid surface of the table on which the mirror had rested, white smolderings came from the wood.) Expressionless he was, and his dry eyes, like the depth of space wrung of all its stars and glimmerings, might have turned a world to stone.

Then, he drew in one breath, and the breeze stirred again through the city, and the demons stirred with it, and the plants and waters and fires of it. They came to life and felt what he felt, like blades in their sides. And none dared cry aloud.

And when he came from his palace, riding one of the black demon horses, its blue hair furled about him like smoke, none dared call to him, or even kneel to him. His passing was like the passage of death, though Uhlume, Lord Death, had never entered Druhim Vanashta.

Azhrarn rode to the limits of his city, and left its spires and pinnacles behind, that were now like rent swords and long bone needles and splinters, and all seethed in the calcified glare that the magic sublight had become, greenish, sickly, aching, the hues of pain.

He rode into the sable countryside, among the silver trees. A mile from the city, the horse stumbled. It sank beneath him slowly, and died of Azhrarn's invisible unexpressed agony.

After the death of the horse, which was not an actual death, since the horses of Druhim Vanashta were no more that half corporeal, Azhrarn went on alone. He strode through a landscape as unnerving as it was fair, and saw none of it. Hillsides clad in crystal blooms, rills and streams which gushed with zircons, a far line of cliffs rosy as if at sunset, but unaltering; he heeded nothing.

In his brain a clock ticked inexorably. It told the hours in the world above his head. It told how the sun of that world stepped toward the horizon.

He may have considered Lord Death, but Uhlume had no power over the dead once they had achieved that state, save those dead which belonged to him. Or Azhrarn may have considered Prince Chuz, but Chuz and his games were like distant objects; difficult to fill the eye with them.

There was a forest whose trunks were black, and from whose black boughs soft black fur was growing, while in the soil between the trees were pale yellow primroses which themselves were luminous, and flushed the trees with light. Into this forest Azhrarn took himself, and wrapped its blackness about him. And the forest commenced to sing, because it could not weep, a melody without any absolute beginning, or any positive end, a melody like air, that, if it might be reproduced, would kill life with sadness.

That was expression, too, for he neither spoke nor gestured. He did not express emotion. His kingdom must express it for him.

But then the sun of the earth above found the brink of the world, and the forest dazzled and snarled as if a meteor had ripped through it. Azhrarn was gone, upward, to Bhelsheved, where men had slain one that he loved.

Stricken abruptly with awareness, the crowd had run away and left Dunizel alone on the exquisite white bridge to the west of the golden temple.

The crowd had indeed, by sunset, deserted Bhelsheved altogether, save for a few idiotic or insensitive ones, who still ambled disconsolately about the colonnades. There were also the priests, who yet dithered in their cells, bleating at a sense of psychic doom. The storm held, too, in the sky, dully booming, casting handfuls of wind against the fanes, and tearing the litter left behind on the streets.

The sun, stepping from the last stair into the place below the world, stabbed one prolonged hellish magenta ray back across the world. Iron purple churned in the east, and blackness, which would presently conquer everything.

The girl lay, her feet pointing toward the sunset's end.

A final flare, and the sun was gone, leaving only its moody embers after it for the wind to sweep up. Night stood instead at the girl's feet, looking down at her.

Night's Master, Prince of Demons, Lord of Darkness—who had been powerless, for all his power, and was powerless now, save to justify one of those other names of his, one of those blacker names.

Then he kneeled and raised her, and stood up again, holding her across his body. What he did was so strange. He leaned and kissed the lids of both her eyes, which then softly lifted, and her glorious lifeless eyes looked out at him in a semblance of awakening. But then the silver lashes drew the lids down again.

He carried her off the bridge and into that garden by the lake where she had come to him when first he entered Bhelsheved. He set her on the cold brittle grass, and then he turned from her, and gazed away across the night-stained water of the lake.

To the Eshva, sorrow was, like love, a rapture, an art. They would swim in sorrow, drown in it, drink and grow drunken, those children of dream and shade. But to the Vazdru, sorrow could only be mended in blood. The Vazdru would seldom mourn, as rarely could they weep. And he, who had come to rule them, more Vazdru than the Vazdru, he could do neither. Small wonder his country must express his agony and despair. For he could not. His pain was inexpressible. Like one that would scream but had no voice, or one who was wounded with some dreadful internal wound that no physician could come at to heal, so he was. Azhrarn who invented carnal love, and cats, and the most profound intricacies of evil, so he was and so he suffered.

His face was so white it seared the darkness like a fire, and his dry unreadable eyes—be glad they are not to be read— made the darkness meager and faded by their blackness.

Aloud he said, but gently: "Bhelsheved I will thrust back into the earth which vomited it. And the lands of Bhelsheved I will leave a bottomless crater that shall not grow one living shoot until ten centuries are forgotten."

The night in the garden seemed to recoil at his words. These were his powers, if he had been powerless before. The night and the soil and the trees and the atmosphere itself knew and believed him, and that piece of the world shrank on its bones.

"Not one smallest, most feeble shoot," he said, so gently, gently. "And of men, not one until twice ten centuries are torn from the pages of the world's book. And many, many more."

Pitch black was Bhelsheved now, and no star showing. The buffets of the storm were stifled, for it, too, was afraid. The lake was without reflection. Not a light or a hope of light anywhere, while he stood and tasted the promise he had made, vintage poison in his mouth.

And then, a light. Unexpected, slender and frail, moving along the margin of the lake, toward him.

Azhrarn looked at that light, and he cursed it, for it evoked a memory of how she had first come to him in just such a way, bearing the firefly lantern along the shore. But at his curse, incredibly, the light sprang up more strongly, as if he had blessed it, and now it seemed to speed toward him.

At the last instant, he knew. He stepped from the trees, and thus he waited, and the shimmering light came up to him, and it was Dunizel, or her ghost, her soul, come back from that misty region beyond the world, to which, in those days, souls expired. And she was like herself, save she was translucent as the thinnest porcelain. The night showed through her, through her young skin, her swan-white hair, through her beauty so faithfully, so pathetically reproduced.

And, "Lord," she said, "I knew you were here and have

come out to seek you." Just as she had said it to him in the beginning.

At that, the pain in him, like the raw edge of a sword, most probably became like the pain of seven swords, and seven acids on their points. He answered her with an anger so cold no live thing could have borne to hear it.

"Be glad, now, White Maiden. You would not obey me, but would cleave to this place, and it has destroyed you, and shall be destroyed in its turn."

"And why will you destroy Bhelsheved?" asked the soul of Dunizel. "Is it to revenge my death?"

"What else," he said, and turned from her. It was not often he concealed his face, save for trickery, and this was not trickery.

"Then," she said, "do not destroy Bhelsheved for my sake. I need no vengeance. I shall live, as you see, though not as formerly. Of all souls, mine is vital and sure of existence, for the soul of the sun visited me in the womb."

She knew herself at last, so it seemed.

"Why will you plead for an anthill?" he said, dismissing her self-knowing, for it no longer concerned him, or he appeared to think it did not. "Those that slew you deserve no kindness of yours."

"For them?" she asked. He voice came between the trees, into the shadow where she had not followed him. "It is not for them, but for you, that I plead, my beloved, you, the truth of my life and always that truth, even beyond the gate of death. For when you strike men and slaughter them, and ruin the earth and lay it waste, then it is some part of yourself you are striking, slaughtering, ruining, laying waste. You are greater than your own kind. You are above them. One morning—and advisedly, my love, I speak of day to you—you will set your wickedness aside like a rich garment you are weary of."

"Do not," he said, "say these things to me, or I will blast this spot with a bane that shall ensure its death ten million years."

"Then, you will blast yourself. And, though I am beyond the world, your pain will become my pain. You will blast me, also."

"Begone," he said. "You merit no pity. You threw away your life."

"My life continues, elsewhere, or here, for maybe I shall come back to the world, in some future time. And if so, the light by which I shall find my way will be the light of you."

"What I would have given you, you put aside. Spilled wine, Dunizel. You never learned its sweetness."

"Then teach it me," she said.

He laughed then, beautifully and cruelly, in the shadow.

"Woman," he said, "you are cobwebs and smoke. Go be lessoned in love by the phantasms cringing in the outer nothingness."

And then her hand came upon his arm, weightless as a leaf, yet he felt it, as if it had been of flesh.

He might see her, even now, her dead whiteness lying between the stems of the trees. Yet at his side he could also discover her, as she had been, standing before him, no longer transparent, but finely opaque, lit only by her inner brilliance. If anything, she was more lovely than she had been, if such a thing is possible, and maybe it is not.

"The soul is a magician," she said to him, "and this you know. But my soul more than another's, since I am the comet's child. And because your blood once mingled with mine. For a space, I can put on the seeming of flesh, but only for a little while, for the hours of one night. Even my soul, which loves you and draws its strength from love, can do no more than that. If you would send me away at once, you have only to close your heart to me. If that is your desire, I will not grieve at it. I will leave you without regret, and love you always."

"Your body is mirage only," he said. "Do you think me such a poor mage I would not know that?"

"My body is composed of love. Love me, and you, even you, will tell no difference between illusion and reality, for in this case they are one."

Then he touched her face with his hands. His touch, like notes of music; she grew at once more vivid, sure and real. No human man could have possessed her as she was. But neither she, nor her love, nor her lover were human.

"The time is too short," he said. "One mortal night."

"No, for you are the master of time. One night may be a thousand years. I fear the joy I will know with you."

"Fear rather the parting beyond it," he said, and it was as if he told her that he himself feared that parting.

"There is no parting," she said. "I am always with you, and I shall be with you, as now, once more in some other age. But do not destroy this place. For without this place, you might have gone by me in the darkness. Put out the light of Bhelsheved, and there may be then some other place, in some later time, where you may not find me."

Azhrarn looked at her, at her face held between his hands; then he bowed his head and kissed her. The earth all about seemed to tell from that kiss that his determination to destroy had been relinquished. Love and hate thrown in the balance, love had outweighed everything, as once before, long ago, and that time he himself had died.

Her body, that was more soul than flesh, meeting with his that was of supernatural atoms, light with dark, their mouths meeting, their hands, even their hair entwining, binding them, caused to flow away from them a delirious ambience as if from the glow or heat of a fire.

The whole area responded, throbbing to that inaudible resonance. Lands also lived. This one had been promised annihilation, and love had woken there instead.

The storm melted, sighing. Stars poured through, seeming to rain upon each other. The scale of love ascended through the earth and away from the earth. Time ceased, as in Druhim Vanashta time had ceased. One night became a thousand years. One act of love became all acts of love, past, or of the future.

And yet, it was as nothing to that other love which might have passed between them.

While in the heart-temple, on its golden chair, unremembered, too small to climb down, the Demon's daughter, wide awake, aware of the currents and the waves of love spinning in the night, and how it was not part of them.

The dawn came to Bhelsheved, as it seemed, reluctantly, and shyly, and pale, as if after many years of sunlessness. The city, opening to that sunrise, had a pure and almost formless look, like something very new, or else something which had been washed clean of all its past, the accretions that had grown up on it. The storm winds had swept the dirt from its streets. The naked trees were like dark silver. Even the desert was serene and stroked with color by the sun. Like a woman who has known a peerless and encompassing love, so the land lay, and so the sun flowed up over the land.

The priesthood had emerged from their cells to stare at the sky. Those remaining by the walls gave thanks to the gods. And the caravans which had been running headlong from the city, driven by terrors they scarcely comprehended, had stopped still in their tracks. They had been spared the retribution of the night. Heaven had protected the righteous. Fooled by the dawn that followed the night of love and sorrow, they had got the story wrong again, and wrongly they would tell it, for a number of years to come.

Nonetheless, Bhelsheved that day stayed mostly vacant. Merely an ancient beggar, scavenging about the four streets, and apparently perturbed at the lack of rubbish, who reached the temple door and unhopefully peered in.

Huge and empty the temple seemed. Only the vague glintings of the morning water of the lake went over its walls, and dappled the sides of the enormous beasts that framed the alter.

Then two turquoises, two twilights, ignited in the midst of the tall throne that had been the harlot's chair.

The beggar started. In the gloom, he could make out no other thing. Suddenly, he recalled the demon child, and squeaking, he hastened from the temple.

On the bridge he caught a glimpse of a young nobleman in a damson robe, but the beggar did not care for the look of him, either, and did not pause to whine for coins.

No one else came near the temple all that dulcet day, though Chuz hung about there, and now and then fish walked out of the lake on their fins.

At sunset, Chuz entered the temple and crossed the mosaic with a cat's-paw tread. He came up to the chair where, throughout the day, the blue-eyed child had lain on its belly, staring at him through the doorway.

Chuz was attired somewhat differently. On his left foot he wore a shoe, and on his left hand a glove of smooth purple cloth. The left side of his face was masked by a half-face of the blondest bronze, a face that matched the fleshly handsome side exactly. His hair was concealed. He was now a most beautiful, if quite abnormal sight.

"Pretty child," said Chuz, to Dunizel's daughter, Soveh, "I will conduct you from this uninteresting fane."

The child, Soveh, lowered her eyes, much in the manner of Chuz himself, though not for the same reason.

"Should you not," said Chuz, "wish to behold your inheritance? Do not be alarmed. I will sheld you from the dregs of the sun, though it is almost out. I waited until sunset, from courtesy to you. I regret your mother and father have been called away on business. As your uncle, I propose to adopt you. In token of good faith, here is a gift."

The blue jewels came up again, and focused on an amethyst one. It was the die.

Soveh did not take the die, but she regarded it, and as she did so, Chuz regarded her, and it might be noted that both his extraordinary optics were covered by sorcerous lenses of white jade, and black jet, and amber, that precisely mimicked a splendid pair of natural eyes. From a slight distance, one might be deceived entirely. Chuz had come out in his best, and no mistake, to woo the daughter of Azhrarn.

But still she did not take his gift, though she glanced at him occasionally, without mistrust or trepidation, while the day's last spangles perished on the threshold.

"This is most hurtful," lamented Chuz eventually. And, perhaps intending to provoke her, he turned his back to her. And found himself face to face with Azhrarn the Prince of Demons, who had that instant come up through the lake and the floor to stand seven paces away.

Chuz did not seem abashed. He smiled delightfully, and the bronze mask smiled with him in complete coordination.

"Well," said Chuz, "I am not, it transpires, to play uncle after all. And I thought you had forgotten her, despite what it cost you to bring her about."

Azhrarn's face was hard to be sure of. Cloud seemed to enfold him. But his eyes smote through the cloud. Few but Chuz would have been ready to meet them.

"You and I," said Azhrarn, "un-brother, un-cousin, are now also un-friends."

"Oh, is it so? You sadden me."

"Oh, it is so. And you shall be saddened, even if I must hunt you over the world's edges to come at you."

"I see you condemn me out of hand. You suppose I incited the stone-worshippers deliberately to attack me, that my toys might be scattered and the lethal thing with them. Yet who permitted the whip to cut his palm and the three drops of his blood to fall and change to adamant?"

"Chuz," said Azhrarn so quietly he was barely to be heard, yet not a mote of dust that did not hear him, "find a deep cave and burrow into it, and there listen for the baying of hounds."

"Do you think I shake at you?" Chuz said idly. "I am only the world's servant. I have done my duty. And you, my dear, have known madness. Did you relish it?"

Azhrarn's face came from the cloud; it was the face of a black leopard, a cobra, a lightning bolt.

"There is a war between us," Azhrarn said. "And I have done you the kindness of informing you."

"I admire you too well to wrangle."

And like a wisp of vapor, Chuz was gone, though somewhere an ass brayed wrackingly, three times.

Then Azhrarn stood looking at the child he had made, and dismissed, and at length returned for. He had been a careless and unaffectionate father, and now he was a remote and frankly fearsome one.

But when he stretched out his pale ringed hand to the child, without hesitation, she set her own hand in it.

"Your name," he said to her, "shall be Azhriaz. All shall know you are my daughter. And each of the petty kingdoms of the earth will belong to you, and you will rule them in the way of what you are or what you shall be."

And then the temple was filled by blackness, and in that blackness he too was gone, and he bore her away with him. And it is said pieces of the moon fell that night and crashed upon the world.

But out on the wide plains of the desert, in the remaining calm of the afterglow, Prince Chuz was walking to and fro over the silken dunes that were still lined with rose, as if the loving dawn had come back again that never could come back.

A little to the east of him, a star had darted out, and sometimes he looked at the star, but he was waiting for another, and presently she arrived.

She walked across the dunes toward him, and her blowing hair was the color of the desert, and her garments were sewn with gold, but the star shone through her forehead. Like Dunizel, this was a ghost.

She was far from the old tower, was Jasrin, the tower she had haunted, and far from the city of Sheve where once she had been Nemdur's queen. And although she was not a soul, but only the lost reflection of one, yet she seemed somewhat astonished to find herself so removed from those known landmarks. But then, seeing Chuz, she recognized him with gladness and unease, and she checked, and just the evening wind moved on about her draperies. And then she lifted her hand and in it there was a bone, the bone of her child which she had inadvertently slain in her envious insane love of her lord.

"No further, Jasrin," said Chuz. "For you may give me the bone now."

Jasrin, or that essence of Jasrin that the apparition was, hesitated there, musing. Memories of hundreds of years of penance may have come to her, a self-imposed and inadvertent penance, when her ghost had lamented, going on with the deadly routine of longing and guilt and misery that had been her life. Perhaps even a memory that the bone had also fled her, as happiness had, fled to Chuz, accusing her of her crime against it. And that this, therefore, was merely a ghost of the bone, as she herself was a ghost of a ghost. And did she now sense her imprisonment was done? Jasrin, who had loved Nemdur and killed her child out of that love. But now another woman had come to Sheve, and loved there a lord more exalted than any king of the earth, and had in turn, by protecting his child, herself been slain. The balance.

"Madness redresses all balances. Give me the bone," Chuz said again. And Jasrin came to him and held out the insubstantial thing, and Chuz took it from her.

And Jasrin smiled, or that paring of her which was stranded there, that smiled, and smiling she was no more. The bone had vanished in the instant she let go of it; that Chuz had finished the gesture of acceptance was simply politeness.

Thereafter, he strode on, his mantle, dyed like the evening, flapping around him, and his blond hair now slipping almost boyishly from its concealment, though the other less appealing hair kept modestly from view. As he strode, the ass's jawbones spoke to him.

"Love is everywhere, and the death of love," they clicked

and muttered. "And time, which is built of the histories of death and love. Death and time I concede and acknowledge."

Chuz, forgetting his eyes, like half his face, were also masked, lowered them.

"But what," demanded the jawbones, with sinister insistency, "is *love*?"

## DAW
## TANITH LEE

"Princess Royal of Heroic Fantasy"—*The Village Voice*

### THE BIRTHGRAVE TRILOGY
☐ THE BIRTHGRAVE                   (UE2127—$3.95)
☐ VAZKOR, SON OF VAZKOR            (UE1972—$2.95)
☐ QUEST FOR THE WHITE WITCH        (UE2167—$3.50)

### THE FLAT EARTH SERIES
☐ NIGHT'S MASTER                   (UE2131—$3.50)
☐ DEATH'S MASTER                   (UE2132—$3.50)
☐ DELUSION'S MASTER                (UE2197—$2.95)
☐ DELIRIUM'S MISTRESS              (UE2135—$3.95)
☐ NIGHT'S SORCERIES *(April 1987)* (UE2194—$3.50)

### OTHER TITLES
☐ THE STORM LORD                   (UE1867—$2.95)
☐ DAYS OF GRASS                    (UE2094—$3.50)
☐ DARK CASTLE, WHITE HORSE         (UE2113—$3.50)

### ANTHOLOGIES
☐ RED AS BLOOD                     (UE1790—$2.50)
☐ THE GORGON                       (UE2003—$2.95)

---

**NEW AMERICAN LIBRARY**
**P.O. Box 999, Bergenfield, New Jersey 07621**

Please send me the DAW BOOKS I have checked above. I am enclosing $_____
(check or money order—no currency or C.O.D.'s). Please include the list price plus $1.00
per order to cover handling costs. Prices and numbers are subject to change without
notice.

Name _____

Address _____

City _____ State _____ Zip Code _____
Please allow 4-6 weeks for delivery.

**Attention:**

## DAW COLLECTORS

Many readers of DAW Books have written requesting information on early titles and book numbers to assist in the collection of DAW editions since the first of our titles appeared in April 1972.

We have prepared a several-pages-long list of all DAW titles, giving their sequence numbers, original and current order numbers, and ISBN numbers. And of course the authors and book titles, as well as reissues.

If you think that this list will be of help, you may have a copy by writing to the address below and enclosing one dollar in stamps or currency to cover the handling and postage costs.

DAW BOOKS, INC. DEPT. C
1633 Broadway
New York, N.Y. 10019